The Ex

THE
EX

ALEX SINCLAIR

JOFFE BOOKS

Joffe Books, London
www.joffebooks.com

First published in Great Britain in 2025

Cover art by Nebojša Zorić

ISBN: 978-1-80573-092-7

To my wife and children — your love, patience, and belief in me give me the strength to keep going. This is for you.

CHAPTER ONE

Eighteen years ago

According to Buddha, every morning, we are born again, and what we do with the rest of our day is all that matters. At least that's what my college professor told me. Then again, he may have been lying to get into my pants. He was known around campus as a man who coerced young coeds into sleeping with him. Regardless, the words he said back then changed my life in ways I cannot explain.

I sat nestled beneath the golden canopy of an old oak tree on the campus quad, my gaze once again fixed on the so-called perfect couple everyone couldn't stop talking about — their glow of love almost theatrical. Perhaps, impossible. She repeatedly laughed at whatever he was saying, throwing her head back like she didn't have a care in the world. All the while, he gazed at her like she was the only star in the night. How romantic.

I wanted to throw up.

What did he see in her? Was she pretty? Yes. Did she have an effortless allure and a radiant smile? Yes. Was she loved by all? Again, yes. But what was perched beneath her polished exterior? Did he know the real her? Or was he just another useful pawn manipulated by her well-crafted facade of innocence? A means to an end.

I saw through it all, even if he didn't.

I wish I could have told him. I wish I could have walked right up to his perfect face and made him understand that she didn't love him. Not in the way I did. Not in the way he deserved to be loved.

She didn't know the real him. His eyes were a deep ocean of intellect that burned with passion every time he spoke. He had grand potential, one that was waiting to be harvested by someone worthy. All he needed was the right person to lift him to new heights. He needed me.

He was mine for a time. He was everything I ever wanted in a man. What we had was special and more powerful than anything her tiny brain could have possibly imagined. But the fates conspired the way they always did and pulled us apart. I wouldn't let it stop me, though. I wasn't ready to let him go.

I'd been watching them for months, studying the way they walked hand in hand through the quad as they shared whispers and joy. Each public display of affection was a dagger to my soul and a constant reminder of what I'd lost, of what should have been mine all along. But things would not stay this way forever. I wouldn't let them.

I had learned her routines, her habits, and most of all, her weaknesses. It was only a matter of time before I found the perfect opportunity to show him the truth, to reveal to him she was not the one. Then he would come to his senses and do what needed to be done. He would be mine again. We would be one, just like we were always meant to be.

They say that all is fair in love and war but fail to mention the bitter taste of envy that coats your tongue while you prepare for battle. Waiting for the best moment to strike was harder than anything else. A constant pain clouded my every waking thought. If I wanted to succeed, I had to sit back and let the love of my life exist in the arms of another.

I could take the pain.

All I had to do was make him see things clearly. If I achieved this, I'd be saving him from a mundane future with a girl who would never appreciate his promise. And I'd only have one shot at it. One chance to get it right. I couldn't go in, guns blazing. I had to take my time and chip away at their foundation until something cracked. Then it would be time to strike.

As they walked away, lost in their own little world, an overwhelming sensation of inevitability followed. Little did they realize what was coming to shake their supposed love apart. Their fleeting connection wouldn't pass the test. Their shallow bond could never compare to my burning need and desire. It consumed me from the inside out, and there was only one cure for my suffering.

One day, he would understand. He would know it was always meant to be him and me. Me and him. Us. No one else. Until such a time came, I would continue to watch, to wait, to plan. Because when it comes to love, sometimes the right path demands the greatest sacrifice.

As I sat there, alone in the shadows of the oak tree, I traced the fresh wound in the palm of my hand. I'd carved it the day prior and would make sure it would never heal. I wanted it to leave a scar. Each trace of my finger sent a signal up my arm and into my head, flirting with the fine line between pleasure and pain. I felt the carving on my palm, sliding my fingertip over the J, then the plus symbol, and finally the N.

J + N. It was such a simple equation, and only I knew the answer to it.

CHAPTER TWO

Present day

> *To our beloved neighbors,*
>
> *As many of you might have noticed, there has been a flurry of activity at our cherished home on Maple Court. After thirty wonderful years filled with countless memories and friendships we will cherish forever, we are writing to share with you all some unexpected news.*
>
> *We never imagined leaving this close-knit community. Our plan was to spend our golden years in our home, the same home where we watched our children and grandchildren grow and blossom. But life, as we all know, often has its own plans.*
>
> *Recently, we received an offer for our house. At first, we dismissed it. How could we leave a place so dear to us? But the buyer was persistent. Their interest in our home was unlike anything we have ever encountered. They approached us with a figure that, quite frankly, we could not ignore. After some deep soul-searching, we came to a decision, one we knew was the right choice for our future. We sold our home.*
>
> *We want to express to everyone in Maple Court our deepest gratitude for the years of laughter, support, and*

friendship you have all provided. Leaving is bittersweet, but we carry with us the spirit of this wonderful neighborhood. We will miss the summer barbecues, the holiday decorations, and the simple joy we received from chatting in the street. We promise to stay in touch and to keep you posted on our lives, for the next chapter of our story is so unexpected.

As for our home's new owner, we hope you will welcome her to Maple Court with the warmth and kindness you've always shown us. We know little about our buyer, as she preferred to keep her affairs private, but we trust she saw in our home the same love and potential we did all those years ago.

Look after each other, as you always have. And to your new neighbor, we have only this advice to impart: Please understand, you have bought more than a house. You are now a part of the Maple Court family.

With all our love and thanks,
Trina and Danny
The former owners of number six, Maple Court.

CHAPTER THREE

I don't want to meet my new neighbor. Don't get me wrong, I enjoy meeting people and learning about their lives and all that, but I'm not in the mood for it today. And if I'm being honest, it's more than just some nerves holding me back. I'm going to miss our old neighbors, Trina and Danny. They were next door to us from the second we moved into Maple Court, three years ago. They were easy to talk to and never complained about a thing. But now, I have to start all over again with someone new.

I'm being dramatic. I know it. But when we first moved into number eight, I set out to keep a low profile. I wanted to keep my interactions with the other people on the street to nothing but a casual wave here and there. At most, I was happy to have a brief chat about the weather and not delve into anything meaningful. My plan was to protect my privacy. I managed to do just that for the first three months, but with enough time and friendly smiles from Trina and Danny, I let my guard down. Before I knew it, Jack, the kids, and I were attending barbecues and dinner parties. I now know everyone in Maple Court.

When we first came to the cul-de-sac, we had a bit of a head start. We already knew one household — the Greenes

— who moved in right before us. David and Ellie have been friends of our families for the longest time, dating back to when Jack and Dave became best friends right after college. Ellie and I get along like we've known each other forever, and their children, Ethan and Olivia, are close in age to our two little devils.

One afternoon, when we were all catching up, David and Ellie mentioned how they had just put a deposit down on an established home in Cedarwood Rock, a small town outside of Seattle, and that there was another house on the market on the same street: Maple Court. We were looking for a place to buy. Actually, we were desperate. We were living in a two-bedroom apartment with Dorothy, our toddler. Not only was she getting bigger by the day, but we were trying to have another baby, so we needed more space – fast. As desperate as we were, we weren't sure about becoming neighbors with our old friends. It somehow felt like we were invading their space. They didn't agree and convinced us to consider it. With their blessing, we inspected the house at number eight. It was love at first sight. A tour of the suburb sealed the deal, and the rest, as they say, was history.

All day yesterday, I watched the moving trucks. Workers with back braces and sweaty brows carted heavy furniture and boxes into number six. I haven't spoken to the new neighbor yet, but I caught glimpses of her here and there as she unpacked. I didn't mean to spy on her through my bedroom window, but she doesn't have any curtains up in the entire house.

I've already heard a few things about her. The rumor mill churns daily on Maple Court. From what I've been told, our newest resident of Maple Court is a woman in her late thirties. She's a similar age to Ellie and me. There's no husband, boyfriend or children to speak of. It's just her moving into a four-bedroom house. One that is in serious need of renovation. And according to the letter Trina and Danny wrote to us all, our new neighbor paid a small fortune for the property. I know little about this woman beyond her marital status, but I find it odd that someone her age would pay through the nose to buy Trina and Danny's house. I don't mean that in a bad way, but the place hasn't aged well.

In typical fashion, our other neighbors, Bradley and Gabrielle Morris, at number ten, have invited every single person on the street to a backyard barbecue. It's being held today at one to welcome our new neighbor.

The Morrises can't seem to help themselves with this kind of thing and will use any excuse necessary to throw a barbecue. That or they are just being their typical nosy selves. Bradley works in IT and is your run-of-the-mill middle-management type, while Gabrielle is a stay-at-home mom with too much time on her hands. Hosting these events seems to be the highlight of their existence. Or perhaps it's just a way for them to stay up to date on any gossip in the cul-de-sac. Year-round, you'll find them in their backyard hosting something — be it a birthday or holiday celebration, they funnel their energy into each event. They have a son and daughter aged ten and twelve who, frankly, seem to be sick to death of having people invading their space.

I desperately want to stay home and skip the barbecue today. But I can't. It wouldn't start me and the woman at number six off on a good foot. Especially when everyone else in the cul-de-sac will be there, showering this newcomer with kindness. So, like a decent neighbor, I'll slap on a smile and push through.

"Honey, have you seen my hat?" Jack yells from the bedroom. I'm in our bathroom getting ready for the barbecue. Dot and Noah are downstairs watching cartoons. Some days, I swear that TV is like the third parent.

Jack continues into the bathroom when I don't answer him immediately. "Bianca? Did you hear what I said?"

"Yes, Jackson," I reply. He hates it when I use his full name. "And no, I don't know where your hat is."

"I put it on the dresser a few days ago. Maybe you moved it when you were cleaning."

"I haven't touched it," I say, keeping my gaze locked on my reflection as I do my make-up. Naturally, my answer sends a rod down Jack's spine.

"Are you sure? Because I'm positive that's where I left it. You do have a history of moving things around."

A scoff escapes me. I don't want to admit it, but he's hit a nerve. "No, Jack. I don't have a history of moving things around. If I ever touch anything of yours, it's because I'm trying to tidy up after a husband who is too lazy to do so himself."

Jack's nostrils flare as he leans toward me. He is about to unload and let me have it as per usual, but Noah calls out to him from the bottom of the stairs.

"Daddy, help!"

Noah is two and a half and is going through a dad-only phase. Basically, if Jack is around, he wants him and no one else to help him with his day-to-day problems. It was cute at first, but the appeal has worn off.

"Okay, buddy," Jack calls back with gritted teeth as he leaves. I can see him doing his best not to escalate things between us while the kids are within earshot. It's what our marriage counselor recommended. I realize I should do my part and avoid antagonizing my husband, but I'm sick of being blamed for every minor problem that exists in this house. Yes, I am here more than Jack. He works full-time as a high school history teacher at Cedarwood Rock High School, alongside David, while I only work part-time at our local library.

If I didn't need to look after the kids so much, I'd spend every free moment at the library. Don't get me wrong, my children mean everything to me. But some days, I would rather be at my job, helping someone locate a book, or surprising them with a recommendation they didn't know they needed. Still, just because I spend more time around our home doesn't mean I exhaust my days plotting new ways to drive my husband crazy. Without much effort, I bet I could find Jack's stupid hat.

Unable to resist, I leave the bathroom and track his Seattle Mariners baseball hat down in less time than it took for him to ask for the damn thing. It's sitting in our walk-in closet, right on top of a pile of his dirty laundry that he's yet to put in the hamper. I roll my eyes and sigh as I snatch up the hat. If it weren't Jack's favorite — one he's had since we were at U-Dub together — I'd throw the ratty thing out.

Jack's frustrations rip through me the way they always do. This is not how I wanted to spend my Sunday. We aren't due at the barbecue for another thirty minutes, but I want us to be ready and on time for a change. It's a running joke how we are always the last to arrive for anything in the cul-de-sac. I shouldn't let it bother me, but it does.

Once I finish my make-up and adjust my hair for the third time, I decide it's time to head downstairs and prompt the kids into action. Wrangling two young children into getting ready is about as easy as it sounds. Before I start prying the kids away from the TV, I hand Jack his hat. "Here."

"Where—?"

"On your pile of dirty clothes. Maybe if you—" I stop myself from continuing my thought and swallow the build-up of frustration that is threatening to erupt like a volcano. I need to try harder and not let the things other people say affect me. Like Dr. Carabello says, 'We can only control ourselves.'

I'm still finding it hard to adapt to therapy again. I'm sure there are plenty of people who benefit from it every day, but I remain skeptical about how long we can suppress our emotions like this. This isn't my first stint of counseling, of course. Years ago, I needed help with a problem no amount of therapy could ever solve.

"Thank you," Jack says, apparently noticing my effort to be civil. He takes his hat and brushes it off. The thing is worn out, but he still looks at it like it's a link to the good old days. I wish he still had the same eyes for me. "What did Noah want?" I ask before my thoughts get the better of me.

"For me to fix his juice box," Jack says with a chuckle.

"Ah, the juice box," I say, using the opportunity to let the tension out of my spine and shift my focus. Our son is forever shoving the straw on his juice box too far in and losing it. We've tried offering to pour his juice into a cup, but he thinks cups are "yucky." Just your typical two-and-a-half-year-old logic.

Moving past Jack, I bend down to my daughter and make sure I have her attention before I speak. When she's watching TV, it's like she's in a trance. "Five more minutes, okay, Dot? Got it?"

"Huh?" she says with a furrow in her brow like I'm speaking Norwegian.

Warding off a sigh, I drop lower and speak to her with wide eyes. "Five more minutes."

"Okay, Mommy," Dot says, giving me her bright, youthful smile. It still melts my heart the way it did the first time I saw it. Of the pair, she is the most obedient. Noah does what he is told most of the time, but he's the most stubborn human being I have ever encountered. Well, maybe the second. His father is the current record holder.

"What are we doing today?" Dot asks.

"We're going next door."

"What for?"

"The barbecue. We told you about it several times already." Dot's eyes dance around while her mouth hangs open. I might as well be explaining to the neighbor's cat how a watch works. "Get ready, please. Wear something cool for a sunny day."

"Okay," she says, bounding away a second later without a care. I wish I could move from one task to the next so effortlessly.

"Daddy," Noah says, charging toward Jack, who thought it was okay to plop down on the sofa and play with his cell phone. Jack groans and doesn't look up from his screen while Noah wraps himself around his knee.

"Come on, Daddy," I say to Jack.

"Alright, I'm coming. Let's get you dressed, little man."

"Yah," Noah shouts, more excited than he needs to be. He takes Jack's hand and walks with him upstairs, clinging on to his stuffed elephant as they go. The thing has been put through the wringer.

Before I go upstairs, I grab a few things we might need while we're at the barbecue. It sounds silly seeing as we are literally going next door, but I like to have some necessities on hand for the kids. Some call it control. I call it being organized.

I head to the kitchen with Noah's old nappy bag. He potty-trained early, so it's more of an uh-oh emergency bag than anything else. Plus, it can hold a reasonable number of snacks for picky eaters, young and old.

While I'm in the kitchen, I notice a shadow from the corner of my eye. It sends a jolt of panic through me until I realize it's our new neighbor moving around inside her house. I spot her through the window, just over the fence. I can't quite see her face, but she's there. She still hasn't installed any curtains, leaving her home open for all to see. We have sheer curtains on every one of our windows that allow sunlight in while offering a decent amount of privacy. Unable to resist, I continue to watch her.

She seems to be in a bit of a rush. No doubt this barbecue is a total pain for her. She probably has two dozen boxes still to unpack and is being forced to meet a bunch of strangers instead. What a nightmare. She walks in my direction while carrying a box and is about to come into my line of sight. I consider staying where I am and letting her see me, but at the last second, I chicken out and duck away.

"Pathetic," I whisper to myself. What am I so afraid of? I might make a friend and have more than a handful of people in this world that I can rely on. Then again, it's probably for the best. I didn't spot any toys coming out of her boxes yet. And the fragile decorations I've seen placed around the house suggest she lives in a child-free home.

We'd have nothing to talk about. The kids are the only things I seem to think about these days. They take up so much of my time — in a good way, of course. But I can't help feeling that a piece of who I once was is slipping away with each year that passes.

What is wrong with me? I'm making up excuses and judging this woman before I've even met her. Just because she doesn't have kids doesn't mean we wouldn't have anything in common, right? I used to live a pretty exciting existence. Jack and I used to go out a lot and have fun. Maybe this woman has some similar stories to share. But no, my damn brain couldn't possibly entertain such a thought. It's as if I want things between us to fail before they start.

I wasn't always this way. I used to be confident and so sure of myself. Making a new friend didn't come with a host of made-up problems. Now, when I meet someone, I look for any excuse to run in the opposite direction. I find flaws that don't exist or exaggerate ones that do. It's not entirely my fault after what happened. But maybe it's time to make a change.

Once the coast is clear, I slide out from my hiding spot and resume getting the bag packed. I can't have this new neighbor seeing me jump out of nowhere like a crazed stalker. Whatever it takes, I am going to introduce myself at this barbecue and attempt to get to know her. Even if it kills me.

13

CHAPTER FOUR

We are behind schedule. I don't know how, but we are going to be late for the barbecue. We are literally going from our house to the one next door, and yet, time has once again gotten the better of me.

The barbecue officially started at one. Despite my best efforts, we failed the simple task of getting ready on time for a damned event that is being held less than 100 feet from where we live.

I thought it'd be helpful to get myself ready before them. Usually, I'm the last one to get dressed after wrangling the kids into action. I wanted to avoid the usual rush to do my make-up and hair before we left the house. But my plan didn't account for Jack and Noah spending twenty minutes in Noah's room playing trains.

"For God's sake," I say to Jack in our bedroom. I'm unable to keep my anger bottled. "Noah should have been ready fifteen minutes ago. Now we're going to be late."

"Calm down," he fires back. "We were just playing. Besides, it's only a barbecue with the neighbors, and it's right next door. It's not like it's an hour away."

"That's beside the point. I wanted to be somewhere on time, and now we're going to be late."

"Whatever," Jack huffs at me as he walks into the bathroom to check his hair for the third time. It's a pointless exercise. We all know he'll be wearing his damn hat the second we're out in the early June sun.

I consider hunting him down for his comment to let him have it, but we're already behind schedule as it is. Besides, yelling at Jack won't make a difference. He is beyond caring about what I think of him. It's not the first time he's dismissed the way I feel, and it won't be the last.

It wasn't always like this. Back in college, we had a passion for one another that could have burned a hole in the sun. I never thought we'd reach the point we're at now. Not after the ups and downs we've been through. Especially not after that night.

I shake off the thought and wonder how much longer we're going to last. We're already hanging on by a thread.

"There, I'm ready," Jack says as he comes out of our bathroom, throwing his arms out.

"Gee, thanks," I force through gritted teeth and a fake smile. He's about one dumb comment away from hearing what I truly think of him. If there weren't a bunch of people next door, I'd shut the door to our room and unload. Instead, I stab my nails into my palms and ignore Jack's petty behavior. Marriage counseling is turning out to be a waste of time.

We take another fifteen frantic minutes to move out the door. The delay causes me to recheck my hair in the mirror upstairs. While I'm there, I add another layer of make-up over the scar on my forehead. I hate looking at the thing but even my distaste doesn't justify the price of costly plastic surgery. And even if it did, the surgery wouldn't take away the lasting pain that sits behind the wound.

Jack is the last to leave and has a cooler full of alcohol in hand. I walk ahead, holding Noah's hand. For once, he doesn't want to be carried. We head along the sidewalk and take the narrow footpath to the house next door. It leads to an unlocked side gate. I take a breath as we go in.

Apart from the new neighbor, it appears we are the last family in the cul-de-sac to arrive. Of course.

"Welcome, Anderson family," Bradley says from behind an oversized grill he's proudly manning. He's wearing a black apron with "Licensed to Grill" printed in white. It's the least embarrassing apron I've ever seen him wear.

I give Bradley a brief smile and a wave as I find a place to put down our things and dismiss the kids to play. There are seven other children here for them to run around with. They are mostly older, apart from Ethan and Olivia, who don't seem to mind our little ones joining in.

I head straight to Ellie, who is standing next to David. The couple is deep in conversation with Renato and Bonita Rodriguez, the family from number seven across the street. The three Rodriguez children are playing soccer with some of the other kids.

"Hi, Bianca," Bonita says, beaming at me. She's a pediatric nurse at the local hospital. Due to her busy schedule, she often misses out on neighborhood gatherings, but not today.

I love knowing she lives close by in case one of the kids has a medical emergency. I say hello and give her a light hug. She's a hugger and squeezes me back twice as hard. Renato also says hello and gets back to his conversation with David. But before long, his eldest son, Miguel, is caught hogging the soccer ball from the other kids, forcing Renato to intervene.

Jack steps up to the rest of us and places down the cooler full of drinks. It's a Sunday, and we both have to work in the morning. "Dave. Ellie," Jack says to our friends, almost grunting the words.

"You're here," Ellie replies to him with a wide grin.

I nod and smile.

Ellie smiles again and brushes at her side-swept bangs. She's had the same look ever since I met her. Her hairstyle matches her personality. Dependable. It's the reason we get along so well.

Ellie is my go-to at all things social in the street. Although I know everyone on Maple Court, some more than others, I still struggle with mingling. I always feel out of place, that I don't fit in with these people. I can't help the voice in the back of my head that tells me to stay quiet and out of the way.

"It's about time," David says with a chuckle, referring to our lateness. He takes a swig of the beer he's holding and receives a soft elbow to the stomach from Ellie. "What was that for?" he asks. "They're late, aren't they?"

Bonita shakes her head and half conceals her smile from us all.

David crosses his arms over his chest, beer in hand. "Jeez, it was just a joke."

"It's fine," I say.

Before things become awkward, Bonita excuses herself from our little group and joins her husband in the scolding of Miguel. Both she and Renato speak to their son in Spanish faster than I can pretend to understand.

Jack mumbles to himself and lets out an exasperated breath. He then opens the cooler and gets out a beer for himself without asking me if I want anything. By way of greeting, he twists the cap off the bottle and says, "Cheers," to David and clinks his bottle against his. David sips his beer and asks Jack, "So, how are things in the Anderson household today?"

Jack puts on his hat one-handed. "Same old, same old," he says. "You?"

"Can't complain."

Ethan and Olivia rush up to their father. "Dad," Ethan says. "Can you play with us?"

"Not right now, buddy. Maybe later."

"Okay," Olivia says, disappointed. Then they run off back to the other kids. Jack stares at Ethan and Olivia as they go and almost looks sorry for them. Ellie shakes her head, then pulls me away.

"So, how are things, Bee?" she asks, using her nickname for me, similar to the Honey Bee, Jack's chosen name for me. He hasn't said the name in a long time. Unbeknownst to her, every time I hear Ellie say Bee, I die a little inside.

"Oh, you know. The usual," I say.

17

"Not at home," she whispers, half turning back to our husbands. "I mean with you and Jack?"

I sigh. Why did I tell Ellie about the marriage counseling? Sure, I wanted to get some things off my chest at the time, but I had to know she wouldn't let it go.

"We're okay," I reply.

"Just okay?"

"You know what I mean. We're fine."

"That doesn't sound very promising."

I want to dive deeper into the whole thing, but there are too many people close by.

"We'll push past it," I offer. Ellie deflates a bit. Her reaction tells me she was hoping for more. I think she's silently wishing therapy will be the magic cure for our marriage. Then she could convince David to try it. It's no secret how much they are also struggling.

Ellie and David's kids are four and six. Life is hard when you have young children. Maybe we're all having marriage difficulties.

On schedule, Gabrielle Morris steps over to us before we can continue our private chat. I don't know what it is about Gabrielle, but we've never gotten along. There's always been this air of resentment I've felt come from her since we first moved in. Like she's just waiting for me to screw up.

"Hi, ladies," Gabrielle says. "How are you both doing on this fine day?"

"Good," I say at the same time as Ellie. We sound like two high schoolers talking to their teacher. Gabrielle is around our age, but she often behaves as if she's ten years older. Maybe more. Ellie isn't close with her either. Like me, she finds Gabrielle to be too rigid, too controlling. She's the head of various community clubs and committees. She's also part of the PTA at the elementary school Dot attends — next door to the high school where Jack and David teach. I don't know how she has the energy to do half of these things.

"We've got plenty of food, so help yourselves," Gabrielle continues with a smirk.

18

"Thank you," I reply, glancing toward the table of appetizers and snacks Gabrielle has no doubt spent hours preparing. "It looks wonderful," I force out. It might sound paranoid, but I swear Gabrielle puts in this much effort just to make the rest of us feel inadequate. Especially me.

"Where's the guest of honor?" Ellie asks before Gabrielle leaves.

"She hasn't arrived yet."

I take a glance around the backyard and realize the woman next door still isn't here. With any luck, she might not come. It's a terrible thought, but I can't help it. The only other guests from Maple Court not in attendance are Iris Harrison and Darell Vargas. Iris is always out of town, and Darell likes to keep to himself. He's never once come to a single barbecue or dinner party.

The thought doesn't bother me. I can't stand the man. I've tried countless times to be friendly to him and wave hello when I see him in the street, but all he ever gives me in return are hard stares. The worst part is he's not like this with everyone. I see him regularly speaking to Renato and Bonita. For reasons I can't explain, he doesn't like me.

Forgetting about Darell for a second, I can't help the thought that our new neighbor will be walking into the backyard alone, surrounded by families who all know each other.

My personal nightmare.

"Never fear, ladies. Our guest of honor, as you call her, will be here soon. No one can resist a Morris barbecue."

We each force a chuckle as Gabrielle moves on. The second she's far enough away, I feel myself unclench.

"My God," Ellie lets out as if she'd been holding her breath.

"She's got a way about her," I say.

"That's one thought. Anyway, I need a drink."

"Me, too," I say, grateful Jack and David have brought along enough alcohol to sink a ship.

As the barbecue carries on, the smoky aroma of grilled meat fills the air along with chatter from the adults. The children carry on laughing and yelling. Bradley's brother and wife soon arrive with their kids to add to the noise and chaos. The sight of them makes me think of Jack's brother, Andy. We rarely see him or his wife and three children. They live on the East Coast.

I make my way to Ellie in the back corner in the shade. We gossip away while we drink vodka mixers. It's not a bad way to spend the afternoon. Dave and Jack glance in our direction every so often. I can only imagine what Jack is saying to his friend about me. I don't want to assume the worst, but he's probably telling David how terrible a wife I am.

It's been an hour since we arrived, and there's still no sign of this new neighbor. But, right as I decide to get off my butt and grab Ellie and myself another round of drinks that we shouldn't be consuming on a Sunday afternoon, a hush falls over the yard, keeping me rooted to my spot.

I follow the collective gaze of our friends and neighbors, my curiosity immediately piqued. There she is, walking through the gate with an effortless grace that seems out of place in our casual backyard setting.

She's stunning. A large sun hat partially obscures her face, while a flowing matching dress drapes around her, enhancing her graceful presence — one that demands attention. As she strides in, an air of intimidating sophistication surrounds her, one that seems almost familiar. Her eyes dip below the line of the hat, and I find two intense orbs I've only seen on one person in my life.

I hope I'm having some kind of crazy hallucination. Our new neighbor is no stranger. Her name is Nicole Stokes. Jack's insane ex-girlfriend from college.

"How?" I whisper.

My eyes dart to Jack, searching for a clue or any sign of what he's thinking. Does he recognize her? Surely, he does. You don't forget a girl like Nicole. Jack is frozen mid-laugh with a beer halfway to his lips. He can't seem to look away from her. His stare stretches and is heavy with unspoken words only I can hear. A flicker of anger registers in his eyes, and I know he's reliving the pain all over again.

I feel a knot tighten in my stomach as a string of agonizing memories also bubbles inside me. Ones I hoped I could forget.

What the hell is she doing here?

CHAPTER FIVE

I can't stop staring at Nicole. I swear to God I'm hallucinating. There's no way she's actually here right now. She can't be our new neighbor.

My eyes dance between Nicole and Jack as the people of Maple Court each go up to her and introduce themselves. They are all smiles and friendly gestures toward this newcomer as if she's the nicest person in the entire world. But they don't know Nicole Stokes. Not the way Jack and I do.

"What's wrong?" Ellie asks. "You look like you've seen a ghost."

It's close to the truth. I never thought I'd see Nicole again. Not after what went down in college. Not after—

"Bee?" Ellie asks, cutting into my thoughts.

"I'm okay," I spit out, knowing the words are meaningless.

"Are you sure? Because your hand is shaking."

I stare down at my empty drink and find the glass jittering in my unsteady hand. I place my drink down on the concrete edging in the corner of the yard. This is our space, and no one ever uses it. The people who come to these barbecues understand the rules. Jack and David have claimed the deck. Bradley likes to sit in his favorite lawn chair and

22

crank out terrible jokes. It's all part of a fine balance. Now, Jack's ex has appeared from nowhere, throwing everything off balance.

I study Nicole as more and more people introduce themselves to her. She has removed her oversized hat and doesn't have a single hair out of place. She's as beautiful as I remember her. And like magic, a wave of jealousy I haven't felt in eighteen years washes over me.

Nicole moves closer to Jack. My husband keeps his gaze locked on her, rage simmering behind his eyes. Rage that I've only ever seen a few times in my life. He hasn't looked in my direction once.

"I suppose we should go say hello," Ellie says as she climbs to her feet.

"What? Why?"

Ellie stares at me with a furrowed brow. "What do you mean, 'why'? That's why we're here. To meet her. Plus, it's the friendly thing to do."

"Okay," I mutter, defeat in my voice. There's no way out. I'm literally backed into a corner. Short of hopping the fence and running home, I'm stuck here.

"Up you get," Ellie says. "I realize this kind of situation isn't your favorite, Bee, but who knows, maybe we'll make a new friend."

It takes everything in my power not to let out a maniacal laugh and tell Ellie what a horrible person Nicole is. I'm sure I'll have a few choice words to share about Jack's ex later, in private, but not now. Not with all these people around. Instead, I need to be civil and not let this upset me. At least until I can figure out what Nicole is doing here.

I climb to my feet with Ellie's help and dust myself off. Before we can cross the backyard to join the group of people gathering around Nicole, I see her looking at Jack. He stares straight back at her, teeth bared. I'm not imagining things. This is indeed Jack's ex from all those years ago. The one who came so close to destroying us.

She doesn't look any different. Nicole still has the same trim figure and glossy hair. Apart from a few wrinkles around her eyes, she looks just like she did in college. But I can tell Jack isn't standing there wondering what could have been. He looks like he's ready to kill her, and I know why.

Ellie loops her elbow into mine. "Come on. Let's get this over with. I'm sure she won't bite."

I shake my head and mutter to myself, but Ellie doesn't notice. She doesn't know who Nicole Stokes is or the hell she caused us. But I do. I know everything about her and the violent way she tried to come between Jack and me. I thought that time was all behind us, but here she is.

Nicole reaches Jack — my husband. He grips the beer in his hand so tight it looks like it might shatter. And to make matters worse, he still hasn't taken so much as a glance in my direction. Why? Is he trying to pretend she's not Nicole? Or is he so dumbfounded by her attendance his brain has shut down?

The knot in my stomach twists tighter. More thoughts and possibilities enter my mind. All I'm left with are questions I can't answer.

Right as Nicole is about to greet Jack, Bradley cuts in and speaks to her first. He's still wearing his apron. Bless him and his desperate need for attention. Bradley talks Nicole's ear off about his barbecue grill and the weather. He's like a little boy bragging about the presents he got for his birthday.

I'm saved. For now. I disconnect from Ellie and bypass the Morris show, doing what I can to avoid Nicole's eyes. They once haunted me and are the kind you never forget.

"Bee?" Ellie calls after me.

"I'll be back in a second," I reply over my shoulder as I rush toward Jack. I won't be, though. Not if I can help it.

Jack notices me for the first time and almost gasps. "Bianca, please tell me this isn't happening," he says.

I pull him away from the group as fast as I can. In a hushed tone, I ask the only question I want an answer to. "What is she doing here?"

Jack shrugs with loathing in his eyes. "How would I know?"

"You didn't know she was going to be our new neighbor?"

"Of course not. Don't you think I would have said something? 'Oh, by the way, dear, our new neighbor is my psycho ex from college.' How stupid do you think I am?"

He's telling me the truth. I can see the shock in his eyes. He's as bewildered by the whole thing as I am.

"What are we going to do?" I ask. But I realize my question is pointless. There's nothing that can be done. Not when every time I try to discuss the past with Jack, he shuts down. Short of spending the next week in therapy to force his hand, I don't know how to handle this situation. My only suggestion is to never leave the house again and make sure we have a thirty-foot razor-wire fence installed on Nicole's side of our property. Seems practical.

Jack shrugs again. "I don't know. This is crazy. Why would she buy the house next door to us?"

It's a good question. And it's one I intend to get to the bottom of. Especially when I think about the letter Trina and Danny wrote to us all. They said the buyer was insistent on securing their home and made them an offer that was way over the market price. Nicole had to have known who her new neighbors would be. I just need to prove it.

I won't let Nicole rip us apart again like she almost did all those years ago. I refuse to let her destroy our marriage.

CHAPTER SIX

Eighteen years ago

Concealed by dim lighting, I was nestled in a corner booth of the café, reeling away from the other patrons. My eyes were fixed on him, on Jack. He was here again, working another shift behind the counter of the poorly named café, The Artful Bean. His hands moved with skillful ease as he crafted yet another latte for yet another pushy customer.

He wore that apron he liked, the one with the faint coffee stains. The one I knew reminded him that these rushed mornings and long days would one day pay off. This wasn't his dream, but the hard work wouldn't deter him from getting through college.

I took a sip of my coffee, the one I had bought from down the street, and poured into a matching to-go cup from The Artful Bean. My coffee was burnt and bitter, but I didn't care. Not when the sweet sight before me blocked my every sense.

The café buzzed with the low hum of conversation. No one looked at me twice. Not when I had a few textbooks out on display, along with my notebook. To them, I was just another student from the University of Washington.

I watched as he laughed with a customer, his eyes crinkling at the corners the way they once did for me. He gave out his easy, unforced chortle, the one that made me feel special. It was something unique that should have been all mine. But my time with Jack was cut short.

After our break-up, he changed. He became someone else. All to fit in with those around him. The ones he thought were more worthy of his time than me. It took me a few days to understand it, but I realized I had come on too strong from the start and had scared him off. It was an unintended consequence of my love for him. At first, after he discarded me, I was angry. I hated him for casting me aside so carelessly. But I soon realized what had happened. He didn't think he was worthy of my affections. That's why we broke up and why he had to back away and pursue people who only saw him for his charms and looks.

I adjusted my hat, pulling it lower over my forehead as I glanced away. Whenever he moved in my direction, I had to take the painful step of avoiding his eyes. It was a delicate dance, this game of hide and seek. I was there to observe him and to be in his presence from a distance, and in that process, I couldn't let him see me. Not yet.

The door chimed as someone else entered the café, and for a moment, Jack's attention was diverted. I used the opportunity to give him my full focus and stare at him with impunity. He greeted the customer with a straight back. Jack had grown more confident and more at ease in his own skin. I had done that for him. I knew it. When we first met, he was still that shy kid not long out of high school who was pursuing a Bachelor of Arts in Education. He was so green. So raw. But I saw the potential in him no one else did. He had so much more to offer, and I needed to be the one at his side to guide him through it all. Unfortunately, we were only together for three months.

Our time would come again, though.

Being close to Jack when we were no longer together filled me with a grief I couldn't describe. During the long conversations we shared, we had divulged our dreams to one another. We had spoken about a time that went beyond college. I could have been more to him than some off-the-rack girlfriend or a summer romance. I loved his soul. But he hated himself more than I could ever comprehend. That's how she had claimed him — Jack's girlfriend. She seized her opportunity without a second thought.

Jack stepped along the counter, forcing me to hold my breath. I was afraid he might notice me. But I wasn't ready to see the shock in his eyes nor to answer the questions that would follow. He wouldn't understand why I was at The Artful Bean, watching him like a shadow. Maybe it was time to leave.

As I gathered my things to go, I took one last look at Jack and committed the vision of him to memory. Watching him from afar had become part of my routine. And for now, that was all I had. We didn't have many classes together anymore. And when we did, she was always next to him, blocking my access to him during the only time we had together. I had no choice but to keep my distance.

I stepped out into the cool Seattle air, leaving behind the sounds of the café. The fight for our love was far from over, but until I took the next step, nothing would change. I recognized what needed to happen. I just had to find the strength to make things right again.

As I walked down the street, I thought about the note I left behind at my table. Jack would find it and read it. Then, he would have no choice but to think about me, about us. It was a simple note, but it contained everything I needed to convey my message.

J + N forever.

CHAPTER SEVEN

Present day

I pull Jack farther away from the rest of the barbecue and take him inside the house

"I can't believe this is happening," I mutter to Jack once we're inside the bathroom with the door closed. Jack is cramped beside me and seems lost for words. He stares at the wall with flared nostrils. Several times he goes to speak but stops himself. Finally, he says something.

"This has to be some kind of sick joke."

"And she hired a moving company to carry in heavy furniture and dozens of boxes to an empty house? I don't think this is some prank for social media, honey. Nicole Stokes is our new neighbor."

Jack shrugs away from me with clenched fists and shakes his head. "After everything she did, why would she come here?"

"I don't know. But her reason can't be good. You remember how bad things were back then, right?"

"Of course I do," Jack says, turning to face me. "I won't ever forget what she did. For God's sake, she should be behind

29

bars or in an asylum. Especially after she—" Jack stops himself short and squeezes his eyes shut. I know what he wanted to say and why he couldn't say it. Eighteen years ago, Nicole should have been locked up, but there was never enough evidence to have her put away. For years, we had to watch our backs, always looking over our shoulders expecting to see her appear. But, for reasons I've never understood, she let us be. So why now? Why has she suddenly appeared?

"Should we call the cops?" Jack asks.

"And tell them what? She was never charged with anything back then, so what hope do we have now? All she's done is legally buy property and come to a barbecue she was invited to. If we call the police, we'll look like the crazy ones."

Jack sighs and steps away from me again. "This isn't happening," he mutters.

I shake my head and lean back against the door, convinced I'm trapped in a nightmare. In the moment of silence that envelops us, I stare at the bathroom's outdated decor. Everything about the space reminds me of Bradley and Gabrielle Morris. It's an amusing distraction, but it soon fades when I hear Nicole outside chatting with the Rodriguez family.

I move to the half-open window at the end of the bathroom and listen in. Renato is introducing himself along with Bonita. I can't see anything, but I can only imagine Nicole's face as she pretends to care. She was always great at faking civility and winning people over.

"So, what brings you to Maple Court?" Renato asks Nicole.

"Well, I've been wanting to buy my own place for some time now. I saw number six online and fell in love."

"Wow, that's, uh, surprising," he says, doing little to hide what he thinks of number six. I'm glad I'm not the only one. "I guess Trina and Danny's house is sort of charming."

Nicole laughs. "I know what you're thinking. It's old and needs a lot of attention, but it's precisely the home I've been looking for. Plus, I love getting my hands dirty."

"That's good to hear," he replies. "I like a woman who isn't afraid of some hard work. If you ever need some help with your renovations or whatever, we're just across the street. Number seven."

"Thank you. That's very kind of you to offer."

I shudder. She's already at it. I can sense it in her voice. The false sincerity. The manipulation. No doubt Nicole is working Renato over, with her full lips and fiery gaze. She might come across as sweet, but these people don't know her the way we do. The way I do.

"What are you doing, Bianca?" Jack asks.

"Listening in. Maybe she'll let something slip."

"She won't. She knows what she's doing. These people have no idea who they're dealing with." Jack mutters some more words to himself.

I pull back a touch from the window and try to think of a plan. I saw the front door on the way through to the bathroom. We could duck out and not look back. Then I could text Ellie to discreetly escort the kids away from the barbecue and bring them home for me. She'd do it if I asked. Then I could lock our front door and set the alarm system. We'd be free and clear. But it's a desperate idea at best, and it won't address our problem.

A thought comes to me, and I work out what we should do instead. Unfortunately, it's as foolish as this day is becoming.

Despite not being asked, I tell Jack my thoughts. "I think we should go talk to her and say hello."

"You're joking, right?"

"Think about it. We're surrounded by people. She can't pull any stunts while we're here. Plus, I know she's spotted us. She knows who we are."

Jack crosses his arms over his chest. "She was staring right at me like it was no big deal."

"Exactly. Was there even a hint of surprise in her eyes?"

"None."

"Which means she moved into number six on purpose. She knew we lived next door."

Jack's mouth hangs open as he takes in my revelation. He paces about then asks, "So what does she have planned?"

"I don't know. But if I had to guess, I think she's here for one reason and one reason only."

Jack leans closer to me, his height ever apparent. "What?"

"You."

"Come on. No way. After all that chaos? After I almost . . . ? You seriously think she's here for me?"

"Yes. Think about what she did."

"That was a long time ago," he shrugs. "Like, over fifteen years. And it didn't end well, did it? There's no way she's been waiting around that long for another chance to be with me."

I glance away and don't say another word. Jack can live in denial all he wants, but deep down he must feel it, too. Nicole is here to take back what she lost. She wants my husband, and I know how far she'll go to get him. "Let's go," I tell Jack.

"Where?"

"Back to the barbecue. It's time we meet our new neighbor."

CHAPTER EIGHT

As we return to the barbecue, it feels like all eyes in the back-yard are on us. In reality, no one cares that we went to the bathroom together. Except David, of course, who makes a childish suggestion that we were in there having sex. If only. I'd take that over the truth.

We settle in beside David and Ellie and try to act natural. Jack gets handed another beer while I'm offered a vodka mixer. I decline. As badly as I could use a drink, I need to keep my wits about me. Especially with Nicole around. Jack accepts his beer and takes a hefty swig right off the bat.

"Are you guys okay?" Ellie asks us both. Our faces are betraying our attempts to act unbothered. I can imagine mine is white as a ghost. I still don't believe that Nicole is here. She's the last person I ever expected to see after all this time.

Jack doesn't answer and takes another swig of beer.

Ellie narrows her gaze at me instead. "Bee?"

"I'm fine," I answer. "Just feeling a little queasy." I do feel sick.

"Okay," she replies with a furrowed brow. She doesn't believe me. I can't get much by her and never have been able to. She always can tell when something is upsetting me. I do my best not to cast my eyes in Nicole's direction. I don't want Ellie to spot me looking at her and connect the dots. Sure, I'm dying to tell my friend all about Jack's crazy ex, but now isn't the time. Until I can make sense of the situation, I have to play it cool.

We gradually slip back into our normal social rhythm and start chatting about all the usual things like work, kids, and local gossip. All the while, I'm putting off the inevitable and trying my hardest to pretend that everything is fine. But my attempt to deny reality doesn't make a difference. Jack and I need to go speak to Nicole. We need to rip that Band-Aid off.

Nicole keeps looking in our direction from across the yard. Even as she speaks with the other guests while holding a drink, she has one eye on us. And it's obvious who is keeping her attention the most.

"Jack," I say with as much subtlety as I can muster. "We should go meet our new neighbor."

"Ah, yes," Jack says, sounding about as natural as he would auditioning for a Shakespearean play.

"We said hello to her before," David chimes in. "Her name's Holly or Henrietta. Something like that."

"It's Nicole, you jackass," Ellie cuts in.

"What did I do?" David chuckles.

Jack doesn't laugh. Instead, he stares at the grass and takes another gulp of beer. He twists the neck of the bottle with his spare hand. I can feel the indignation at the mere idea of being in the same backyard as Nicole, but we have to do this. We have to get ahead of whatever comes next.

"Thanks," I say to Ellie, pretending I've never heard Nicole's name before. Then I face Jack and tilt my head, gesturing for him to come with me.

Jack sighs, and we trudge toward his ex. I can't believe this is happening. Nicole sees us coming, and I swear a smirk comes across her lips. Maybe I imagined it. I can't help but assume the worst about her. The only reason for her to be here is to make me suffer. It's working. She steps away from every-one else at the party as we approach, giving us some amount of privacy.

Jack drags his feet and mutters some vile things behind me. He's not one for cussing, but he's not holding back right now.

We come to a stop a safe distance from Nicole. From the dress she's wearing, I don't think it would be possible for her to be hiding a gun or a kitchen knife underneath her outfit, but you never know. For years, I feared that one day she would appear from nowhere and attack one or both of us after what happened. But time passed, and the threat became less and less likely. But now that threat is here, staring straight at me.

"Jackson, Bianca. Long time," she says. Her words flow as casual as a conversation about the weather. You'd swear we didn't share the past that we do. There's an air of confidence about her that reminds me of the girl we once knew in col-lege. Knowing I need to match her energy, I step forward and speak first.

"Nicole. It's good to see you." I regret my words instantly. It's not good to see her. But I couldn't think of what else to say. I couldn't lead with anything too outrageous like, "Why the hell are you here, and what do you have planned?"

"Nicole," Jack says to her through gritted teeth. He adjusts his hat and takes a swig of beer without breaking eye contact. I swear he is close to snapping and hurling the bottle at her face.

"I suppose you're both wondering what I'm doing here."

"The thought had crossed our minds," I say.

Nicole chuckles. "Tell you what. Why don't we find somewhere nice and quiet to talk? I can explain everything."

I turn to Jack. His shoulders are tense, and one of his eyes is twitching. He shakes his head, but I grab hold of his forearm. "It's okay," I whisper. He exhales and lets some of the stiffness out of his neck. He gives me the tiniest of shrugs.

I refocus on Nicole and force a smile. "Sounds like a plan. Maybe in the back corner would be ideal." There aren't too

35

many other options right now, and I don't want to go somewhere where people can't see us.

"Lead the way," Nicole says with a warm smile. It's one that meets her eyes and seems genuine. How is that possible? How can she swallow so much hatred and act so normal around us?

As I cross the yard with Jack at my side and Nicole trailing behind, I can't help but wonder if she has changed after all this time. Is it even feasible? Maybe she's a born-again Christian who has started over. Or maybe she's fantastic at acting and is planning on punishing us in as many ways as possible. Wherever the truth lies, this is the longest walk of my life. I feel like I'm being marched to an open grave.

We reach the far corner without incident and are away from the other guests. Enough so none of them can hear us. I sweep my eyes over the barbecue and spot Ellie staring at me with a curled lip and a furrowed brow. She knows something isn't right, and I'll need to explain it to her later somehow. One problem at a time.

"I'll go first," Nicole says, grabbing my attention. "While I can understand your, let's call it apprehension, I just want you both to know that this is nothing but a giant coincidence. I had no idea that the two of you lived at number eight." She points to the fence where our house is. Immediately, I want to shout and ask her how the hell she knows we live at number eight. "And before you ask, Gabrielle knocked on my door yesterday and invited me to this barbecue. It was very kind of her. She not only invited me here, but she took it upon herself to tell me the names of everyone in the street and where they live. I'd forgotten half of them until she told me that Jack and Bianca Anderson live next door at number eight. You can imagine my shock."

"Yes, we can," Jack says, finding his voice.

Nicole gives him an awkward smile that twists my stomach. Just having her glance in his direction is enough to fill me with an old jealousy.

She continues. "Let me say this one more time: I had no idea the two of you lived here. I didn't even know you were married. But when Gabrielle said those names, I knew it had to be the same Jack and Bianca I knew in college. What are the odds?"

"A million to one," I blurt. Nicole gives out a muffled laugh. Then a silence falls over us, leaving us staring at one another. I refuse to look away. She's going to crack any second and show me the real her.

"So what now?" Jack asks, breaking the quiet. "We act like everything is peachy keen? Do we wave to you in the street and complain about the traffic over the fence?" His breath quickens. I grab his wrist to soothe him.

"I don't know," Nicole starts, avoiding Jack's heated gaze. "But I think with some time and effort, we can all make this work."

"Screw that," Jack spits, his voice raised. "You can sell your house and move."

"Calm down," I mutter to him.

"Okay. Sorry."

I give Jack a few moments to pull himself together. When we stare at Nicole, I find a casual smirk hidden beneath an artificial layer of concern. She's loving this. I'll bet this barbecue is going exactly as planned.

"Jackson," Nicole starts. "We all share a past. You don't have to remind me. I haven't forgotten a thing. But I've moved on, and if you're willing to do so, we can keep the past where it belongs. I won't bother either of you."

"Are you serious?" I ask.

"Yes," she says, peering into my eyes with an intensity I can't match. "We can exist peacefully with one another. We can be neighbors. I only ask one thing of you both."

Jack and I exchange a look.

"Please don't tell anyone about our history. I want to get along with everyone in the cul-de-sac, and the best way to do that is if we give each other a fresh start." Nicole holds out her hand for me to shake. "What do you say?"

37

CHAPTER NINE

Nicole stares at us, waiting for an answer. She is offering to leave us alone if we agree to tell no one about the past. The more I think about it, the more I realize how threatening her proposal is. If I'm interpreting her correctly, she's promising to make our lives a living hell if we breathe a word about our time at college to anyone in Maple Court. She didn't outright say as much, but I can read between the lines.

"Tell you what?" Nicole says, retracting her hand. "Take some time to think about what I'm saying. I know you don't believe me, but I'm not the same person I was in college. Everything that happened then was a lifetime ago, and that's where I'd like to leave it. I don't want to sell the house I've just moved into, so take a day to think this through, okay?"

I cross my arms over my chest and close my eyes, needing a second to process what she's asking of us. She makes it all sound like a business deal and nothing personal. When I open my eyes again, I simply say, "Okay." This is all I'm prepared to give her right now.

"Thank you, Bianca," Nicole replies, touching me on the arm as she beams at me. My breath tightens as I fight off the urge to flinch. Then she walks away from Jack and me like she hadn't just upended our lives.

"What did you just agree to?" Jack asks.

"Nothing. She wanted us to say something, so I did."

Jack steps in front of me. "You can't seriously be thinking about agreeing to any of that bullshit?"

"No. Not a chance. I was letting her talk. We can never be friendly neighbors. Especially after what happened to—"

"Don't say it," Jack utters, the corners of his mouth tightening. I realize my mistake and scold myself internally. We never talk about her.

Jack still hasn't processed what we went through. Despite not wanting to, I've tried to talk about it with him countless times, but the conversation never goes far.

I stare across the yard at Nicole and wonder what plans she has inside that head of hers. If she got Jack alone, what would she tell him? Without effort, Nicole joins a chat with Gabrielle and Bradley. Within thirty seconds, they are laughing along with her. Nicole's always been confident. But it always felt fake to me, like she was playing a role. She always came across as so sure of herself, even with complete strangers. And soon, she'll have the people of Maple Court eating out of her palm.

"We should head home," Jack says.

"Yeah," I agree. I can't look away. Not until I see Ellie heading toward us with concern in her eyes. Her expression is screaming at me. She wants to know why we were off having a heated and private conversation with Nicole. We haven't agreed to keep the secrets of the past from everyone yet, but if Nicole sees me talking to Ellie in hushed tones, she'll suspect the worst. Seeing that I don't know what any of this means, it will be best to keep Nicole happy. At least for now.

"I'll grab the kids," I tell Jack. I keep my head down and walk right past Ellie.

"Hey, Bee, I was about to—"

"Sorry," I say, throwing a smile her way. "We need to head home. I'm not feeling well."

"Oh, okay. Let me know if you need anything."

"Sure, thanks," I say over my shoulder. I call out to the kids and struggle to pry them away from the fun they've been

39

having. Jack swoops in on a crying Noah and picks him up while Dot drags her feet and eventually listens to me.

"Why do we have to go?" Dot groans.

"Because Mommy said so."

"But that's not a reason."

"Dot, I swear to God," I say through gritted teeth. I hate speaking this way to my child, but now is not the time for disobedience. I receive glances and stares from almost everyone at the barbecue and am forced to explain.

"We have to go, sorry," I say to Bradley and Gabrielle. Nicole is standing behind them, keeping her focus on me.

"Why?" Gabrielle asks, staring at me with an upturned lip.

"My stomach is playing up."

"So sorry to hear that," Bradley says. "We could watch the kids for you while Jack takes you home."

I don't mean to, but I glance at Nicole. The thought of leaving my two babies alone makes my stomach hurt. "No, it's okay. We've all got a busy day tomorrow. I'm sorry we're leaving so early." Jack says nothing and avoids any scrutiny while I exchange looks with Gabrielle. The thought of anyone leaving her precious barbecue early is an apparent crime. I don't care, though. We need to go. Every time I look at Nicole, her eyes drag me to the past. She sends a bout of anxiety to my core that I haven't felt in a long while.

I ignore the stares and head for the back gate while holding Dot's hand. She hesitantly walks alongside me.

I don't glance back as we leave. I don't so much as exhale until we're inside our own home with the doors locked and the curtains pulled shut.

CHAPTER TEN

Eighteen years ago

It was a blissful summer day. I sat alone on a bench at the edge of the quad and soaked it all in. This bench was one of my favorites — not just because it had the most shade or because it was out of the way, but because it had a perfect view of Jack's favorite place to lie in the grass.

Resting a finger on the shutter button of my Canon EOS 10D camera, I readied myself. The telephoto lens I had paid a small fortune for poked out from the sanctuary of the backpack I had sitting between my legs. Because I couldn't look through the camera's viewfinder, I had to guess where my subject would be. But I had gotten decent at keeping Jack in the frame. Practice makes perfect.

The campus of the University of Washington, or U-Dub as the students loved to call it, teemed with the usual midday flurry. A sea of students, each absorbed in their own world, rushed to their classes in the historic buildings while others lounged on the campus lawns, deep in discussion. My world was narrowed to one focus: Jack.

There he was, sitting alone on the grass. He had textbooks fanned around him. He picked up a book and even

41

from this distance, I could see his eyes scanning and absorbing the knowledge the text held while sunlight crowned him and cast a soft glow over his skin.

I watched and waited, holding my breath for the perfect moment to arrive before I clicked the shutter. It was an anticipated agony I both loved and loathed.

Something in his studies made him laugh, so my finger responded, clicking the button. The sound of his happiness broke through the distance and reached my ears. I knew his laugh better than anyone else's in the world and could hear it in my mind. It was so genuine and rich. It always sent waves of exhilaration right through me.

Another student, an acquaintance from his class, joined him to study. They spoke for some time until Jack tapped a finger in his open textbook, no doubt helping the student in his selfless way. I captured this moment with a press of the shutter button. The camera caught Jack's compassionate side with perfect lighting and focus. Later, I would print the photos of Jack out and label them all "J + N." Then I would trace the lines of his features in the quiet of my dorm room. The best shots would make it into the photo album I'd been working on. The rest would go into a box. The process took hours, but it sent my mind back to our time together as if we were never apart.

More laughter came my way from Jack's lips. I was caught up in the moment and watched as his face radiated with carefree joy. The camera whispered as I clicked the button again and seized another honest, unguarded nanosecond in his existence.

His laughter belonged to me. Why did I have to share it with anyone? Stealing these moments from a distance rendered their value fleeting at best. How strong was lightning in a bottle compared to a full, untethered storm?

The photos were a poor substitute for the real thing, but I wouldn't stop. I couldn't stop. For now, this was the only way we could be together. And it was just a diversion from our story. A minor setback. We would be whole again.

I clicked the button as another person arrived to join the study group. But this young woman wasn't just some other student. It was *her*.

Her presence doused me with ice. She approached Jack with a smile and sat down beside him, intertwining her hand with his. And soon, it wasn't just their fingers that had merged, but their laughter too. A pang of something sharp and bitter ripped through me. The button clicked again and again as I stabbed it. Through my lens, I captured an intimate world that was once my own. And as I did, I swear, a dark and heavy cloud came over the campus.

I looked away, unable to swallow the pain for another second. Why her? There was nothing special about this shrew of a woman. She would never give him the devotion he deserved. She would never sacrifice for him the way I could. Was he so blind?

I captured one last photograph. One where their foreheads were pressed together — a picture of a blossoming romance to the common observer but pure nausea to me.

I placed the cap over my camera's lens and pushed the unit into my backpack. A hollow ache took over as I came crashing down from the rush. I had taken enough photos for today.

Reforming my focus, I witnessed the acquaintance depart, leaving Jack and his supposed girlfriend to be alone. They soon kissed one another, lying on their sides like lovesick puppies as if no one were watching. But I was watching. I was sitting there by myself, observing the man I'd lost, one kiss at a time.

Their affection continued. I sat there for a long time, frozen in a rage. I should have closed my eyes at the very least, but I needed the pain to center my goals. What didn't kill me would only make me stronger.

I couldn't continue like this, like a silent spectator to a life that I no longer possessed. No, this passive observation, this shadow of a relationship, it wasn't enough. It would never be enough. I needed her gone.

It was risky. I trembled at the thought of the consequences. Yet, the idea of doing nothing, of watching Jack drift further into her arms, was unbearable. I needed to act and stop telling myself I was going to do something. It was time to step out from behind the lens.

I gathered my things to leave while my mind raced with the possibilities. I would not be a forgotten nobody in Jack's life. Just that nameless girl in college he once dated. Today marked the end of my silent vigil. It was time to return to the light and into his world again, no matter the cost.

With one last glance at the lovebirds, I stood up. My steps were hesitant at first, but with each stride, I knew I had found my resolve. I was no longer an observer. However it needed to happen, I would make Jack mine again. Forever.

CHAPTER ELEVEN

Present day

I can't believe this. How did things go from our family needing to attend a barbecue at the Morris household to us coming face to face with Nicole Stokes?

I'm standing in the kitchen of our home, staring at the window I had watched her through earlier. The curtain is now shut, but I can still picture her walking around Trina and Danny's house, knowing that Jack and I are close by.

"Do you think she knew we lived here?" Jack asks me from the other side of the island bench in our kitchen. We've been in the room since we got home after putting the kids down in front of the TV with a snack. We're each drinking strong coffee to help push the alcohol out of our systems. Sober is the only way to handle this Nicole situation.

"Of course she did," I say without looking at him. I sip my instant black coffee and stare at the tiled floor. Jack continues, "So you're saying she bought a house, paid way too much for it, all so she could move in next to us?"

"Why else would she have done this?"

He shakes his head. "I don't want to know."

"I'm sure we'll find out soon enough." I drum my fingers over my mug. "We can't accept her proposal."

"You mean her weird offer?"

I nod and pace the room, sipping my coffee some more. On the surface, her offer doesn't sound weird. Not to someone who isn't aware of what happened in the past. But for Jack and me, what Nicole is presenting to us is nothing short of devious. "It sounds ridiculous," I say. "Does she honestly think we can go along with the idea? It's not like we'll ever trust her, right?" I already know the answer to my question, but I want to make sure Jack agrees.

"Never. Not in a thousand years. She's a lying, manipulative psycho."

We're on the same page. Thank God. The last thing I need is for Jack to think about the past and wonder if maybe, just maybe, things could have been different between him and Nicole. I'm sure the thought has crossed his mind once or twice over the years. No one likes to think they made such an awful calculation about a person they once cared for. It makes you doubt your every thought.

Jack sighs and scratches his head. "God, why now? Why so long after everything? Maybe this is all a strange coincidence."

I move up to him and place my coffee on the bench. I wrap my arms around his shoulders and make sure his eyes are on mine. "We both know this isn't a coincidence. And whatever it is she's up to, we'll get through it. I promise."

Jack nods and pulls me in tight. We haven't held each other like this in months. We might have been together for a long time and are going through a rough patch, but I miss these moments.

We pull away from our embrace and look each other in the eye.

"What happens now?" he asks.

I take a second to think, then shake my head. "I still don't know. But what I do know is that I need to fold some laundry and make dinner. We should put the kids to bed early. Will you help me?"

46

"Happy to."

Normally, such a request is met with groans. But after we came face to face with Nicole today, Jack seems to be on my side for a change. She could be the catalyst that saves our marriage. The irony isn't lost on me.

We spend over an hour putting clothes away. Jack forgets where half of the items go, as usual, but he does his best. Then we get dinner started. Seeing that the kids pigged out at the barbecue, I don't make them much. I throw together some meatloaf while Jack chops up vegetables to be boiled. Anything they don't eat will be leftovers for the week. Once dinner is on, Jack helps me herd the kids upstairs. Dot is old enough to take a shower on her own, so we let her use our bathroom. Noah, though, needs to be supervised. I ask Jack to handle Noah's bath while I lay down on our bed and scroll through Instagram while Dot showers. Most days, I'm entertained for at least ten minutes before I grow bored, but today I can't concentrate at all. Not after seeing Nicole again. It still doesn't feel real or even possible that she's here. I want to believe that she has changed, and that she hasn't done all this to punish me, but nothing else makes sense. The only plausible reason she is here is Jack. He was an amazing catch. I might sometimes act like I've forgotten, but deep down, I believe he still is.

We've drifted apart in recent years and have had our share of problems. Back in college, though, we were inseparable. I still remember lying on his bed in his dorm room without a care in the world. But life had other plans for us.

As I'm watching some pointless video on my cell phone, a text pops up on my screen. I almost have to look twice when I realize who it's from.

"Nicole? What the . . . ?" I say, stifling the curse word I was about to let out. Sitting all the way up, I hunch over my phone with wide eyes. My hair is blocking my view, so I brush from my view over my ear. Why is Nicole texting me? How the hell did she get my number? It's not the one I had in college. I read the text.

Hi, Bianca. It's Nicole. I got your number from Gabrielle. I just wanted to say that it was nice seeing you and Jack again today. I hope we can come to an understanding about the past and maybe become friends. I appreciate that the very idea seems impossible given our history, but I'm willing to try it if you are. Also, I just wanted to say again I didn't know that you and Jack lived next door. If I did, I would have reconsidered buying the house. Anyway, sorry for the long text, but my offer still stands. Please reply to me when you can. — N

"Are you kidding me?" I say out loud. My hands shake as I re-read the load of crap Nicole sent me. She can't mean a word of it. In fact, the more I think about it, the more I'm convinced she is lying. She's acting the part of someone innocent and forgiving. The question is why? What's her endgame? And more importantly, what's it going to cost me if I sit back and do nothing?

Not knowing how to respond, I call out to Dot and tell her I'll be right back. Then I rush to Jack. When I reach the bathroom down the hallway, I find him sitting on the floor next to the bath with his cell phone out. He never does this. Even though Noah is old enough to handle the water, Jack prefers to stay alert. I see Jack reading a long text on his cell phone and realize what's happened. "She sent you the same message, didn't she?"

"Yeah," he says through gritted teeth. "The damn Morrises gave out our numbers. This is just great."

"Are you okay?" I ask, knowing how hard this is on him.

Jack ignores the question. "Does she seriously think I can ever forget what happened? She's lucky I didn't . . ." He trails off. I could easily guess what he wanted to say, but I know he won't complete his thought. If he did, he'd have to think more about a past he wishes he could forget. Soon, he won't have an option but to face it. "What do we do? Can we move?" he asks.

"Move?" I stammer. Noah looks up at me. I have to hold back and check my tone. The last thing we need is for Noah to think anything is wrong. He's a sensitive little boy. I take a breath and speak to Jack as calmly as possible.

"Forget the fact that we'd be letting her get to us before anything has happened, where would we go? This area is perfect. Ellie and Dave live two houses over. We both have stable jobs here. Your parents are within an hour's drive. We've built a life here."

Jack shakes his head. "Sorry. I was talking out loud. It's a dumb idea."

"It's not," I say as I move closer and sit down beside him. "We're just desperate. I guess we thought the past would stay where it belonged."

"Yeah," he says, staring off into the distance. And I can see it as clear as day: he's thinking about Nicole, about their time together. I should tell him to block her number, to never speak to her in person again. It would be as much to protect her as it would be to prevent him from doing something that would see him thrown in prison for the rest of his life. But if I stop Jack from communicating with Nicole, what will she do next?

"What do we write back to her?" Jack asks.

I focus on Noah while he plays with a rubber ducky in the bath. "I'll say to her that we won't tell anyone about college, that we'll do what we can to make this work."

"What? Why?"

"It's just what I'm saying to her. It doesn't mean that's what we'll do. I don't know what this all means yet. Until then, we need to play her game and let her think we're on her side."

"Okay," he says. "I hope you know what you're doing."

I push up from the side of the bath and unlock my cell phone. As I leave, I glance over my shoulder and say, "Me too."

CHAPTER TWELVE

After we eat dinner and get the kids off to bed, I'm wrecked. The vodka mixers and chaos at the barbecue finally catch up with me. I'm about ready to fall asleep on my feet.

I go to bed early. Jack stays up to watch some action film he's been dying to see on Netflix. Beats me how he has the energy or the focus to do so right now.

"Don't be too late, okay?" I tell him.

"I won't," he calls, waving me off without taking his eyes away from the screen. Things are back to normal already.

The kids have been tucked in for an hour or two and haven't made a peep.

I trek up to bed with heavy footsteps. All my joints ache, making me feel ten years older. It's not like I've run a marathon today, but the stress of everything has put a knot into my shoulder blades. I need a massage. Unfortunately, I need to take Dot to kindergarten and Noah to preschool in the morning. Then I have to put in a half day at the library from ten until two, pick up some dry cleaning for Jack, and pick up both kids again from kindergarten and preschool at separate times and separate locations.

Just like a certain orange tabby, I hate Mondays. But the show must go on. I scroll through my cell phone in bed for twenty minutes, knowing I should be reading a book instead, until I've only got less than two per cent battery left. With heavy eyes and a foggy brain, I plug in my phone to charge and fall asleep faster than usual.

Sleep eventually evades me. I start to toss and turn until my sheets tangle around me. An unwelcome darkness envelops my mind like a thick, suffocating blanket.

I'm standing in our backyard in the dead of night, but there's something different about it all. The air feels heavy, like it's been charged with an ominous energy. I sense someone's presence, like a shadow, lurking just beyond my field of vision. I spin around to catch a glimpse of them, but it's like chasing smoke with a net. I can't see who is there, but I know who they are. She's always there. My heart pounds in my ears and almost deafens me.

Then the crying starts. That familiar begging sound I've heard before. It twists into a cruel mocking. It's coming from everywhere and nowhere, surrounding me and closing in. I want to scream and run, but my feet are buried in mud while no sound escapes my lips. The voice pleads with me.

The ground beneath my feet blurs into motion, and I'm no longer in my backyard. Instead, I'm walking on a dark, winding road. The crying gets replaced by the distant hum of a single roaring engine. A set of headlights appear on the road ahead and narrow their beams at me. Someone is behind the wheel of the car. And out of nowhere, I find myself also in a car, driving.

I want to steer away from the approaching death, but I can't. I'm not in control. The driver in the other car wants me dead and is determined to crash into me. I try to exit my car, clutching at the door handle and window buttons, but they won't function. I'm stuck inside.

The lights ahead grow brighter as the distant engine howls louder than before. Then the crying returns. Right as our two vehicles are about to slam into one another, the screech of tires against asphalt fills the air.

We crash. The collision is so visceral; I feel it in my bones. Metal crumples and glass shatters over my face. For a moment, time stands still and is suspended in a heart-stopping silence.

I jolt awake and gasp for air while the remnants of the nightmare cling to my consciousness. The room is silent and safe, but the feeling of dread lingers. It's a persisting cloud that refuses to dissipate, even as I tell myself for the third time that it was all just a dream.

I sit on the edge of the bed with sweat coating my forehead as I regain my breath. "Not again," I whisper. I haven't had that nightmare in years. But I'd be lying if I thought Nicole's sudden arrival wouldn't come without consequences.

With a shaky hand, I reach out and fumble for my cell phone. I yank its charging cable free and watch the screen light up. The brightness of my lock screen stabs at my throbbing retinas. It's a photo of Jack and me with the kids at our sides as we visited Santa at the mall last Christmas. It amazes me how fast my children are growing up. The sight of them calms my racing heart.

I lock my cell phone after seeing that it's close to one in the morning. It's technically tomorrow, but the new day is still a long way off. I settle back into bed, hoping I haven't woken Jack with my thrashing, but then I realize something. There's no one snoring beside me. I reach out and pat the bed on Jack's side. He's not there.

In the dark, my eyes dance around with possibilities. He's not in the toilet. I'd be able to see the light from the bathroom shining in my face. He never shuts the door. Jack is not in this room at all. So, where the hell is he?

My mind runs amok. Has Nicole done something? Has she made her move already? I'd made sure to lock every door and window in the house and set the security alarm. She couldn't get into our home without us knowing about it. I need to calm down and think about things rationally. Jack has probably just fallen asleep on the sofa. It's not like he doesn't do it every other night.

I get up and leave my bedroom. I tiptoe down the corridor to avoid waking the kids. I don't even make it to the stairs when I realize the light to Jack's study is on. Not the main light, but the desk lamp. What is he doing in there at this time of night?

I should turn around and leave him at it, but this nightmare has me all confused. I just want to make sure he's okay.

Quietly, I shuffle along the carpeted flooring and inch closer to Jack's study. When I reach the door, I lean around and find him sitting at his desk with his back toward the door. He's looking at something, but I can't tell what. I inch a bit closer, careful to avoid creating a shadow.

I see him holding a small cardboard box covered in dust. From the open box, he retrieves a dusty Polaroid photograph and holds it up. It's of a person I can't make out from this distance. Not just any person. A woman. After a long gaze, he places the Polaroid back into the box with care and retrieves another. Again, it's another dusty photo of a woman. I squint and see the same person from the last photo, only this time she's cuddled up close with a guy. Who are these people?

These stills can't be of Jack and me. Neither of us has ever owned a Polaroid camera. At least as far as I knew. The only form of printed photos we have are hanging on our walls. The rest are all digital.

Jack holds up the box a little higher, allowing me to read what's written on the side.

College

My hand flies over my mouth to smother any sounds I might make. Why is Jack looking through an old box of Polaroids from college? A box I didn't even know existed? I should confront him and find out what the hell he's playing at, but a voice in the back of my head says stop. For once, I listen to my advice and step away, hiding around the corner.

I can't say anything to Jack. In fact, I'm better off finding out where this trip down memory lane leads, because the last time I checked, we didn't keep old boxes of hidden memories from one another.

With every bit of willpower I have, I retreat to bed. Ten minutes later, Jack comes to bed and fumbles around in the dark. I pretend that I'm out like a light. When he slides into bed, he doesn't press up to me the way he usually does. He doesn't even wrap an arm around my waist or kiss me on the back of the neck. Despite having problems in our marriage, we still manage to hold each other at night. Maybe he's too busy thinking about whoever it was that was in those photos.

No matter what, I need to find that box. I need to find out who he was staring at like that. And I don't know if I can handle what it will mean when I do.

CHAPTER THIRTEEN

The rest of my attempt to sleep is a disaster. I wake up every few hours in a sweat from a fresh nightmare. Each time, I'm back in the same place, but now Jack is in the dream, silently watching my demise as I'm hunted down. Crying and begging fill the air in every vision. Each time I wake, I find Jack beside me, snoring. The sound of him asleep tempts me to go to his study and search for that box. But it's too risky. I'm better off waiting until I have enough uninterrupted time in the morning.

I eventually sleep, but it comes at a cost. I don't hear my first alarm, and when the second one dares to wake me, I turn it off along with the remaining two. I only wanted to rest my eyes for a few minutes, but time gets away from me, and I fall back asleep. I'm not a morning person.

When I finally get up, I'm running late. Jack has already left for the day to his early Monday morning meeting before school. As per usual, it means I'm left to whip the kids into shape on my own. Getting Noah and Dot ready for pre-school and kindergarten is no easy feat. The second I have Noah on task, Dot is asking me a random question or can be found playing with a toy. I push through the headache that's

55

throbbing in my temples and swallow the urge to scream. What's worse is I'm desperate to look in Jack's study and don't have time to do so. Not unless I want both the kids to be late.

Before long, I have Noah and Dot out the door. As we scramble toward my Subaru Forester parked in our driveway, I catch sight of Darell Vargas across the street at number five. He's a self-employed maintenance worker who leaves his messy work truck on the parking strip at the front of his property. He's got a beer belly and dresses like he hasn't showered in months. Frankly, I'm surprised anyone hires him. I often spot him loading up his truck as we leave each morning, but not today. Instead, he's mowing his overgrown lawn. He sees me heading to my car and stops what he is doing to stare.

I think about waving and decide to err on the side of caution. I'm not a hundred per cent sure, but he may have found out who it was that complained about his overgrown lawn. I didn't report him directly to our Homeowners' Association. Instead, I may have mentioned something to Bradley and Gabrielle, who, with enough encouragement, are sticklers for the HOA rules. I could tell Darell's unkempt lawn was annoying them both and that they needed a simple push in the right direction.

Typically, I like to keep to myself and don't care about the way other people in the street choose to present their homes, but I'm ninety-nine per cent sure Darell was the one who clipped my car when I parked it in the street last month. I approached him directly after it happened and looked him in the eye. When I asked if he knew anything about the incident, he practically laughed at me and walked away, saying nothing. He must have worked out I had no proof and knew he would get away with it. Given the way things have been between us since we first met, I thought he was my worst neighbor. I guess I was wrong.

"Mommy?" Noah asks, grabbing my attention.

"Sorry, honey. Mamma was daydreaming." I load the kids into the car and decide to forget about caution. As Darell begrudgingly mows his lawn, I throw him an overly friendly wave and toss him a smile. He can think what he likes about me for all I care. Maybe this will remind him to take better care of his front lawn and to be more alert when he drives.

As I back out into the cul-de-sac, I slam on the brakes when I spot a car parked in Nicole's driveway. And it's not some random vehicle either. It's an old black Audi A3. Of all the cars in the world that could have been parked in her driveway, I never expected to find an old black Audi A3. What kind of sick game is she playing? If Jack saw this car on his way to work . . .

This A3 might not belong to Nicole. With any luck, it's just someone visiting her. In all the confusion yesterday, I don't think I saw anything parked in her driveway. Only a moving truck. Still, this can't be her car. There's no way.

She knew I would see it when I backed out of my driveway.

With little time to spare, I rush the kids to school. Since her school is the closest to the house, I drop Dot off first, so I have to unload Noah from the car to walk Dot inside before traveling five minutes down the road to Noah's preschool. He's good for most drop-offs, but every so often, his lips quiver on arrival and his eyes get watery. Then there's a fifty per cent chance he'll burst into tears when I try to leave.

"I'll be back before you know it, okay?"

"Okay, Mommy," he says, putting on a brave face. He knows how to break my heart. If we didn't need the money, I'd quit my job and keep him at home until he was older.

Once I climb back into my car after dropping both kids off, it's almost nine. I'm not due to start my half day at the library until ten, and there's a decent café close by. Ellie doesn't work Mondays, so we like to meet up for a quick coffee and a chat before I head off to my shift. Ellie texted me earlier to confirm if I'd be at the café. No doubt she is desperate to learn the truth about what happened at the barbecue yesterday. It's going to be impossible not to say anything. In all honesty, I'd rather be home alone with some time to search for the box

Jack was poring over last night, but then again, I'm terrified of what I might find. Maybe a good chat is the better option.

Last night, I was too far away from Jack to determine who was in the Polaroids he was gazing at, but I think I can guess. It sounds impossible considering how much he hates her, but I have a feeling Jack was looking at old photos of himself with Nicole. Photos he felt the need to hide from me. Could there still be something there, despite everything that has happened? They were in a relationship. Young love can be hard to forget. Surely, though, he couldn't look past how it all ended?

Ellie sends me a new text saying she's almost at the café. I look forward to the day when Noah is in the same school as Dot.

Ellie's two are enrolled at a different school than the one Dot attends. I had wanted to send Dot to the same school, but it was more convenient for her, and soon Noah, to attend the same one where Jack teaches. If Jack doesn't have any meetings, he's able to take Dot to school and bring her home.

Ten minutes later, I meet with Ellie at Cinnamon Whispers Café. The place has a terrible name, but they serve a decent cup of coffee. Plus, one of the baristas always gives us a discount. I think he has a crush on Ellie. The man is almost half her age, but that and the fact that she is married doesn't seem to stop him. I figure it's harmless, so I've never told Jack about it. If I did, I know he would feel compelled to tell David. Those two share everything. It wouldn't surprise me if Jack had blabbed about Nicole to him already.

"Hey, you," Ellie says, brushing at her fringe as I find her inside the café at our usual table.

I say hello and drop into my chair with a heavy sigh, placing my bag at my side. I only have about thirty minutes before I'll need to get myself to work. Despite the short time, these thirty minutes are crucial for me today, especially after the crappy night I had. What I do at the library isn't taxing, and I really enjoy it most days, but when I combine it with everything else that needs doing on a Monday, I'm left drained by sundown.

Ellie has already ordered for us both, seeing as she knows what I like, so it doesn't take long before we receive our coffees and some freshly baked croissants.

"So," Ellie says, leaning down in a hushed tone. Here it comes. "Tell me everything about Nicole."

I hate always being right. But I also should have known better than to meet Ellie at a café after yesterday.

"Well?" Ellie presses. "Dish."

I shouldn't say anything. We did promise Nicole that we would keep the past in the past. But Ellie's my best friend. I have to tell her what's going on. At least some of it. "If you don't want to get into things, that's fine. But I know you guys have all met before. The expression on your faces said it all. I wouldn't be surprised if—"

"She's Jack's ex," I blurt. Regret fills me in a heartbeat. I could have gone with anything else. But I came right out and said that Nicole is Jack's ex. Idiot.

"Jack's ex?" Ellie asks, beaming. "Are you serious?"

"Yes," I say, slumping down.

"That's wild. Oh my God. Now she's your neighbor."

"Apparently."

Ellie chuckles to herself as she stirs her latte.

"Is this funny to you?"

"I'm sorry, Bee. I don't mean to laugh, but what are the chances, right?" Ellie stares at me. I try to hide my thoughts from her.

"Wait," she continues. "You don't think it's a coincidence at all, do you? Oh my God."

I hold my stare for as long as I can, but it's like holding my breath underwater. I have to look away before she gleans more from my apparent stress. I have the urge to spill what I know and tell my friend about the darkest time in my life, but instead, I say, "It's a cruel coincidence. Nothing more."

Ellie stares at me for a beat longer. "Well, that's a relief, I suppose. So which ex is she?"

Again, I have to tread carefully. Ellie knows that Jack dated a few people in college. We've spent years talking to

59

each other about our lives. It's one thing for people to learn that Nicole and Jack were together in the past, but it's an entirely different can of worms for them to hear the rest of their awful history. I settle on something simple.

"Just an ex. I don't know much about her, sorry."

"Oh, okay. As long as she's not that one who, you know . . ."

"It's not her."

"Good. That would be awful."

I force a smile. "Yeah." I may have told Ellie some details about Nicole in the past. To keep things simple, I never mentioned her name. And there are a lot of details I kept out. Things only a few people know. I shouldn't have said a word, but I couldn't help it. That time of our lives was riddled with drama.

I avoid Ellie's gaze for as long as I can. But when I glance up at her, she's staring right through my facade. She knows there's more to the story.

"So what are you going to do?" she asks.

"Nothing. She's our neighbor. That's all."

"For now. What happens if she makes a move on Jack? I mean, why else would she buy number six?"

"Maybe she likes to renovate old places?" I say, forcing a shrug.

"Uh-huh, sure."

I take a gulp of my coffee and wonder how long it will be before everything with Nicole comes out. Word travels fast in Maple Court. I could make Ellie swear on her two children to keep this between us, but she wouldn't be able to resist. At the very least, she would tell David — assuming he doesn't already know. Then, they each might tell one other person. Given how nosey some of our neighbors can be, it wouldn't be long before everyone found out that Nicole and Jack once dated. Then they would learn about the rest of the sordid saga.

We chat for a while more about work and our husbands' annoying habits.

Ellie tries to extract more out of me about Nicole, but I stand firm. She knows I'll cave soon enough. The truth is, I don't want it all to come out. If Nicole would sell number six, leave this place, and never contact any of us again, it would be the best outcome for us all. I don't want to think about that time, or Nicole, or—

The alarm on my cell phone buzzes, pulling me from my thoughts. I'm out of time and need to run. I tell Ellie to do her best to keep what I've told her so far to herself. She promises to guard my secret, but I sense a glint in her eye that tells me otherwise. It's a problem for another day. Right now, I need to rush to the library. Hopefully, working for four hours will take my mind off my problems. The library is one of the few places where I can manage such a feat.

As I head to my car, a shudder runs down my spine. The feeling spins me around in all directions. I can't explain it, but I swear I'm being watched. No one is nearby, though.

I see the hint of a dark car rush by me, but I don't take in its details. Not wanting to take a chance, I hurry to my car and scramble inside. I make sure the doors are locked once I get in.

Is this how things are going to be from now on? Am I doomed to spend the rest of my life looking over my shoulder? Nicole seemed so relaxed when we spoke. Would she really try to harm me now?

Maybe.

Or maybe I'm letting the past control me. Still, I need to be careful. If Nicole is watching me, she's learning my routine and the places I go. Besides, it wouldn't be hard for her to come between Jack and me. Our marriage is fragile. I just have to pray that Jack still hates her enough for it to never happen.

CHAPTER FOURTEEN

Eighteen years ago

The corridor was silent, save for the faint buzz of an overhead light. My heart hammered in my chest and echoed in my ears as I stood outside the dorm room — Jack's room.

His door loomed before me. It was a barrier to his world. One I had once crossed into freely. Now, I was nothing but a stranger who needed permission to enter.

I took a heavy breath and steadied my nerves. I shouldn't have been afraid. Deep down, I knew this was what he wanted. Everything he was doing was a test to see if I was worthy of him. No other possibility made sense.

I slipped a copied key into the lock, one that took me long enough to acquire without Jack's knowledge. The barrel and key turned with a soft click and unlocked the wall that separated my life from his.

After I stepped inside Jack's room, I closed the door gently behind me. I needed privacy and time alone to be here. I didn't want some concerned nobody interrupting me.

The room was as I remembered it — lived in with that unmistakable scent of books, laundry detergent, and a hint of cologne. Jack's scent. I inhaled the aroma and exhaled a shaky breath as I was flooded with memories. It was like a drug I could never get enough of. I could have basked in his space all day and breathed only his air, but I had little time. Jack and his roommate were in class, and sometimes students left lectures early.

My eyes roamed the room and took in the single beds that sat opposite each other. One was neatly made and undoubtedly belonged to Jack's boring roommate. The other was Jack's and was in a state of disarray. The sight brought a smile to my face despite the circumstances. This chaos he lived with made him feel more real to me than anyone I'd ever known. But then again, he wasn't always this way.

My gaze landed on Jack's desk. It was cluttered with textbooks and scrawled notes. I picked through each one and saw his thought process and his ambitious ideas. Promise existed on those pages. I recognized Jack would achieve remarkable things. And I believed he would one day leave this campus, shape minds, and make the world a better place. I would be by his side when that day came.

My hands stopped when I found what I wanted. Among the disorder of Jack's desk, I discovered a photograph sitting in a simple frame. It was of him . . . and her — that bitch from the quad. The girl he thought he loved. But he didn't know what it meant to love a person. Not yet.

Something inside me tightened. An intense disdain overtook my soul as I stared at her in the picture. She was smiling and gazing up at him as he held her, her eyes full of adoration. This moment of intimacy was frozen in time, and I wasn't a part of it. It should have been me in this photograph, but this girl had stolen my place and was now sharing a life with Jack that used to be ours. What happened to our photos? What happened to our captured moments? Had they all been destroyed?

I snatched the frame from the desk and was ready to smash it to the ground. But I stopped when I saw his eyes staring at me. My fingers traced Jack in the photograph as I covered her with my thumb. I would return to this frame soon enough.

I placed the photo down and stepped away from his desk. As I did, I brushed against Jack's hoodie that was draped over his desk chair. Taking a moment, I folded it for him. It was a minor act of care I knew he would notice. Once we were back together, I would show him how to be neat again. This slob he replaced me with was a bad influence on his organizational skills. Her laziness was rubbing off. I needed to act fast to save him.

I slipped a note into the front pocket of the hoodie, just like the one I left him at the café that read J + N forever.

Looking around, I memorized the details of his half of the room and sucked in a last breath. It would have to quench me for some time. I could only do this every so often without someone noticing. Once I was done, I crept out of the room and locked the door behind me.

As I walked away, I was overrun with guilt and longing. I had crossed a line today; I knew it. But in the silence of Jack's space, amidst his absence, I hoped what I had done would keep our connection alive.

Soon, I wouldn't have to sneak into his room when he was away. This would be our space once more, and she would never enter it again.

CHAPTER FIFTEEN

Present day

After what felt like an endless day of work and running around, I drive the kids home and have an hour at my disposal before I need to start on dinner. Jack won't be home until at least five, as he has some scheduled planning time after school on Mondays. With a hangover chasing him all day long, I'll bet he is regretting how many beers he had yesterday.

We've got less than two weeks left before the summer break starts, which means the usual routine will soon go out the window until it's time to take Noah back to preschool. We like to keep his routine going, so he doesn't get the big break like Dot and Jack do from school. I will also need to put in extra shifts at the library since we run special programs over the summer break. Fortunately, Jack will be available to help at home.

When we pile in through the door, Noah and Dot still have bundles of energy to burn. I'd love to dump them in front of the TV for long enough to poke around Jack's study, but I can only pull that trick off so many times before my motherly guilt sets in. Besides, I missed them today.

The kids each tug at my arms and heave me toward the back door. "Mommy, let's play outside!" Dot yells with wide eyes. Noah jumps up and down in agreement, eager to drag me to the backyard as well.

"Okay, okay," I tell them. I smile, trying to let the warmth of their excitement melt away the concerns I have about Nicole and Jack and that damn box. With any luck, the kids will keep my thoughts occupied.

"Outside we go," I say.

We rush through the door that opens to our backyard. A cool embrace of the Seattle air greets us. It's not as warm as it was yesterday, being early June, but the summer is only beginning. The kids soon overload me with play. I'm commanded to do this and that and act out all kinds of scenarios. Within twenty minutes, I'm sapped of energy and need a rest. Noah and Dot continue to play and make enough noise that a passerby would assume there was an ax-murderer in the area. The thought inevitably makes me think about Nicole.

I stare at the fence we now share and shudder at the thought of how close she is to us, to my babies. Where do Noah and Dot fit in with her plans?

As the sun gets lower in the sky, I take Noah and Dot back inside. They complain as if they've been locked in a cage all day, but I still need to make dinner and get on with the rest of our nightly routine. Plus, I can't leave them out here alone. Not anymore.

As I pull the door to the backyard shut, my cell phone rings. It's Jack. "Hey, honey," he says. "Have you started making dinner yet?"

"I was just about to. Why? Is something wrong?" As I ask, I remember him in his study last night. I can't forget the way he was gazing at those Polaroids.

"Nothing's wrong. Dave called me a few minutes ago. He said he wants to head out for a drink."

"Right now? Didn't you two spend enough time drinking together yesterday?"

"We did, but . . ."

"But?" I ask, holding back on anything more. The therapist said we should never assume the worst about each other which, unfortunately, is easier said than done.

"I probably shouldn't be telling you this, but he's going through some . . . stuff."

"Stuff?" I think about Dave at the barbecue yesterday. He seemed to enjoy himself well enough. And Ellie didn't appear to be anxious about anything major. She was only concerned with the secret she knew I was hiding. Dave might as well have been at home.

"I can't get into it," Jack continues. "It's private. But trust me, he's not his usual self today. I thought maybe it would be best if I took him out to a bar for a few hours. We won't be too late."

"You thought? You just said that he called you, that this was his idea?" I ask the question with a flat voice, working hard not to become emotional.

"Sorry. That's what I meant. I was just trying to keep things with Dave under wraps. You know how he is."

I hold my phone away from my head for a second and ask myself a silent "what?" Dave isn't like anything. He's Dave. If I were to describe Dave in one word, it would be apathetic.

I return the phone to my face and wait for Jack to speak again. He doesn't make a sound like he's waiting for me to give him permission to go out. "Okay, then," I say. "Have a nice time, I guess. I'll leave your dinner in the oven."

"Thanks, honey. You're the best. Love you."

"Love—"

He hangs up before the end of my reply is even uttered, leaving me holding my cell phone to my ear. I lower the device and stare ahead with only one thought on my mind: is Jack lying to me?

CHAPTER SIXTEEN

With the possibility of Jack lying to me still fresh in my mind, I get dinner underway. I cut up some vegetables for the steak I had planned on making — the steak that I left out to thaw just for him. It's his favorite meal, and it's now going to go to waste.

The kids are in the living room watching TV. I held out for as long as I could. Either way, I need them occupied so I can make dinner in peace and hopefully distract myself. Don't get me wrong, I love Dot and Noah more than anything else in this life, but some days, they have more words for me than I can process. And today is not a good day for my patience to be tested.

As I stand at the island bench chopping the vegetables, my eyes focus on the window to my side. The curtain is still closed the way I left it, but behind the material, Nicole lives there. I can't help but imagine she's in her home right now, staring at me through her open windows with a sneer. Is she thinking about the barbecue yesterday? How she rattled my cage?

Once or twice, I've taken a quick peek through my bedroom window upstairs to see what Nicole is up to. She still hasn't put a single curtain up in her home, so it's easy to spy on her. Not that I want to.

Thoughts of Nicole make me think of my husband. Why do I think Jack lied to me on the phone? And in such a lousy way? I don't know what he's really up to, but something tells me Dave has nothing to do with it. There were holes in Jack's story, and I don't know what I should do.

I've been in this position before.

"Ow," I yell when the knife slices my thumb. The pain is instant and blood flows from the cut a second later. I drop the sharp blade on the bench and grab hold of my thumb, squeezing it tight. I wrap a nearby dish towel around the wound to stop the bleeding. It's not an elegant solution, but it does the job.

With one hand, I fumble for the first-aid kit we have under the kitchen sink and slap a bandage onto the cut. The pain, in its own way, is a distraction, but it's not the one I was looking for.

As I stare at the blood that has leaked through the dish towel, all I can think about is Jack. Is he meeting up with someone, a person who isn't Dave? Is he meeting up with Nicole?

"No," I say, shaking my head, almost laughing. Jack hates her. He wishes she was dead. He wouldn't be out there hooking up with another woman. Not again.

It pains me to think about it, but Jack has been unfaithful in our marriage. I like to think of the whole thing as a moment of weakness, one I have since forgiven him for. Unfortunately, it was only a short while ago. Surely, he hasn't slipped again? He promised me it was a one-time mistake that would never happen again.

"Mommy?" Noah asks, seeing me hurt. "You 'kay?"

"Oh, Mamma's fine, baby. I just have a little boo-boo. Nothing to worry about."

"That blood?" he asks in his fractured toddler speak, squirming at the sight of the dish towel. The tiniest pinprick is enough to fluster him.

"Yeah, honey. But I'm okay. I'll be fine."

"Yucky," he says with a smile. Thankfully, injuries on other people don't seem to bother him as much. I ruffle his hair and beam at his sweet innocence.

"Mommy, I hungry," Noah says, moving on from the incident like it never happened.

"I'm making dinner. It won't be long."

"But . . . I hungry."

"You'll survive, baby. Why don't you go watch some more TV with Dot? Before you know it, dinner will be ready."

"Okay," he says, half-deflated. He runs back to the living room as fast as his little legs can take him. If I could, I'd keep him at this age forever. Sure, there are days when he is difficult and throws a tantrum for next to no reason, but when I stare into those beautiful eyes of his, my heart melts.

I go back to making dinner with a throbbing thumb. Cutting what's left of the vegetables becomes a painful task, but I push through it. The kids are having chicken nuggets instead of steak. With my steaks and vegetables ready to be cooked, I have everything in place. But the same nagging thought comes back to me. One that seemed impossible only a few days ago. What if Jack really is meeting with Nicole?

I sit down in the kitchen and try to remember if I saw the black Audi A3 in her driveway when we got home. Why didn't I think to look for it? Not that the car would have told me much. She could have it parked in her garage — if it's even her car to begin with. The very idea of Nicole owning that vehicle is downright absurd. Besides, I have a much easier way to see if Nicole is home.

I step away from my dinner preparations and move closer to the kitchen curtain I've kept shut since we rushed home from the barbecue. As I reach out to touch the material, thoughts of college and the hell Jack and I went through enter my mind. If Nicole catches me spying on her, what will the repercussions be? Do I want to find out? Do I want to go through it all again?

I stop my trembling hand and take a breath, leaving the curtain alone. There is another way to see what Jack is up to. And it doesn't involve Nicole.

CHAPTER SEVENTEEN

I cook the steak and vegetables, then pick up my cell phone. With a sore thumb, I type out a message and send it to Ellie. Being as subtle as I can, I joke in the text about how Jack and Dave can't seem to get enough of each other, and that I can't believe they wanted to go out to a bar after yesterday. As I wait for a reply, time slows to a crawl. Without thinking, my thumb lifts to my mouth. I attempt to bite a nail and stop when pain shoots through my entire hand, reminding me of the damn cut.

"Ow, ow, ow," I let out before sucking in air through my teeth. The knife sliced through me with ease. And all because my own thoughts distracted me.

"Come on, Ellie," I say as I pace the length of our island bench and stare at my unlocked cell on the surface. She could be busy doing a million different things. Or maybe Dave is at home already, leaving her to wonder what the hell I'm on about. I could be putting her in an awkward position. But I don't care. As painful as it might be, I need the truth.

The woman Jack risked our marriage for appears in my thoughts. At least the concept of her. I never saw who she was in the flesh, but Jack slept with someone else. The bastard went behind my back and betrayed me in the worst way possible. Most days, I try to imagine it never happened, that such a thing never happened.

I don't know how we survived it, but we did. We came through. Hell, I came through. And for what? Lately, all we seem to do is fight. I'm sure I'm harboring some resentment, but I do my best to keep going. And not only for my sake, but for the kids. I don't want them to go through a chaotic divorce at such a tender age. I did when I was young, and it was awful. At first, I thought it was great. I got more presents for my birthday, and both of my parents acted like my best friends. I never got into trouble for anything.

Putting thoughts of divorce aside, I love Jack. I always will. In fact, I couldn't imagine what my life would be like without him. Even so, I can't go on if he is doing what I think he's doing. And with Nicole? No way. I must be delirious. He hates her more than he's ever despised another human being. How could he want to be with someone who wronged him in such a horrible way?

My phone buzzes. It had better be Ellie texting me back. I snatch my cell phone from the bench and find her name on my lock screen. Thank God. I read her reply.

Thankfully, it's nothing sinister. She knows all about the after-work drinks. According to her, it was Jack's idea. I shake my head. Apparently, Dave is also a terrible liar. I guess they really wanted to go out for a drink after work and wanted to avoid a heated discussion with a disapproving wife.

"Pathetic," I say with a chuckle. Then I close my eyes and remember to breathe. There's nothing to worry about. Well, there's still the matter of the box in Jack's study, but I'll figure that out later. Jack won't be home for a few hours, so I have plenty of time to investigate.

I make dinner and serve it to the kids, Jack's plate left in the oven. I doubt he'll touch it when he comes home, whatever time that may be. When he drinks at night, even if it's only a few beers with a friend, he doesn't like to have dinner.

The kids chat and poke at their dinners, as usual. Noah is a terrible eater on a good day. He makes a mess of things and only eats half of his chicken nuggets. I try to make him eat a few mouthfuls of vegetables, but it's like pulling teeth. At the barbecue, he was more than happy to eat junk all afternoon.

After dinner, I go through the usual frantic mess of bathing Noah while Dot showers. After an hour of hell, I take them to bed. Then I tidy up the kitchen and living room.

Doing it all on my own, as I did this morning, is an immense effort. I take a long shower to unwind and dress for bed. By the time I fall onto the sofa in the living room, I'm beat.

I check my cell phone and see no messages or calls from Jack. He's still out with Dave. At least I hope it's Dave. There's still a part of me that has doubts. Would Dave help Jack do the unthinkable to me? We had only been in Maple Court for a few months when Jack cheated, but I have no reason to think Dave was involved.

I think back to that time. We had just conceived Noah. Despite it being a planned pregnancy, he didn't take the news well. It wasn't like we couldn't afford it. For whatever reason, he went off the deep end and settled his feelings by spending a night with some whore.

"Everything is fine," I tell myself, knowing I need to put the idea of Jack being unfaithful out of my head. Besides, I have a mystery to solve. As much as I'd love to relax on my own for the evening and read a book, I should go to Jack's study and look for that damn box.

For all I know, the pictures in the college box could be ones of us. Maybe Jack went back through our digital collection and had them turned into Polaroids. I'm not sure if such a thing is even possible. Most likely not, but it's a hope worth clinging to.

I turn the TV on to drown out any noise and head upstairs with my cell phone in my back pocket. I shouldn't be doing this, but I need to know. It still feels unbelievable that she's here. After all the crap that went on in college, you'd think she'd be reluctant to speak with us. The police handcuffed her in public. Everyone on campus found out about it.

Even though Jack isn't home, I move as quietly as I can upstairs. I don't want to disturb the kids. Noah will be out like a light, but Dot might still be wide awake in her room, reading books or playing with her dolls. I can't have either of them stumble in on me searching through their daddy's things, so I do a quick check in each of their rooms and find them both asleep.

When I reach my husband's study, I head inside and close the door.

I don't want Jack to think I've been in his study, so I take my time to shift and move things around. Like a spy in a cheap movie, I note the angles of things like his chair and laptop. I try hard not to disturb anything. Not that Jack is all that observant.

Inside one drawer, I find an item I had forgotten was there: the bracelet Jack has kept for eighteen years. It's a simple piece with a single letter charm attached to it. My hand reaches out to touch the letter, but the thought of touching the "K" sends a chill down my spine. I haven't thought about Kara or seen this bracelet in a long time. And for good reason. The drawer slams shut as a result. I have enough to deal with as it is.

I don't find the box. It's not in his desk or up in the storage compartment along the side wall of the room. He either keeps it somewhere else or it's vanished into thin air.

After twenty minutes of checking the same spaces repeatedly, I start to question my sanity. Did I walk in on him looking at photos from a box marked "college" last night? Or was that all part of my nightmare? I swear to God I was awake.

Sitting at Jack's desk, I'm nearly ready to give up when I notice something is off about his chair. Jack's desk chair sits on a chair mat, but it seems to sit up higher than it should. I stand and roll the chair to the side, then move the plastic square. Once I do, I find an extra section of carpet that has been placed under the square. And it looks like it was recently moved out of position.

74

It couldn't be this simple, could it? I run a hand through my hair and drop to my knees. Taking a corner in both hands, I roll the carpet away and find what appears to be a small trapdoor that's inset into the existing carpet. It's no bigger than a foot wide in each direction. And there's no lock. Just a handle that fits into the lid to create a flush surface.

"You've got to be kidding me," I let out. Am I dreaming again? Is this another nightmare?

With a racing pulse, I reach down and loop a finger through the trapdoor's handle. I lift it with no resistance. There isn't some hidden lock or failsafe. It's just a door covered by a matching off-cut piece of carpet. I clean this house week in and week out, yet I've never noticed this before. What else has escaped me?

As I lift the door, my cell phone rings in my back pocket, startling me enough to fumble my grip. The trapdoor slams shut and makes a thudding noise. Hopefully, the kids haven't heard the racket.

Stumbling, I retrieve my phone and discover Jack is calling. This is early for him. "Crap." Is there a nanny camera in his study I wasn't aware of? Is he calling to let me know he's caught me in the act?

My cell phone ignores my questions and continues to ring. I need to answer so Jack doesn't think I've been snooping around the house while he's out. Not that a missed call would mean such a thing. I'm overthinking this.

"Hi," I say. "Is everything okay?"

"Hey, babe. Sorry to bother you, but I left my keys at school."

"Your keys?" I ask, confused.

"Oh, right. You don't know. We got an Uber home. Had too many drinks to drive. I mean, we had too many drinks and left our cars at work. I forgot my keys. Can you let me in when I get there?"

"Uh, yeah. No problem," I say, staring at the trapdoor.

"Should be home in a minute or two."

"What? Already?" I let out, not meaning to.

"Yeah. Don't you miss me?" he asks, his words slurring.

"Of course. I guess I thought you'd call or text when you left the bar."

"I know, I know. Please accept my humble apologies."

I let my phone drift away from my face as Dave laughs in the background. At least I now know Jack was out with him, getting drunk on a Monday night.

"We are in Maple Court," Jack says. "I will see you soon, my love."

He hangs up on me before I can protest. I have to hurry to put Jack's study back in order, then rush down to the front door. But the trapdoor stares at me, begging to be opened. It would only take a second to see what's inside.

My fingers hover over the trapdoor.

CHAPTER EIGHTEEN

Eighteen years ago

The corridor was silent. The only sound I heard was the faint buzz of an overhead light. My heart raced, its beats echoing in my ears as I stood before yet another barrier — a door that led into her world, Jack's pathetic girlfriend. This was her dorm room.

I steadied my breath, knowing I had the right to be here. This was all part of his test. Jack's test. He wanted to challenge me to discover how far I would go. And I would prove myself worthy. What Jack and I had was unbreakable. His current entanglement was nothing but a detour in our path to perfection. Soon, it would run its course.

I stole her key when she was in class. With a disguise on, I sat next to her during a lecture I wasn't supposed to attend and waited for the right moment to strike. It was an extreme risk to take, but one worth taking.

I didn't bother to make a copy of the key like I did with Jack's. I wanted her to know that someone had taken her keys. That she wasn't safe simply because she was dating my Jack.

The key slid into the lock and turned with a whisper of a click, unlocking the door. Ever mindful of her roommate, I opened the entrance an inch and peeked inside. There was no one inside. As planned, both girls would have been in class.

I stepped into the room, easing the door shut with practiced ease a moment later. I was getting good at this. Jack would have been so impressed. If only he could see me. If only he were watching through the window from across the way, he would understand what I was capable of. Then again, maybe he was watching.

In an instant, the room assaulted my senses. Unlike Jack's familiar chaos, her mess was jarring. It was a harsh reminder of the influence she held over him.

Her clothes were strewn about without care, her books were piled into haphazard towers, and amidst it all, there was a scent that was distinctly not Jack's. It was foreign and invasive, and each breath sent a pang of nausea through me.

My eyes, though, were ever drawn to the evidence of Jack's existence here. I found my target on her desk. It was as cluttered as the rest of her disgusting world.

Between the chaos, I saw it — a photograph. Just like one I had discovered in Jack's room. A perfect copy. But this one ignited a firestorm of loathing within me. There she was again with that damn smile, captured in a moment that should have been mine. A whore's smile. My fingers itched to tear the image to shreds, to erase her presence from Jack's life. But I paused, the rage simmering into something cold and calculated. Destruction was easy and quick. Instead, I took the photograph and shoved it into my bag, leaving the frame. It was now mine. A trophy. A token and a promise of the deliverance to come.

I didn't leave any other sign of my existence. No note slipped into a hoodie — no words that were a declaration of my intent. If I did, she would have known what true fear was.

As I made my way out, locking the door behind me, adrenaline coursed through my veins. Today, I had crossed a line from which there was no return. But it was in the fight for Jack — the fight for us. In that time and space, nothing was off limits. Nothing was too extreme.

The photograph in my bag felt like a weight. I would keep it as a reminder of the battles to come, of the war I needed to wage. Not only against her, but against the very idea of Jack choosing another person over me.

He would understand, in time. He would see the truth of my actions, and the depths of my love. And she — she would be nothing but a forgotten nobody in our story.

As I blended back into the anonymity of the corridor, the echo of my footsteps reminded me of the path ahead. Every step required purpose. A single one out of place could spell the end. I wouldn't fail him. Not again. For the promise of our future, I was ready to face any storm.

CHAPTER NINETEEN

Present day

I can't help myself. I lift the trapdoor all the way open despite having no time. Jack's Uber has already arrived and is idling in the street. Jack and Dave's voices fill the night as they noisily climb out of the car and laugh with each other. I should be down there, disabling the security system and unlocking the front door for my drunk husband, but instead, I'm here, staring at an empty compartment that's been built into the floor of Jack's study.

"What the hell?" I ask myself, trying to make sense of my findings. There's nothing inside the trapdoor. Just a void.

With no time to think, I shut the compartment and roll the carpet square back into place. Then I refit the plastic, reposition Jack's chair as best I can, and pray there's nothing I've forgotten to reset in the room.

Trying not to make noise, I rush downstairs and disable the security system. Next, I fumble to unlock the front door. When I open it, I see Jack and Dave chatting away at the end of our driveway, loud enough for every household in Maple Court to hear them. I head out to the tipsy pair, knowing I need to get Jack inside and David home to Ellie before someone complains.

"Have a good time?" I ask them as I make my approach. My hands are wrapped around my body and tucked under my armpits to fight off the cool breeze.

"There she is," Dave calls out. He seems fine considering what Jack had to say about his emotionally needy friend before.

"Here I am," I say, ignoring Dave as I stare at Jack. He's got a relaxed smile on his face, and the tie he wears to school is missing. They've definitely been out drinking. It's a relief, but the feeling doesn't last when I think about what I found in Jack's study. Or, more importantly, what I didn't find.

The hidden compartment looked big enough to store the "college" box he had out in the middle of the night. So where is it? And why did Jack feel the need to move it? My questions make me wonder if he heard me sneaking around when I stole back to our room last night.

"Hey, honey," Jack says, stepping closer to me. He plants a kiss on my cheek that is enveloped in a cloud of booze. It smells like he's had more than a few drinks.

"Hi," I say, half holding my breath. "Did you have fun?"

Dave throws his arm around Jack's shoulders and points a finger at his chest. "Do not let this man take you out for a drink. You'll end up drunk." Dave bursts out laughing at his own joke, and Jack joins in. I pull away from them both and walk toward the house.

"Goodnight, David," I say without glancing back. I'll be dealing with Jack for the next hour or so until he either passes out on the sofa or our bed. As usual, he'll be extra chatty and will most likely make a move for sex. After discovering that strange hiding place in his office, I'm not in the mood.

Jack and David joke some more before Jack finally stumbles inside after me. He shuts the front door too hard and knocks into a wall on his way to the kitchen. When he finds me, I'm making him some coffee. He needs to sober up. We're

81

not in our twenties anymore. Two days in a row of drinking could see him home sick from work. The school won't be thrilled about him taking time off so close to summer break.

"I'm starved," Jack says, much to my surprise.

"Your dinner's in the oven. I can heat it up for you."

"No need. Some days I like it cold, you know?"

"Okay," I reply, unsure why he would want to eat cold food. I shake off the thought and figure it's the alcohol talking. Jack often says dumb things when he's drunk. I fetch his dinner and ask him again if he wants it heated.

"No, no, no. This is perfect. Just the way it is. Like you, my love."

"Thanks," I say, dragging the word out. I'm unsure how to take a compliment where I'm likened to a cold dinner. I set his plate down on the bench with a knife and fork. "Let me pour you some coffee."

"Water's fine," he says. "No need to go to the trouble."

"If you say so," I grumble as I take a glass from the cupboard and fill it with water from the tap. I set it down beside his plate and can't help but feel annoyed about the coffee. I know water is important for dehydration, but I also want him to sober up.

"So, get up to anything interesting while I was out?" he asks, picking up his plate of food like a kid eating a slice of birthday cake.

Halfway to the fridge, I freeze. "Uh, not much," I say. "Just got the kids off to bed. Watched some TV. The usual." I keep walking to the fridge and open it. Inside, I retrieve a jug of filtered water for myself.

"What did you watch?" Jack asks with a mouth full of food.

Crap. The TV is still on, and I don't remember what channel I had it set to.

"Oh, nothing. I mostly was on my phone, to be honest. I had the TV on for the background noise. Guess I missed you."

"Aww," Jack says, half swallowing his food. He's asking me a lot of questions. Usually, after a night out with Dave, he talks about himself or 'the idiots at work.' He's never all that interested in me. Why does he want to know what I've been doing?

"Well, I'm here now," he says, placing the meal down on our island bench. He opens his arms wide for a hug. I move toward him and accept his hug, his powerful arms as wrap around me and squeeze tight.

Normally, this is my favorite place to be. Even when Jack pisses me off, I still want him to hold me. It makes me feel safe. But right now, I don't trust him. He's keeping secrets from me again, just like when he was cheating. His behavior is as suspicious now as it had been back then.

Jack always claimed that his cheating was a spur-of-the-moment thing. He'd gone out one night, not with Dave or anyone else, but alone. He'd told me he was going to a teacher's conference for history teachers. But the event was being held at night on a weekday. Something didn't add up. The naïve wife that I was, I gave Jack the benefit of the doubt and believed him. But when he got home, I found a smudge of lipstick on his neck. I could also smell another woman on his clothing. He didn't even try to hide it.

I confronted him right then and there. Without much prodding, he admitted everything. There was no teacher's conference. He'd gone out to a bar and met a random woman. One thing led to another, and he slept with her at some cheap hotel, paying cash for the room.

"It was a one-time thing. I swear," Jack had said. I barely remember what came out of my mouth after his pathetic excuse, but it involved a lot of swearing and yelling. He begged and pleaded for my forgiveness, dropping to his knees like a pitiful worm. I refused to hear what he had to say and was ready to file for divorce. Then Dot came out from her room, rubbing her eyes as she asked me what was going on. I tried to explain to Dot why Mommy and Daddy were yelling without telling her much. If it wasn't for that forlorn expression on her face and the baby in my belly, I would have left Jack without a second thought.

Over the next three months, I forgave him. We repaired our relationship one strand at a time. It wasn't easy, but I did it for the kids more than anyone else. I had opposition along the way. My mother had a firm opinion on the matter, but her bias was understandable considering my father had done the same thing to her. Ellie told me it would be a deal breaker if Dave ever did something so stupid, but she understood why I chose to stay. Even my co-worker Sophia weighed in on the issue, encouraging me to kick Jack to the curb. I probably shouldn't have told her about it, but I couldn't help myself. It took my all not to listen, but the thing that sealed the deal was the annoying fact that I still loved him.

I still do. I always will.

"Let's go to bed," Jack says. I feel his voice rumble in his chest and can't resist. Maybe I'm overreacting to everything. Maybe I need to let the past stay where it belongs and not let my experiences throw me into a state of paranoia.

"Okay." I smile up at him. He kisses me and it deepens into something more. Something heated. He lifts me up to an empty section of the island bench and cradles my head in both hands. His tongue is on mine, and I don't tell him to stop. Despite my fears and concerns, this is the most passion I've felt from him in months. I know he's been drinking, but I don't care. We need this. I need this.

Jack looks at me like I belong to him and no one else. He drags me upstairs and takes me to bed. We make love the way we used to, back before the kids, back before we had responsibilities and a mortgage to consume our waking thoughts.

For twenty minutes, I forget all about Nicole, one-night stands, secret boxes, and hidden compartments.

CHAPTER TWENTY

"Wow," is all I can utter when we finish. Jack and I are on our backs, sweating and panting.

"That was—"

"Amazing," he says, finishing my sentence.

"Yeah. Where did that come from?" I don't mean to ask the question out loud, but it escapes my lips.

"I don't know. I can't explain it. Well, I do know, but . . ."

"But what?" I ask, turning to face him in the half-light. He still sounds a little tipsy, but not as much as he was before.

He glances at me and appears almost shy. "Promise you won't get mad?"

"Okay. I'll try."

"Okay, as in you'll try not to get mad, or okay, you'll promise?"

"Both."

Jack chuckles. "All right. Here goes." He takes a deep breath. "After seeing Nicole yesterday, it got me thinking."

I sit further upright with my eyes wide open. Every word he just spoke has me on edge, ready for anything. Jack continues.

"She came so close to destroying us in the past, I believe she's here to try again. And even if she's not, even if this is all some crazy coincidence, these last few days have made me realize how much I don't want to lose you. Ever."

I shuffle closer to him and place an arm on his bare chest. "I get it. I really do. She was responsible for the worst time in our lives. And now she's back to do God knows what. I don't trust her. No matter what she says or how she acts."

"We can't. Not now. Not ever."

Jack's words help me to breathe again. I let a moment of quiet pass over us before I speak again. "We've been drifting apart lately. I can feel it. I'm sorry if I've contributed to it in any way."

"No, I'm sorry. It's my fault. I've been a shitty husband for far too long. You deserve so much more. I need to focus on what's important and get my act together. Especially after the hell I put you through."

His concerns fill me with a hope I haven't felt in a long time. Maybe we will survive this rough patch. But first, we have to endure Nicole and whatever it is she has planned. She doesn't want there to be peace between us. She's here for revenge.

My mind drifts back eighteen years to the night we never speak of. The one I simultaneously want Jack to open up about but also never to discuss. It's an excruciating way to live, but I've never been able to think of a better way to deal with it all.

I wish I could erase that part of my memory. No matter how hard I try, it won't go away. The screeching tires and shattering glass are always there. They creep into the forefront of my mind and threaten to ruin our time together. I push it all down as far as I can before it forces its way back up. Then I kiss Jack and tell him how much I love him.

Jack tells me he loves me, too, and I pull myself closer and rest my head against his chest. The beating of his heart calms the swirling darkness inside me. For the briefest of moments, my fears fade away. With any luck, I won't be having any nightmares tonight.

Sleep finds Jack within minutes. I won't be far behind him. Who knows? My nightmares might actually stay in the recesses of the dark where they belong.

* * *

I am rejuvenated when I awaken at six the next morning. I'm convinced I could take on the world before breakfast. That, or at least figure out this Nicole and Jack situation. And, of course, the damn box of photos.

I still don't know who was in those Polaroid pictures. I could take a solid guess, but I don't want to be right. It doesn't matter. I have no clue where Jack hid the box. I only hope that Jack has destroyed it. Maybe that's why he needed to go out for a drink last night with Dave. To say goodbye to the person in that box.

Jack is already up. I don't understand how he bounces back after two days of drinking. I'd be out for half the day if it were me. He's probably gone for a jog to clear his head before school.

I take a shower and get dressed. I tie my hair into a pony-tail, seeing as I'm not working today, and slap on a minimal amount of make-up. All I have to worry about is getting the kids off to where they need to be and coming home to clean the house. I'm not in the mood for it, but who knows, maybe I'll come across a certain box or its remains.

If Jack has destroyed the college box and the memories that it preserved, it will do him some good. It might help him let go of that time. It won't make him forget what happened. But it will allow him to concentrate on the future. Our future.

Once I'm ready for the day, the kids stir from their rooms and find me in the kitchen. I don't know how, but they wake up around six thirty every day.

"Morning, my babies," I say. Dot tries hard to hide her grin while Noah beams at me. He's my sweet angel and will continue to be for a few more years. Dot, however, is realizing there's a world outside of Mommy.

"Are you guys hungry? Would you like some chocolate pancakes?"

"Yes, yes, yes," Noah screams, while Dot stares at me with a wrinkled brow.

"You don't want chocolate pancakes?" I ask her.

"I do, but you said we can't have them on a school day."

"I did say that, but you know what? Life is short. Let's have some today. This is the happiest Mommy has felt in a long time."

Dot gets on board with the idea and charges around the room with Noah, who is celebrating way too hard. He is always trying to coax his sister into a game of something.

I direct the kids to continue their fun in the living room while I make chocolate pancakes from scratch in the kitchen. I'm no baker, but I can bake a cake when I feel like it. I've never had that natural instinct I've heard so much about for the whole stay-at-home mom side of things. But I do what I can to get by.

I create a colossal mess making the children a sugar-filled breakfast. The disarray can be sorted out later. I'm still buzzing from last night and don't want to spoil my mood.

Jack comes home partway through breakfast, covered in sweat. He grabs a pancake and kisses me on the cheek. He chomps it down in a few bites, then heads upstairs for a quick shower before school.

After the kids and I finish eating, I clean their faces and help them get dressed and ready for the day. I'll be glad when the summer break starts. We'll be able to sleep in for a few weeks before Noah goes back to preschool — in theory, of course. In reality, I'll have two children up at six thirty each morning and a bored husband at home with me. I'll miss the school routine in no time.

Jack finishes getting ready, then rushes out the door as his Uber arrives before I can ask if he has time to take Dot. I should have arranged it with him sooner. After last night, though, I can barely remember my name.

"Come on, Dot," I call at the base of the stairs with Noah at my side. For once, I've got his backpack on him. It's way too big. He's not as tall as his sister was at this age, but I'm sure he'll catch up. Jack was the same, according to his mother.

We hardly see Jack's parents these days, despite them only being an hour away. They are always off on another overseas holiday. They could never travel when they were young, so they seem to be squeezing it all in before they get too old.

My parents aren't together and each currently resides out of state. Sadly, they rarely visit their grandkids. It's a shame. Dot and Noah would love them to be in their lives more. Especially my mom. She always brings a smile to their faces on those rare occasions when we spend time with one another. My father though . . . that's another story.

"Coming," Dot says as she charges down the stairs, finally ready.

"What were you doing up there?" I ask as I guide her along, prompting her to keep my pace.

"Finding the right bow for my hair," she says, pointing at her head. I don't have to look to know that she picked her favorite pink bow.

"Very nice, honey," I say, happy I can still speak to her with a hint of sarcasm. One day, Dot will work out what I'm doing and use it against me.

We head out the front door, ready to face the day. I set the security alarm on the way out and lock the house. When I walk to my car, I spot Darell across the road, loading up his truck. I give him an enthusiastic wave just like yesterday. He sees my sarcastic gesture and glares down his nose at me the way he always does. He doesn't return my hello. Instead, he regards me with a smirk on his lips. He seems rather pleased with himself for some reason. The image of him happy sends a shudder down my spine. Dismissing the creep, I continue to my car.

"Mommy?" Noah asks, using his concerned voice. He's by our mailbox and has probably stepped on a bug.

"What's wrong, baby?"

"What's that?"

"Huh?" I let out as I look where Noah is pointing. His finger is pointing toward the mailbox. The flag is up, and there's something dripping out of the front. Something that looks like . . .

"What is it?" Dot asks as she rushes past me and reaches for the mailbox.

I swat her hand away before she touches the blood that's dripping from the box. My stomach twists as my breath catches in my throat. "Don't touch that. Please, get in the car. Take your brother with you."

"But what is it?"

"I said get in the car, dammit." I block Dot's view of the mailbox. I didn't mean to yell at her and immediately feel guilty.

Once the kids climb into my car, they no longer have a good view of the mailbox. I turn around and make sure I block their views.

With hesitation in my hands, I reach out and open the mailbox, lowering the lid slowly. Inside, I find a pool of blood. The sight of it makes my toes curl. Fortunately, there's no dead animal that goes along with it. Only a folded note. Glancing over my shoulder one last time to make sure the kids can't see, I retrieve the scrap of paper and unfold it.

There's only one word crudely written on the blood-soaked note.

CHAPTER TWENTY-ONE

"Confess?" I whisper to myself, reading the bloody note left in my mailbox. I've read it three times over now. What the hell does it mean?

Then something clicks. I glance up at Darell, who is still loading his truck with a smile. Did he do this to me? All because he had to take care of his stupid front lawn? It sounds like the kind of petty crap he would pull, especially when I think about every interaction I've ever had with the man since we moved onto Maple Court. I don't know what I did to piss him off, by I swear to God he hates me.

I have half a mind to storm over to Darell and unload, but I need to get the kids off before we're late. Plus, I can't leave this disgusting goop in the mailbox for Jack or anyone else to find.

With little time on my hands, I lock the kids in the car to keep them safe and rush back to the house so I can grab a sponge and a pair of gloves. I unlock the front door and disable the security system, cursing to myself with every breath.

I don't even know if it's blood in the mailbox or something else, but it has to go. The thought of leaving it there makes my stomach churn.

With my arms extended and my head as far back as possible, I clean the liquid. I wipe it all away, sparing Dot and Noah from the sight of it. Then I scrub my hands with soap three times in the kitchen sink before heading back outside. Needless to say, the buzz Jack gave me last night is gone.

When I reach my car, I unlock it and climb inside in a hurry. I relock the doors and take a moment to think. Why would Darell do this? I know we've had a lot of differences over the past three years, but why would he go this far? Just because I made the objection about his front lawn? I wasn't even the one to lodge the complaint with the HOA, but he worked it out. Unless . . . unless it wasn't him.

As if reading my mind, Nicole appears in my driveway with a bright smile and a wave. "Hi!"

"Jesus," I let out.

"Mommy said a bad word," Dot declares.

"I'm sorry," I whisper to my daughter. "It was an accident." I face Nicole and smile reflexively.

Nicole continues to grin at me while finger waving like we're best friends. The sight of it makes me want to puke. As I keep the grin plastered on my face, I realize how close I had been to leaving home. If she'd shown up ten seconds later, I'd have been gone already.

"Do you have a minute?" she asks, her voice muffled by the glass of my Subaru.

I turn on the engine to lower my window enough for her to speak to me and nothing more. Nicole steps up to my side of the car, maintaining her smile.

"So sorry to bother you, but I was wondering if I could ask you for a favor?"

I stare at Nicole with an open mouth. Is she the same person from college? It doesn't seem possible. It's like someone has wiped her memory clean. Has she forgotten everything that happened? There's no way.

Nicole is playing me, thinking she can win my trust. And the second she has it, she'll use it against me. Well, two can play at her game. "What do you need?" I ask.

Nicole ignores my question and glances into the backseat at the kids. She smiles at them like she's known Dot and Noah for years. "Hi, guys. Are you off to school now?"

"I'm in kindergarten," Dot says. "My brother goes to preschool."

Noah stays silent. He's wary of strangers, thankfully.

"Wow, that's so cool," Nicole replies.

"What did you need?" I ask again, gripping the steering wheel tight. I'm desperate to keep this unhinged woman away from my children.

"Oh, sorry. I got distracted by them. They are so cute. I can see you and Jack in their faces."

"Thank you," I say, forcing the words through my teeth. Her comment unnerves me.

Nicole stares at them for a long moment and then faces me again. "I was wondering if Jack had a screwdriver set I could borrow. I have some things to put together and seem to have lost my tools in the move."

I glare at Nicole, unsure what answer to give. I could say yes or no, or lie and say we don't have any tools, but she would see right through me. If I say no, she might take it as a slight. But if I say yes, I'd be lending Jack's tools to the last person in the world he'd ever want to loan something to.

"It's okay if you can't," she says. "I understand."

"No, it's fine. I was just trying to remember where we keep them."

"Probably in the garage, I'm guessing," Nicole chuckles.

"Uh, yeah. That's right. Of course. When do you need them?"

"Right now, if that's possible. Or after you drop the kids off. I'm happy to wait. Do you have anywhere else you need to go today?"

I study Nicole's eyes and wonder if she's probing me for information. Is she trying to work out what I get up to each day? Or does she actually want to become friends? I know where I'd place my bet, so I have to play this right.

"I need to take them to school. Then I can drop over those tools. Will that work for you?"

"Yes, perfect," Nicole says. "Thank you so much. It's a big help. I'm sure my tools are somewhere in the house, but I can't find them."

"They'll turn up," I say, glancing away from her. Eye contact is the one thing I should focus on, but I can't stand being this close to her. All I think about when I see her eyes is Kara.

"Well, you'd better get moving. I'll be waiting. Bye!"

With a nod, I say goodbye and roll up my window. As I drive out into the street, I lock my eyes on Nicole in the mirror. She doesn't look away, tracking us as we go. What in God's name is she up to?

CHAPTER TWENTY-TWO

Eighteen years ago

Jack,

I watch you, day in, day out, pretending to live a life that doesn't include me. You act as if I never existed in your world, as if I wasn't your world. But I see through it all, Jack. I see the truth you're trying so hard to hide. And not just from me, but from your girlfriend, too. You've become more secretive, more evasive, as if you know I'm watching. But do you truly think you can hide the truth from me? No.

Behind closed doors, you may think you've found solace. You might trick yourself into believing this new venture will give you what I once did. But we both recognize that's a lie and a deception to shield your fragile ego. What you are undertaking will never compare to what we had. Or what we will have again. I see you in your dorm room, doing these things you don't want anyone to find out about, and it tears at my soul. It cuts me like a rusty blade. Yet, despite it all, despite your attempts to forget me, to bury us beneath many layers of your own self-loathing, I find it within my soul to forgive you. Yes, Jack, I forgive you because I love you.

I love you, Jack Anderson. More than you could ever comprehend.

You must realize I have eyes on you at all times. And still you attempt to conceal this shame from me and hide it away from my view. But I see it. And I'm here to say it's okay.

I know you're confused. You've been caught in a web of your own creation and now you can't escape. But I can cut through the chaos and set you free. You just have to accept that my love for you will never fade the way theirs will. We share a bond that time, distance, and even your new secret girlfriend can't break.

Yes, I know all about her. The one you keep from the other. You both thought you were being so clever, that no one would ever find out you were seeing two girls at once. That's no easy feat, but I guess it confirms what I already knew. You don't love either of them. They are nothing to you.

But make no mistake, Jack. My love is not weak. It's not passive. It's a force and a brewing storm that's ready to sweep away everything that stands between us. Secret or not, they both are a problem. And I can only hold back this tempest for so long. As they say, something's gotta give. And when it does, I will cleanse it all. Anything that doesn't belong in our world will be washed away.

So, consider this a promise, Jack. A promise of what's to come. The day is near when your secrets won't be able to protect you. I will no longer be a shadow in your periphery. I will reclaim my rightful place by your side, and they will . . . well, they will be nothing but a distant memory, a whisper swallowed by my rage.

Actions have consequences, Jack. And the path to our reunion might get a little dark, but every challenge I will overcome will be for us. It's all for our love.

Until then, I'll be close by, watching, waiting, and loving you like no other.

Forever and always yours,
Your true love,
N.

CHAPTER TWENTY-THREE

Present day

As I go about the process of dropping off the kids, I debate telling Jack about Nicole's request. I know how angry he'll be to hear it, but worst of all, he'll think I'm being stupid. The truth is, I want her to trust us. Even if it's all a game, we need her to believe it. If we shut Nicole out, then this whole situation might turn ugly and go beyond our control. I can't let that happen again.

After I finish my drop-offs, I find somewhere to park my car so I can have a minute or two to think and breathe. I can't do so at home — not with Nicole waiting for me to return so she can borrow Jack's screwdriver set. Allegedly. She could be telling me the truth. Or it might be a fantastic excuse for me to drop into her place while I'm all alone and vulnerable. How hard would it be for her to attack me inside her new home?

I need to drop off the set at her door, then leave. Afterwards, I can watch her from my bedroom and spy on her through my curtains. I'll soon see if she does, indeed, have some furniture to put together. Of course, that could be what she wants me to do. Maybe she wants me to find her in her house.

"God," I say out loud. I sound paranoid. And really, can anyone blame me? This is way more than what I need right now. I have enough on my plate with the kids and my marital issues. Nicole has seriously complicated things with her presence.

The bloody note comes to mind. I still don't know who put it there. It sounds like something from a Mafia movie. Maybe the note was meant for another mailbox. It couldn't have been from Nicole, could it?

There's no point denying what I already know.

Deciding to keep faking it with Nicole, I get my car rolling again and head home. It would be so easy to text her and say I got called into work or something else, but I doubt she'd believe me. Then again, maybe that's exactly what I should be doing.

It sounds nuts, but nuts is where we're at. I can't give her those tools. Even though it would be a great way to show Nicole that I trust her, I'm going to tell her I got called into work. And if I do, she'll think I'm not home. And if she believes I'm out and that no one else is there, then she could use the opportunity to break in. It's a wild idea.

I pull out my cell phone and send the text.

[Bianca] *I'm so sorry, but I've been called into work for an emergency. If you can wait until later, I can drop those tools in. No one will be home until around 4 or 5.*

I'm laying it on thick, I know, but there's no time for subtlety. I want Nicole to think she has the whole day free to enter our home and snoop around. If she's moved in next door to finish what she started eighteen years ago, I'm sure breaking into our place will be high on her agenda.

I receive a text a minute later from Nicole.

[Nicole] *No problem! I'll drop by when you're home again.*

I lean back in my seat and let my phone hang free in my hand. This idea is a long shot. Nicole might have no plans to break into my house but I know she's up to something. Of course, even if she breaks in, I won't be able to prove anything. We don't have cameras. Just an alarm system.

Oh, crap. The alarm. I can't remember if I set it again after I cleaned the blood. I was in such a hurry. Did I even lock the front door?

I close my eyes and retrace my steps in my head. At no point in my memories can I recall setting the alarm or locking the front door again. I was so focused on getting back to the kids.

"Dammit," I yell, slapping the dashboard. "Stupid." Frustration seethes from me as I stare around where I'm parked and mutter to myself some more. What the hell was I thinking? Nicole can easily walk inside my house now. And I just told her I wouldn't be home.

CHAPTER TWENTY-FOUR

Still in my car, I re-read the text I sent Nicole and her reply. I stare at the words, shaking my head at the mistake I made. Her reply makes me want to throw up. I realize I have little to go on, but she's so fake and underhanded. If she wants me to believe that she's changed, then this level of composed happiness is not the way to win me over. I'll be damned if I ever become friends with such an artificial person. She can smile and pretend all she wants, but I know the truth.

I think about the damn alarm system I forgot to set and shake my head. This isn't the first time I've forgotten to turn it on. Jack is constantly scolding me about it. If he comes home before me and sees it not active, I'll receive the standard lecture. Maybe it's time to invest in some security cameras instead. They would be more reliable than my memory. And perhaps some hidden cameras for inside the house just to be safe.

Still sitting in my car, I have a decision to make: rush home to set the alarm and lock the door or stay out. I could try to sneak back to secure my house, but Nicole might catch me. Then I'd have some explaining to do. Nicole would then ask to borrow Jack's tools. I'd be put on the spot with no choice but to hand them over to her. Maybe I need to stay away for a few hours — at least for now.

It's going to put a dent in my plans to clean, but oh well. I hate cleaning. Besides, I can use the time to go purchase those security cameras I thought about. Jack won't argue about the cost, especially if I say it's to keep a close eye on a certain neighbor.

When I reach the store, I'm a touch out of my element. I'm not averse to technology, but I'm also not an expert. I want a simple set-up — something that a child could install. And that's what I find after some help from a young sales associate who is all too keen to "hook me up," as he so elegantly puts it.

With several battery-powered outdoor cameras in my possession, ones I should be able to install myself, I feel better prepared for anything the next few weeks or months might bring. I even bought some of the indoor models that are easy to hide. I doubt Jack will notice them. For God's sake, he struggles to find his hat in the laundry hamper. I don't want to spy on him, but he is sneaking around with old boxes of photos. I still have trust issues brought on by his cheating.

The cameras are all accessible via an app I have to pay a subscription to, but the fee will be worth its weight in gold if I capture Nicole doing something illegal. My only problem will be installing these cameras with Nicole around. I'll need to position them in such a way that they aren't so obvious. Not that it will matter. The second she sees a camera installed in a place where none had existed, pointed straight at her home, she'll know it's for her.

With the gear in my possession, I decide it's time to head home. But I can't drive up to the front door — not after telling Nicole that we'd all be out until four or five. And I can't roll up in my Forester if I want to catch her snooping around while she thinks no one is watching. I need to creep into the cul-de-sac like a ghost. In Maple Court, that's no easy feat. As much as I love the place, we live in a nosy community.

Someone is always watching. With any luck, these same eyes will be keeping a watch out for Nicole venturing into places she doesn't belong.

I pull my car to a stop one street over from home and climb out. As I enter Maple Court on foot, it hits me again how much of a shot in the dark this idea is. Even if Nicole does something unneighborly, the chances I'll catch her in the act are slim to none. If I had half a brain, I'd turn around now and head back to my car. The cameras will be enough once I install them.

For some reason, though, I keep walking and don't stop until I'm halfway along Maple Court. There was a time when I was able to think on my feet without getting confused or doubting myself. I guess those days are over. Or maybe Nicole is tripping me up. Her sudden closeness in our lives is throwing me off my game. I feel so useless around her. I guess I can't forget what happened in college or pretend things never got as bad as they did.

"Is everything alright, Bianca?" Gabrielle says to me from her front yard, pulling me from my thoughts. She's got her gardening gloves on and has dirt all over them. From the conversations I've had with neighbors in the street, Gabrielle spends hours per day tending to her damned flower beds. She's a stay-at-home mom with kids that are old enough to take themselves to school. She might do a lot of extra activities in the community, but she seems to have a lot of time on her hands.

"I'm okay. Just coming back from a walk."

"Oh, I didn't see you leave," she says doing little to conceal the contempt from her voice.

"Right," I say, glancing toward number six to check if Nicole is around. I don't spot her or a black Audi A3. When I face Gabrielle again, she's studying me with suspicious eyes. "Maybe you had your head in your flowers when I went by. Well, I better be going."

I turn to go back to my car and realize my mistake two seconds too late.

"I thought you said you were coming back from a walk?" Gabrielle scoffs. I don't need to turn around to know that her hands are on her hips. Has this woman got nothing better to do than to spy on me and hand out my cell phone number to people without asking? I turn back.

"Yes, you're right, but it's such a nice day. I think I'll go for a second walk."

"Right," she says, dragging the word out.

I don't wait for permission to leave and start back toward my car before Mrs. Morris drags me into the nearest confessional. The woman is one of the more annoying people in the cul-de-sac and, of course, she's my neighbor. I have a psycho ex on one side and Gladys Kravitz on the other. And people wonder why I don't like to leave the house.

When I take a quick glance over my shoulder, I find Gabrielle standing there, hands still on her hips, watching me as I go. I mutter some unpleasant words to myself and pick up the pace. But before I'm clear of the cul-de-sac, I spot Nicole at the front of my driveway, glaring right at me. She probably saw the entire exchange.

This day is falling apart, and it's not even lunchtime.

CHAPTER TWENTY-FIVE

My heart rate spikes as I turn away from Nicole. I don't stop moving and quicken my pace, praying in ignorance that it wasn't me she was staring at all the way down the street. She could have been looking at Gabrielle, but I doubt it. The unhinged stalker was waiting for me.

Nicole has caught me in a lie. What happens next will all depend on my ability to keep a level head. I just need a plan to sort this all out. I can't undo the lie, but maybe I can steer it in a direction that works to my advantage. All I need to do is piece together a story that covers my tracks and puts me in a better position than before. Simple, right? Wrong.

"God," I groan, wondering how I always find a way to make things worse. Ellie would love to hear all about this, I'll bet. She found it hilarious that Jack's ex had bought the house next door. If only she knew the rest of the story. She wouldn't be laughing.

I need to keep Nicole under control. To do so, I have to mix together the right amount of truth and lies until what I say sounds believable. Nicole was under the impression I was at work. So why did she catch me walking partway down the cul-de-sac only to retreat again? And at a time that was long before I was due to be home?

An idea comes to me, and it's as basic as it is feasible. Plus, it should work in my favor. I'll text Nicole and tell her Gabrielle thought she heard someone breaking into my house. I rushed home from work to check it out but didn't want to spook a potential burglar who might be in my house stealing my valuables. That's why I was on foot. But when I got there, Gabrielle said it was a false alarm. I'll tell Nicole that I saw her as well, but I didn't have time to say hello. I needed to head back to work.

It's far from perfect and could easily be proven to be a lie, but it might make Nicole think twice about doing anything to my home while I'm away, provided she hasn't already strolled in while my front door is unlocked, and my security system is disabled. I don't know if she was watching me as I struggled to clean up the mailbox.

I run over the idea in my head one more time and wonder if Nicole will buy any of it. She's met Gabrielle. She knows that the woman and her husband like to get involved in everyone's lives. Gabrielle contacting me over a suspected burglary is entirely within reason. I hope. In reality, Gabrielle would probably love to see someone break into my home just to screw up my week. Delivering the bad news would be the highlight of her day.

I reach my car around the corner and check over my shoulder to see if Nicole has followed me. I don't spot her or anyone else, so I climb into my Subaru and lock the doors. As I sit in the driver's seat, I let out a long sigh and lean back with closed eyes. All I want to do is go home and crawl into bed, but I'm stuck like this for hours. If Ellie wasn't working right now, I'd ask her to meet me somewhere for a coffee. Maybe something stronger. It's for the best that I can't see her. I'm feeling vulnerable and open to spilling everything I know about Nicole.

A car rushes by me in the street. I almost don't notice it until I take in the color. It's black and shaped just like the Audi A3 from eighteen years ago. But it can't be the same car. Can it? I need to get a grip.

What was Nicole doing at the end of my driveway? Had I caught her coming or going? Whatever the case might be, it felt like she knew I was coming. Especially when there was no reason for her to be out in the street at that exact moment. Our driveways aren't close together. Was she putting another blood-soaked note into my mailbox?

I have no way of knowing if she was responsible for the first one, but it can't have been anyone else. Darell is a lazy man. Writing a note, even with one word on it, would be too much effort for him. And playing around with blood would not be Gabrielle's style. The fact Nicole appeared immediately after I found the puddle of blood is suspicious as hell. It was like she wanted to see how frazzled the note would make me. It certainly did its job.

"Confess," I say out loud.

Deciding I need to be anywhere but here, I start my car and drive. I don't have a particular destination in mind, but I want to put some distance between myself and home to clear my head. I wish I had been called into work.

After ten minutes on the road, I find the nearest freeway and fly down the entrance ramp until I'm in the left lane, doing twenty over the speed limit. Sometimes when I'm alone, I like to do this. I don't know why, but the faster I go, the more in control I feel. My engine roars louder than normal in response.

The past comes into my mind again. I'll never forget Jack's face when he arrived on the scene and found her. The EMTs had to pry him off Kara's body and hold him back as he wailed. All I could do was bear witness as he broke down.

The 2006 black Audi A3 was a big part of that night. Just like the model I saw in Nicole's driveway. What kind of psychological terror is she trying to hit me with by showing up in Cedarwood Rock in that vehicle? With any hope, the car I saw in Nicole's driveway was there by chance and for a short time only. Just a cruel coincidence. I haven't found the courage to ask Jack if he's seen it around. He mustn't have. The mere sight of it alone would have sent him into a rage.

Red and blue lights flash in my rearview mirror, reminding me where I am and what I'm doing. A police officer is charging up behind me. I check my speedometer and remember how fast I'm going. I tap the brakes to slow down, but it's too late. The police officer pulls me over.

I find the shoulder and come to a gradual stop. How can this day get any worse?

CHAPTER TWENTY-SIX

Eighteen years ago

I didn't send the letter to Jack. I couldn't. As much as I wanted him to read those words, I just had to get them out of my head and onto the page — for my eyes only.

I wandered the campus late one night, lost in a sea of thoughts. Cool air nipped at my neck, pushing me to pull my coat tighter around my body. The chill never sat well with me. It wrapped its icy fingers around my skin in an unwelcome embrace that only Jack's big arms could shake. I loved when he held me.

I rubbed at the healing cut in the palm of my hand. The pain when I etched "J + N" into my skin with the knife I kept in my bag was nothing compared to the thought of never reclaiming what I'd lost. The chill seemed to sting at the deeper areas of the carving on nights like these.

There was a purpose to my nomadic roaming. This wasn't some aimless stroll around the campus. There was only one reason I was subjecting myself to the harsh environment. I was waiting for her: Jack's shameful secret.

The complex scenario Jack had made for himself with his two girlfriends was impressive in its own right. Primarily, it sickened me, but I needed to respect the way he pitted the two women against each other. They had become romantic rivals, but only one was aware of the other. I discovered this secret in my observations and had been fighting to keep myself on track ever since. Jack certainly wasn't making things easy for me with this latest test, but I had a mission to fight through. One I could not fail. One that had become more important than anything before it.

I could have told his public girlfriend about his secret one, but I would only have driven him deeper into the arms of the one he'd been keeping hidden away. Their bond would only strengthen.

Jack's secret flame, the one whom I needed to fear the most, played the role of an innocent girl all too well. I watched her from a distance and felt the weight of the unspeakable betrayal she committed every time she met up with Jack. She knew what she was doing. The very thought poisoned me. And not because I was concerned about either of Jack's girlfriends or their pathetic lives, but because Jack allowed it all to happen. Not allowed, no. He welcomed this behavior. It must have excited him.

Had I been wrong about Jack? Had I misread the kind of man he was? Or had these women corrupted his mind? The latter made more sense than any other possibility.

The night had draped the campus in shadows as I followed her. That trim figure of hers swished about the dimly-lit paths without care. She was heading toward the old part of the university, a secluded spot favored by students who sought solace away from prying eyes. Students like her. All the while, she was unaware of the danger that lurked close behind.

My footsteps were silent, like a phantom about to haunt her world. She stopped in her path to answer a call on her cell phone and sat on a bench that held no light. Her silhouette was bathed in the silver glow of the half-moon.

The venom within me boiled over. My hands balled into fists. This was my chance to unleash my fury and convert it into a focused rage she would never forget. It would be the last thing she ever saw.

I stepped closer, the distance between us shrinking with each beat of my thundering heart. It was like a drumbeat of impending revelation. Her time with Jack was up — expired. And she didn't know. But just as I was about to step out of the shadows to strike, voices pierced the night.

A group of students were headed our way, their laughter carrying through the frosted air. The opportunity to confront her slipped through my fingers. I recoiled into the dark with a seething that threatened to reveal me. But maybe, if I held my breath and waited, I would get another chance.

She rose from the bench and left, continuing her conversation as she headed away from the dark and back into the light. The interrupting voices faded and stranded me with a throbbing headache of unspoken pain. They had saved her and had stopped me from committing an act there was no returning from. I didn't know if I was supposed to be grateful or devastated.

I made my retreat. The campus, with its creaking ivy-clad buildings and ancient trees, shielded my tortured steps. It was the only observer to the night's near-misdeed. But I wasn't done. This wouldn't sway me. I just needed to do things the right way.

Jack's deception had set me on a collision course with these supposed girlfriends, but fate, it seemed, had other plans. For now, my zeal would have to wait for another day. Until then, Jack's secrets would remain with me and continue to be a silent pact between the shadows and my heart.

CHAPTER TWENTY-SEVEN

Present day

The police officer doesn't hold back. I'm subjected to the humiliation of a very public sobriety test and am issued a fine that numbers in the hundreds — one that I won't be able to pay without Jack noticing and questioning. Not unless I dip into the bank account he doesn't know about. I hate to touch that money, but it's better than explaining why I was speeding.

I'm not ashamed to admit it, but I've been hiding money from Jack. I opened a secret bank account when I found out he had cheated. I deposit money into it whenever I can and have a balance of around $3,000. It's not much, but if things ever fall apart between us, it'll come in handy. Divorce can be expensive.

I stop off at the next exit on the highway to grab a bite to eat. There's a gas station with an In-N-Out Burger. It isn't my favorite establishment in the world, but I'm ready to eat. Besides, I still can't go home right now if I don't want to raise suspicions with Nicole.

That reminds me I need to text her. As I sit at a booth inside the In-N-Out Burger with my phone out, I bring up Nicole's name in my contacts and open the last message she sent me. It's hard to believe she's a contact in my phone. I never thought I'd see the day.

I type out a lengthy message to Nicole about the supposed break-in at my place and Gabrielle's nosy part in it all. Once I reach the end of my tall tale, I realize it's too detailed and needs to be chopped down. The best way to keep a lie straight is to use as few details as possible. I don't usually lie, but it's a necessary evil. We all do it. Lying to Nicole makes me nervous. Considering the damage she wreaked on our lives, I wonder if it's a good idea to test her intelligence in such a way.

After cutting down my text, I send it to Nicole and place my cell phone on the half-cleaned table.

Nicole texts me back, saying she understands and for me not to stress. She sends a follow-up text telling me to forget about the screwdriver set, claiming she has found a solution of her own. I go up to the counter and order a cheeseburger meal, then take it back to my booth to eat. As I finish my food, I'm hit with a wave of regret. Eating an unhealthy burger and fries isn't the way to deal with stress. Silently, I wish again that Ellie wasn't working. I'd give anything to be out somewhere with her. When we both have the time, we enjoy a nice lunch and a shopping spree. It's been a while since we've done that. Lately, the only time we've spent together has been our brief meetups at the Cinnamon Whispers Café or when the Morrises host a barbecue.

She used to come over a lot when we first moved in. We'd have coffee and chat for hours at a time while Jack and Dave were at work. She was so helpful when I was pregnant and when Noah came along. I felt so lucky to have her close by. But time and life are pulling us apart.

Lately, she's been working more and more hours at her medical receptionist job. Any time I ask her to do something, she's already taken on an extra shift. Ellie hasn't confirmed it with me, but I think she and David are having money problems.

Jack recently confided in me that David had lost a significant chunk of their savings to a cryptocurrency scam. I didn't understand the finer details of it, but knowing David, I can imagine he saw a shortcut to quitting his job as a teacher. Unfortunately, it didn't work out in the slightest, so now Ellie is forced to put in longer hours so they can get back on track. For all of Jack's shortcomings, I doubt he would ever take such a financial risk.

As I'm about to leave the In-N-Out Burger, a familiar face strolls into the establishment. One I never expected to see here, of all places. Darell Vargas stares at me from across the way, spotting me the second he walks in. Is he following me? Is he taking his hatred of me to a new level?

Darell mutters under his breath and shakes his head as he moves up to the counter. He's apparently here to order some food. The only thing I've ever seen him consume is alcohol on his front porch.

I don't know why, but the sight of him sends a jolt of emotions through me. I come to a rushed conclusion and charge straight up to Darell and let him have it.

"What the hell was that thing you left in my mailbox? You think that was funny?"

Darell's palms raise in defense as he steps back. "I don't know what you're talking about, Bianca. Leave me the hell alone." Darell faces away from me and acts like I'm not there.

A scoff escapes me as I cross my arms over my chest. "Do you seriously expect me to believe you after all the crap you've pulled with me since I moved in?"

"Believe what you want," he says over his shoulder. "I didn't do squat to your damn mailbox, got it?"

Unable to accept his lies, I step in front of him to see the look on his face. It will tell me everything. "Out with it," I say. "Why did you write that word? What was it again? Confess? I mean, if you're going to hurl a threat at someone, at least use more than one word."

Darell shakes his head again and stares at me with a furrowed brow. "For the last time, Bianca, I don't know what you're talking about. Now get out of my face before I call the cops." His voice roars loud enough for everyone in the building to hear. The few employees and customers in the place all stare at me.

It takes a second, but I realize Darell is telling the truth. He seems to be genuinely confused by my line of questioning. I don't say another word and back away. I rush to my booth and make sure I have my things. Then I scramble out the door and jog back to my car without looking back.

As I climb inside my Subaru with tears in my eyes, I'm forced to accept that Darell never had a thing to do with the bloody note. I guess I knew that before I'd accused him and was desperate for a simple answer. There's only one other person in Maple Court who would have a reason to leave me such a note, and she claims she no longer needs to borrow Jack's screwdriver set.

CHAPTER TWENTY-EIGHT

Nicole was the one behind the mailbox threat. Nothing else makes sense. I guess the sight of Darell threw me off when I saw him at In-N-Out Burger. It was also the use of the single word "confess" that got to me. Like him, it was a lazy message. So, who else besides Nicole would leave a one-word, blood-soaked note in my mailbox on Maple Court? No one. Unless it was an unfortunate case of mistaken identity, I'm convinced Nicole was behind the idea. The question is, though, what will she do next?

It's early days, but I feel like we are stuck in a sick game of cat and mouse. Nicole has already caught me and is now playing with her food. I can't let her take a bite, though. She came close to it once before. I won't let that happen again.

After falsely accusing Darell, I wipe the sobs from my eyes and head home. I don't give a damn if Nicole spots me. She already knows I've been lying to her. She can deal with the fact that I know what she's up to. Maybe I need to project some confidence and let her see that she won't win — not without a fight.

When I reach Maple Court, a thought about the note comes to me. I haven't told Jack about it. I didn't want to

115

while he was at work. He doesn't need the extra stress. And the more I think about it, the less I want him to know in general. Jack hates Nicole more than I do. When he found Kara dead that night, he lost his mind. And there was only one person to blame.

Jack confronted Nicole with a white-hot rage I never knew he was capable of. It was a display I pray I'll never witness again. If Jack thinks Nicole left a blood-soaked note in our mailbox, he might do something irrational — more than any dumb thought I might have. The last thing I need is for him to get arrested for attacking Nicole. These things are best handled with a level head.

I roll into my driveway and don't find a black Audi A3 at number six. I also don't spot Nicole or anyone else lurking around, so I hit the remote button for my garage door. It works on the third try.

If I don't delay, I can hide my car inside. Nicole has probably heard me pull in, but I don't care. As long as I can avoid seeing her, I'm happy.

I tap the gas and rush into our garage and hit the remote again. As the garage door lowers, I send a text to Jack asking if he can leave early and bring Noah and Dot home. He replies a few seconds later with a thumbs-up. Our garage is rather cramped. When I climb out, I'm forced to squeeze along a narrow space between my car and the wall with my handbag, phone, and bag of security cameras. I almost fall over but manage to exit my car and make it into the house in one piece.

I sigh as I close the door and head into the kitchen. I place everything down on our island bench and take a moment to stand back from my pile. The day has depleted me, and it's far from over. While I have the house to myself for a few more hours, I've got work to do. And I'm not talking about cleaning.

I can't install the external cameras right now — not with Nicole living next door with no curtains blocking her view. But what I can do is set up the three internal cameras I bought to hide around the house. I need them to keep an eye out for next-door intruders and potentially Jack.

I want to trust my husband, but recently he's given me reason to doubt his commitment to our marriage. Finding him rummaging through secret boxes late at night will do that to a person. Not to mention the hidden storage he never told me we had in his study. It's possible he isn't aware of its existence. It was empty, and we didn't build this house, but even so, something doesn't add up.

I place three motion-activated cameras around the house in vents. I go to the effort of covering up the little LED lights each unit has to show that the system is recording. This way, Jack won't have a clue he's being watched. "Watched" isn't the right word. "Observed?" That sounds just as sinister. One camera goes into Jack's study while the remaining two go into the kitchen and living room. The range on each camera is limited at best, and the vent grilles block a lot of the view, but my mind feels slightly more at ease knowing they are there. I will install the external cameras later — maybe once Jack gets home and I feel safe enough to do so. He could help me and get the job done nice and fast before Nicole notices.

A wave of fatigue washes over me after I have the internal cameras online and accessible via my phone. I decide to go upstairs to take a quick nap before Jack and the kids arrive. Even if I can only get in twenty minutes of sleep, it will do wonders for me. I should be cleaning, but my fatigue outweighs my guilt.

As I ready myself to climb into bed, I think about the view concealed by my closed curtains. I shouldn't, but I creep up to the drapery and take the smallest of peeks over to Nicole's home. I find her straight away. She's at the edge of her living room, by the bay window, putting together furniture like she said she would be. Maybe she was telling me the truth before. Or maybe this is all for show. I don't know. Either way, I should pretend she isn't there and go take a nap.

I'm about to let the curtain fall back into place when I spot something in front of Nicole that sends a lump into my throat. It's Jack's screwdriver set. It has to be. He doesn't own some generic brand of screwdrivers. His father gave him an expensive set of Wihas one year for his birthday. He had them inscribed with his name. I'd recognize that set anywhere. And so would anyone else on this street. Did Nicole break into our garage and take them? And after I told her I couldn't help her? Unsure if I'm going crazy, I rush downstairs to the garage. My car is in the way, but I manage to sneak around it enough to reach the array of tools we have on the back wall. As I suspected, Jack's screwdriver set is missing. I didn't think to look for it when I got home.

In a rage, I storm back inside and rush into the kitchen to check if Nicole is still where I saw her. The missing tools means she's broken into my home exactly like I thought she would. And I guarantee she knew I'd spot her through her open windows using Jack's tools. This is all part of her game.

I peek through the kitchen curtain and see Nicole still in her living room, using Jack's screwdrivers. I've got her now. I'll prove why she's really here. There will never be peace between us. Especially considering she tried to kill me.

With my phone ready to record Nicole, I yank open the front door and rush outside with heavy footfalls, muttering to myself as I go. There are too many emotions coursing through me, but I don't care. Nicole is going to feel my wrath today. With any luck, she might move. If she doesn't, I don't know what I'll do.

I stomp the length of my driveway and turn the corner into number six. When I reach Nicole's front door, the fury that fueled me leaves my body all at once. What I find stops me in my tracks and makes me question my every belief.

CHAPTER TWENTY-NINE

I stare at Nicole's door with an open mouth. What I'm seeing can't be real, and yet, I know I'm wide awake. With soft feet, I move closer to it, closer to the giant hunting knife jammed in her front door. But the knife isn't the only thing sending my pulse racing. It's the note hanging from the blade, pinned to the door. Just like the one I found in my mailbox today, it's covered in what appears to be blood. I read the words that have been scrawled out:

Lies breed chaos

"What in the hell?" I mumble. There's no one else around, so I move closer to the knife and try to make sense of things. It's just like the one we received in our mailbox. Could this have been Nicole? Could she have done this to her own door? All to make herself look like a victim?

If that is the case, then I need to remove this thick blade and note before anyone else sees it. I grab the handle of the knife and give it a pull right at the same time that Gabrielle Morris strolls around the corner to number six.

"Oh my God. What are you doing?" she yelps at me.

I face Gabrielle and see her eyebrows shoot upwards, creasing her forehead with lines of disbelief. She must think I did this. What kind of cursed timing is this?

"This isn't what it looks like," I say, not that I expect her to believe my innocence.

"I should call the police," she screeches.

I turn to see Nicole standing in the now-open doorway. "Is something wrong? Oh my God!" She jumps, turning her accusing eyes to mine. "Who did this?"

"It was Bianca," Gabrielle spits out, stabbing a finger at me. "I saw her."

"No, you didn't," I shout, unable to remain calm. Whether or not she believes me, I can see from the look in her eye that she is going to use this situation to her advantage.

"Yes, I did. I saw her, Nicole. She had her hand on that knife."

A sigh escapes me. "I was trying to remove it."

"It's okay," Nicole says, surprisingly.

"What's going on out here?" Ellie asks, emerging from number four.

"Are you serious?" I mutter. *Can this situation get any worse?*

Gabrielle wastes no time blaming me. "Bianca shoved that knife and note into Nicole's door."

"I didn't," I stammer.

Ellie stares right at me with an open mouth. For a fleeting moment, she looks almost as if she believes her. "Ellie, I swear I didn't do this." I gawk at her with pleading eyes. I shouldn't have to explain myself like this. Especially to her.

"I'm calling the police," Gabrielle repeats, yanking her cell phone from her back pocket.

"That's not necessary," Nicole says.

"But Nicole—" Gabrielle starts. Nicole holds up a hand to silence her. "It's fine, Gabrielle. If Bianca says she didn't do this, then I believe her."

Gabrielle doesn't say another word, which is unlike her. While Nicole inspects her door with Gabrielle close by, Ellie moves over to me. She narrows her gaze and whispers, asking if I did this. I shake my head and reply, "I found it like that. I swear."

"Okay," she replies, giving me a slight nod. And I can tell she believes me. Thank God.

"Then who did it?" Gabrielle asks. I stare at Nicole. Despite receiving the same kind of note in my mailbox, I'm ninety-nine per cent sure she did this to herself. It would be the perfect cover to her schemes. "Maybe it was a prank," Ellie offers. "A lot of younger kids now are doing crazy things to get likes and views online."

"Are you serious?" Gabrielle fires back. "There are pranks, and then there's committing crimes. Whoever did this was trying to send a message. I'm not sure what this 'lies breed chaos' means, but it sounds like someone doesn't want Nicole here. We need to find out who did this and contact the police." Gabrielle's eyes settle on me once again.

"That's not necessary," Nicole repeats, but this time there's an urgency in her voice. Maybe this wasn't her. From what I can tell, she wants to pretend none of this has happened. If that's true, then I have no idea who did this.

"Okay," Gabrielle says. "I won't contact the police . . . for now. How about we all go inside and have some coffee?"

"Oh, no need for that," Nicole says.

With the mention of people going inside Nicole's home, I remember why I came storming over to her house in the first place. The damn screwdriver set. I can't keep up with everything that's going on in this court. "A round of coffees would be a great idea," I say, supporting the idea.

Gabrielle shoots me a dark glare, still convinced I'm guilty. Or perhaps it's more of a hope that this was my doing. Then she'd have a solid reason to turn everyone against me. I throw her a smile, hoping it will show her that this is all a strange misunderstanding. Gabrielle has never liked me and never will. The feeling is mutual. It all started when we first arrived, and I declined her offer of a welcome barbecue.

"Seriously, I'm fine," Nicole adds as she clutches her front door, suddenly not fazed by the giant knife sticking out of it. "It was probably some kids messing around. The message doesn't even make sense."

Gabrielle steps back. "I can assure you that none of the children on this street would ever do such a thing. No, this is something else. Frankly, I'm very concerned and think you need to take this seriously."

"She's right," Ellie says. "I've never seen a knife this big in my life."

"Definitely," I add. "We should go inside and make sure you're safe. We wouldn't want anything bad to happen to you."

Nicole stares straight at me after I utter these words, and in a flash, I catch a glimpse of her contempt for me. I'm not surprised the truth finally reared its head. I just need to keep chipping away at the surface until everyone can see what's underneath. The second we get inside, I'll make my move.

Nicole doesn't protest as Gabrielle guides her inside her own house. The living room is near the entrance — the same living room that has Jack's stolen tools in it. It'll be interesting to hear what lie she concocts to explain herself when I pretend to notice the tools for the first time.

All four of us walk past the knife and note into what used to be Trina and Danny's home. Inside is a sea of cardboard boxes and household items divided into small piles.

"I'm so sorry for the mess," Nicole says, rushing ahead of us as if she has something to hide. "You've only just moved in," Gabrielle says. "Cut yourself some slack. Now, show me what you've got in the kitchen to work with."

As Gabrielle continues to make herself at home, I navigate my way around a stack of boxes and find a half-finished set of drawers. Beside the work-in-progress, I spot Jack's Wihas. Bingo.

"Care to explain yourself, Nicole?" I ask, standing close to the screwdriver set before she can attempt to sweep them away. I'm not going to waste another second.

Both Gabrielle and Ellie look at me with lowered brows. But soon, they will see the real Nicole Stokes and understand exactly who she is.

"I'm sorry," Nicole says. "I thought that—"

"You thought it would be okay to break into my house and steal Jack's tools. And after I had said I wouldn't be home to lend them to you." I stand firm with my arms crossed over my chest and tilt my head, waiting for her full confession.

"What are you saying, Bianca?" Gabrielle asks me.

I shift my focus to the busybody of Maple Court and point at Jack's tools. "Those Wihas are Jack's. Nicole asked me if she could borrow them earlier, but I had to go to work. Apparently she thought it would be okay to just go into our garage without permission and take them." I stare at Nicole. "This is the kind of person who has moved in here." This is my only card to play, so I'm not holding back.

Nicole won't look me in the eye and instead stares at the floor. She's backed into a corner and has no way out. No lie will save her now.

Gabrielle steps into my line of sight with a creased forehead and an open mouth. Let's see what she has to say about her new neighbor now. "Bianca, I think you've got the wrong idea here."

I let out a heavy sigh. It's no surprise Gabrielle is going to defend Nicole. Especially against anything I have to say. This might be harder than I thought. Then again, the evidence speaks for itself.

"It's okay," Nicole says, touching Gabrielle on the arm.

"No, it's not. She can't accuse you of something so heinous."

"I'm not accusing," I say. "I can prove it. Look." I point down at the screwdriver set. "Those are Jack's. You've all seen them at one time or another."

Gabrielle inches toward me. "Why don't you take a closer look?"

"I will," I reply as I bend down to pick up the closest screwdriver Nicole has been using. Once I have it, Gabrielle rotates the tool in my hand.

"This belongs to Bradley. These are his screwdrivers." Gabrielle taps a label down the length of the screwdriver's handle. And sure enough, the name Bradley Morris is there for all to see.

I drop to the floor and inspect the rest. Every tool has a label with the name Bradley Morris on the handle.

This isn't happening.

CHAPTER THIRTY

Eighteen years ago

Dear Jack,

Do you ever stop and wonder how we got here? How the simplest of moments — the brush of a hand, the sound of your laugh — can leave such an enduring mark? I think about them constantly. The world is full of noise, distractions, and changing people clamoring for attention. But to me, you're the one constant in the chaos, the one thing that makes sense.

I know you think I'm strong. You've said it before, probably not even realizing how much those words meant to me. But if I'm being honest, you've always been my strength. Every smile you've given me, every bit of kindness — those are the things I've clung to when everything else felt like it was slipping away.

That's why I can't stop. I can't give up on us. I know you don't see it yet. Not the way I do. You're so focused on what's in front of you, so distracted by two people who don't understand you the way I do. They'll never know the real you, Jack. Not like I do.

I'm sorry about the other day when we bumped into each other. It was my fault I dropped my laptop. Not yours. I was so caught up in my own head that I didn't realize what was happening until it was too late. And like the stand-up guy that you are, you offered to replace it for me. Even though you can't afford to. But maybe it was supposed to happen. Maybe it was fate, pushing us back together, giving us a reason to talk like we used to.

The coffee you took me out for wasn't just coffee. It was a promise. I think you felt it too. The way you looked at me across that table. There was something more underneath. We each felt it. You can't deny me that. And I know you're afraid. I am too. But fear doesn't matter when the truth is this clear.

I'll wait for you, Jack. However long it takes. I'll fight for you, even if it means pushing past the people who don't want us to be happy. None of them matter. None of them ever will.

One day, you'll understand. One day, we'll look back at all of this and laugh, shake our heads at the wasted time and pointless obstacles. And when that day comes, I'll be here, just like I've always been.

Always yours,
N

CHAPTER THIRTY-ONE

Present day

I don't understand what just happened. One minute, I had Nicole right where I wanted her. The next, I was being made to look like the bad guy.

After falsely accusing Nicole of stealing Jack's screwdriver set, I apologize in as few words as possible and leave number six to rush back home. Ellie follows.

"Hey, wait up," she calls out.

I wave her off without looking back. I need to go back inside my garage and make sure I'm not losing my mind. Those damn tools were missing. I know it.

"Bianca," Ellie says again.

"Go home," I mutter as she catches up to me.

"Not until you tell me what's going on."

"You won't understand," I say, fumbling for the keys in my pocket. The garage door fob has been on the blink. One second it works, the next it doesn't. Of course, the second I need it to function, it refuses to do its only job. "Piece of junk," I shout.

Ellie grabs my wrist. "Hey. What is this? What's got you all bent out of shape? You haven't been yourself since Nicole got here."

I look Ellie in the eye and feel like I'm about to burst into tears. I want to tell her everything, but I can't.

"It doesn't matter," I say, shrugging her off. The garage door finally opens.

"It does matter. Whatever is bothering you, you know you can talk to me about it, right?"

"Yes, but this is bigger than you could imagine," I say as I duck under the rising door. Again, Ellie follows.

"Come on, Bee. It's me. I can handle anything you have to say. You know that."

I shake my head and say nothing. Ellie has no idea. None. If she only knew half of the truth, it would be too much. And she thinks she can handle who I'm dealing with.

"Why did you think Nicole stole something from you?" she asks.

I ignore her question again and squeeze my way around my parked car in the garage. I work my way to where Jack keeps his screwdriver set. Again, I see empty space where it should be. "It's not here. So, where the hell is it?"

"What's not here?" Ellie asks once she reaches my location.

I exhale with both hands on my hips. I might as well tell her now. Well, as much as I can stomach. "Jack's screwdriver set. I thought Nicole had taken it."

"Why would you think that?"

"Because she asked to borrow it."

"She did?"

"Yeah . . ." More follows. I go into detail about my story of why Nicole couldn't borrow the tool set, keeping my words consistent. I only give Ellie the information she absolutely needs. "So, when I couldn't find Jack's set, I guess I assumed the worst."

Ellie nods, giving me her usual delicate smile as she reassures me everything will be fine. "I'm sure Nicole will understand," she offers.

A sardonic laugh escapes me. "I'm sure she will," I say, keeping the sarcasm flowing. "I'm sure she'll understand that this is all some unfortunate misunderstanding."

Ellie stares at me with pity. I glance away and think about Nicole. The whole incident leaves me wondering if she knew that Jack and Bradley had the same set of tools and figured she could play a little mind game with me. The hunting knife with the threatening note left on her front door was a clever touch. I'll give her that. God, it was a stroke of genius. Especially when Gabrielle caught me touching it. Nicole must have seen me coming and called Gabrielle to rush over at the perfect time. Or maybe they are working together. I sound insane, but something is going on.

"Are you okay?" Ellie asks.

"I'm fine. I just wish I knew where Jack's tools have gone. At least then I could make sense of things."

"Come on," Ellie says. "Let's go inside and grab a coffee. Gabrielle wasn't wrong to suggest having one earlier. It'll help calm you down."

We share a smile and walk back inside to the kitchen. I make us both coffees and ask Ellie about her day. We sit at my dining table as she tells me about work and the kids as per usual. I'm tempted to ask about David's supposed issues, but I'm positive what Jack said to me was all a ploy so the two of them could go out drinking.

"Hey," Ellie says. "I just had a thought. Why don't you call Jack and ask him about the tool set? Maybe he moved it somewhere. He might have loaned it to someone."

"That's a good idea," I say. "But what if he hasn't seen it? Then he'll think I've lost it or that it's been stolen. I don't want to bother him with this. Especially if he thinks Nicole had anything to do with it." I realize my mistake two seconds too late.

"What do you mean? Why would he care if Nicole had taken them?"

"He wouldn't. Forget it."

"No. I know she's his ex, but there's more to it than that, isn't there? It's pretty damn obvious. So tell me, who is she to you?"

I struggle to avoid Ellie's questioning gaze, but she moves closer to me, demanding an answer.

I don't know what to say.

CHAPTER THIRTY-TWO

Ellie doesn't let up, even when I stand from my dining table and try to walk away.

"You need to tell me something, Bee," Ellie pushes. "If you keep me out like this, it means you don't trust me. And if you don't trust me, then why are we even friends? Just because of the guys?"

"You don't understand," I say.

"I know I don't. But that's only because you won't tell me anything. Unless you give me something to go on, I'm in the dark here."

I shake my head, then face away from her. It's easier than seeing her face.

"Fine, I'm going," Ellie says. "If you don't want to—"

"She's not just Jack's ex," I spit out, turning to her. "She's the psycho one."

"The psycho one?" Ellie asks with a raised brow.

"From college. The one I once told you about. I never got into the finer details, but she is that unhinged girl. She . . . she was the reason Kara died."

Ellie stares at me with an open mouth. "Oh, wow. That's, uh . . . I don't know what to say."

I grab my head and squeeze. "This is why I've kept you in the dark, Ellie. Until Nicole showed up here, Jack and I never spoke about Kara or what happened back in college. But now . . ."

"Nicole is your neighbor."

"Yeah. So you can understand why I'm a little off the rails when I'm around her."

Ellie doesn't respond, and we soon fall into a stunned silence. All the while, I can't help but wonder what I've risked by telling her as much as I have. What if Nicole finds out about this conversation?

"I won't say anything to David," she says, as if reading my mind. "I didn't even tell him that Nicole is an ex. I don't know what Jack has said to him, but he won't hear about any of this from me."

"Thank you. I appreciate it. Until I can figure out a better way to handle this situation, it's best for me to keep it to myself."

Ellie nods in agreement, but her eyes seem absent. She must be trying to take it all in. "God, this is so screwed up," she says. "What is Nicole doing here? And why was she so determined to move in next to you guys? If it was me, I'd have called the moving company and put up a for-sale sign already."

"Of course you would. You're normal."

Ellie chuckles, and the sound of her warm laughter brings me back from the edge. Only a few inches, though. I still feel like I'm tugging at a loose strand in my clothing that refuses to snap. Instead, it continues to unfurl and tear away more of my sanity with each attempt I'm forced to make.

"So, what now?" Ellie asks.

I shrug. "I guess I should try to find out what happened to Jack's screwdriver set."

"Want some help?"

"I'd love some, but I'm sure you've got your own problems to deal with. I'll bet Ethan and Olivia are waiting for you."

Ellie shrugs this time. "There's always something that needs sorting out at home, but it's not a problem. Dave's mom is over. She dropped in for another one of her unscheduled visits. She can handle the kids for a while longer."

"Georgia's there? Oh, God, I thought I had problems."

Ellie nods, sucking in a breath. "She's giving me her usual level of 'constructive criticism.' Apparently, the way I fold laundry is wrong . . . again."

We laugh and sit back down at the table. Before long, we are talking about the normal things that fill our days and weeks. It takes my mind off Nicole for a few minutes and makes me feel grateful to have Ellie so close by. She's always been there when I need her. I've always found it hard to keep friends. But with Ellie, it's never been much effort. We understand one another.

She met David not long after the guys became friends, and she and I hit it off right away. The four of us have spent a lot of time together. We'd go out drinking, to the movies, to restaurants, and many other places. We had so many late nights together before the kids came along.

We all have a lot in common. We each married our partners and attended each other's weddings. We each had children. Ellie and David had kids before us because of some infertility issues I was having.

The meds I was on for several years were messing with my ability to fall pregnant. It wasn't until I dropped my anxiety tablets that Jack and I could conceive Dot. After she came along, I got back on those pills and had to repeat the process for Noah. I haven't been on the tablets since, but this week is making me want to rush out and see my doctor again.

Ellie stands from the table and ushers me to do the same. "Come on. Let's go find that screwdriver set. It can't have gone far. Maybe Jack was using it to build you something for your birthday."

We both laugh at the prospect. Jack likes to think of himself as a capable handyman, but he is forever making messes with any DIY projects we attempt. He has a decent set-up in the garage, but it's wasted on him.

As Ellie and I go through the garage and search through all the usual places, nothing jumps out. We split up and each take a quick walk around my house and hunt through every room. I get notifications on my cell phone when we trigger the internal cameras I installed, so I quickly disable them. I will need to work out a way to avoid getting three hundred alerts per day from Jack, myself, and the kids simply existing in our own home.

We meet back in the kitchen. I apologize to Ellie for the various messes she would have come across in the house, but she waves me off with a scoff.

"I would kill for a messy house right now. Georgia won't stop cleaning. We can't so much as leave a glass on a coaster when she drops in. She even leaves me notes around the place, like telling me to my face isn't good enough. Can you believe it?"

We both snicker at Ellie's misfortune until an important piece of information rushes into my brain: the note. The one I found in the mailbox. No one knows about it. Well, apart from Darell, kind of. But I think he was confused by what I had to say. After seeing his reaction when I confronted him today, it's clear he had nothing to do with it.

Ellie continues to help me look for Jack's tools out in my backyard. The entire time, I debate if I should tell her about what was left for me in my mailbox. I got rid of the note as soon as I could. Short of digging it out of the trash, it will be hard to show her. Plus, I don't want Ellie staring at me with those same doubtful eyes she had earlier. Nothing is worse than having a person you trust with your life lose faith in you.

Ellie stands on the deck with her hands on her hips and stares at my backyard. "Doesn't look like the set's out here. And I'm starting to doubt if David borrowed them, either."

"It's okay," I say. "Thanks for trying. I'm sure it'll turn up."

"It will. I know it." She lets out a sigh. "Well, I suppose I should head home then. Back to Georgia."

"Unless you want to stay a little longer?" I suggest. My reasoning is less than pure. I still might tell Ellie about the bloody note. I haven't convinced myself which way to go.

"I'd love to, but if I don't go back now, the woman will cut me out of our family photos and move in."

"Oh, God," I say, failing to stifle a chuckle.

Ellie matches my expression, but underneath I can see just how challenging she finds her mother-in-law to be. We all agree that Georgia means well, but sometimes she takes things too far and oversteps her bounds.

We wander inside. Ellie doesn't have anything with her. No phone or keys. It's one advantage of living so close to one another. As she heads for the front door, I open my mouth to speak, to tell her to stay so I can fill her more, but I can't seem to find the right way to start the conversation.

"See you later," Ellie calls out, waving as she closes the front door.

"Bye," I whisper to my empty house, wishing I had told her. Deep down, I know letting her go is the smart move. Whoever left that disgusting puddle of blood and note in my mailbox wanted me to make a big fuss. They wanted me to tell everyone I knew and cause a stir. Why else make the message so vague? I mustn't have reacted the way they'd hoped, so they upped the game with the knife at number six.

I've got news for this individual: I'm not playing their game. Be it Nicole or someone else, I won't go down without a fight.

135

CHAPTER THIRTY-THREE

Having wasted my day, I rush to get dinner started and attempt to make a dent in my normal household chores. Jack won't care when he gets in with the kids. He won't notice the disarray unless he doesn't have enough socks or underwear available. It's frustrating. I could bust my butt all day long and scrub the floors until I could see my reflection in them. He still wouldn't notice or thank me for the effort.

When Jack and the kids come through the front door, Noah and Dot charge into the kitchen and shout, "Mommy!"

"Hello, my darlings," I say as Dot wraps her arms around my stomach and Noah does the same around my hips. There's such a big height difference between their ages, but when I look down, all I find are two sets of shining eyes that are filled with love.

"Hey, honey," Jack says, dumping his work bag down at the end of the counter. It will stay there until he needs it in the morning, or until I move it to the hook by the front door where it's supposed to go. I've given up telling him where to put his crap.

"Hi," I say, avoiding Jack's gaze. His screwdriver set is still missing. I wasn't the one to lose it, but it feels like it's my fault it's gone. For all I know, Nicole could have taken the thing and hidden the set somewhere in her disaster of a home. After my meltdown before, I can't go over there and ask.

"Ugh, what a day," Jack says as he grabs a beer from the refrigerator. He pops off the cap and takes a swig. You'd swear he'd been working construction all day and not teaching history to teenagers. Also, I'm surprised he's drinking alcohol again after the last few days. Is he developing a problem, or is he stressed about Nicole?

Jack sighs and mutters to himself.

"Did something happen?" I ask, taking the hint.

"Don't get me started."

"Go play, guys," I tell Noah and Dot. "I'll call you when dinner's ready." The kids charge off upstairs. I don't want them hearing what their father has to say. He often forgets where he is and whose impressionable ears are close by.

Jack collapses into one of the kitchen stools with a weight pressing down on his shoulders. "You know, it's not even the content," he starts. "I love history. I love teaching it. But some days it's like hitting my head against a brick wall trying to force these kids to give a damn about anything that happened more than five minutes ago."

While listening to Jack, I keep busy with dinner, stirring a pot of marinara sauce that's simmering on the stove. The aroma of garlic and herbs fills the space, offering something for my senses to focus on other than Jack's complaints. Next to me, the spaghetti pasta is ready to be combined with the sauce. It's a meal I've made a hundred times before.

Jack takes another sip of his beer. His eyes stare off into the distance as he continues. "There I was today, right in the middle of discussing the Civil Rights Movement, something I thought would engage these kids, and what do they give me? A sea of blank faces. No questions or reactions. Just indifference."

I've had the day from hell, but I recognize it's my job to pay attention and show that I care. I move to stand beside him, placing a comforting hand on his shoulder. The tension in his muscles eases a touch. "That sounds really crappy, honey. But don't give up. You're making a difference, even if it doesn't always feel like it."

Jack shakes his head. "Maybe."

I don't know what else to say, so I force a smile. All the while, I want to unload and tell him everything. He starts again before I get the chance — not that I want to tell him anything that might set him off.

"One kid said that he didn't need to learn what I'm trying to teach him. He said he could Google it if he needed to. It's like everything we've learned as a species, every struggle and triumph we've experienced, is worthless unless it's being shown to them on TikTok."

I return to my cooking, going between the kitchen bench and the stove top. Jack pauses for a moment, then drains the last of his beer, setting the empty bottle on the counter next to his bag with a heavy sigh. "And then, to top it all off, I had a meeting with the principal during my lunch break about budget cuts."

"Budget cuts?" I ask.

"Yeah, budget cuts," Jack confirms, with a hint of bitterness creeping into his tone. "They're considering slashing our funds, maybe even cutting a position. It's like they think history is optional."

I can't help but feel a spark of irritation. Why wouldn't he lead with this important piece of news? I force my annoyance down and try to extract more from him. "Surely, they see the value in what you do? You've been at this school for a few years now. How can they justify cutting the department?"

Jack gives me a non-committal shrug. "It's all numbers to them. They think it's better to reallocate resources to the STEM programs. It's all so they can boost their results. Or so I've heard."

"Okay. Who would they be firing first?"

He looks over at me but avoids my eyes. "I don't know."

"You don't know?"

"Look, I wish I could tell you more, but there's nothing I can do. I don't have a say in any of this."

"That's not good enough, Jack," I snap, the words spilling from my mouth. "You can't take this lying down. You need to show them they're making a mistake."

Jack stands from the chair and throws a hand in the air. He pulls the refrigerator open again and fetches another beer. "How? The principal hates me. The last time I went to her with a concern, she shot me down in flames. She won't listen to me over some district school board jerk. The way she told me about the cuts today was so matter of fact. She strongly hinted that there was nothing more to be said about the issue. Of course, she tells me this right before the end of the semester."

I glance toward the open kitchen door, toward the stairs, and hope that the kids are far enough away. I don't mind them hearing the occasional cuss word, but Jack is getting upset. Plus, he's already on his second beer.

He twists off the cap and sits back in the chair. Jack leers at me like his bad news is all my doing and says, "And how was your day?"

It doesn't seem like he cares. Still, the question is enough to rattle me. "Um, yeah. It was fine. Better than yours, I suppose."

"Really? Dave texted me. He said something weird was going on at number six. You know anything about that?"

"No," I blurt. Then I turn away from Jack to conceal my face and continue to stir the sauce. It's the only way to hide what I know from him. I remind myself to thank Dave the next time I see him — with a slap in the face. Then again, how did he know something weird was happening at number six? Ellie wouldn't have said a word, would she? He could've heard it from someone else. People on this street gossip.

Jack sighs at my brief answer and gets out of his chair. "Are you sure? Because Dave said Gabrielle stopped in after work for a chat with Ellie."

"And?" I ask with as much confidence as I can. Of course it was Gabrielle. She felt the need to make the situation worse. She can't help herself. With any luck, Ellie kept her under control.

"And the two of you share everything like a couple of sisters," Jack says.

My grip on the wooden spoon in my hand tightens. "I was here, sorry. I didn't hear anything happening at number six." I don't turn around, but I feel Jack's eyes boring into the back of my head. He lingers in the kitchen for a moment before he leaves the room, beer in hand. He knows I'm lying.

I hate misleading him like this, but I don't want to tell him anything about today and rile him up more than he already is. He can't know about the note in the mailbox, or the missing screwdriver set. He'll probably hear about the knife in Nicole's door soon enough. The rumor mill on Maple Court will see to it. Learning about a vague threat made against Nicole will probably bring a smile to his face. All I care about is what she may or may not have done to us.

If Jack thinks Nicole had anything to do with our mailbox or his screwdrivers, I know he won't be able to help himself and will charge over to her house and shout her down. Then the police will be called, and God knows what might happen then.

The only time I've seen Jack lose control of his anger is with Nicole. When he found out about what happened to Kara, he promised Nicole, in front of several people, that he was going to kill her. He almost got arrested himself.

Losing Kara damn near destroyed him. Back before the crash, he was close with his sister. They were only a year apart in age and both went to the same college. Most people loved her. It's part of the reason he refuses to talk about that night or mention her name.

Kara enters my mind more than I like and makes me wonder what things would have been like if she were still alive. I guess I'll never know.

Jack returns to the kitchen, pulling me from my thoughts. He's still holding his beer in one hand, but in the other, he grips his screwdriver set. As casual as anything, he places it down on the counter and walks away before I can say another word.

CHAPTER THIRTY-FOUR

Eighteen years ago

Alone in the dimness of my room, the weight of my thoughts bordered on suffocation. In the silence, my mind traveled back to a day that now seemed like another lifetime ago, back when Jack was mine. We had driven off campus, escaping the mundane routine of college life for a day by the beach. It was a long drive — the farthest we'd ever gone.

The memory of the trip felt so vivid. I could still taste the scent of the ocean mingling with a cool breeze as the sound of waves crashed against the shoreline. Jack stared at me with eyes full of a love so pure it made my heart ache. We had laid down on the hood of his car, shoulders connected as we watched the sun dip below the horizon. The twilight framed our love in a moment of raw perfection. I'd give anything to reclaim those seconds. I'd burn half the world if it meant I could end this pain that plagued my every breath and have him back again. So, maybe that's what it would take.

As the saying goes, the only way forward is through.

I'd reached a point in time where my only salvation, my only chance at a cure, was to remove the distractions from

Jack's life. Both of them. But I couldn't be so careless as to attack from the shadows of the campus and pray no one saw me. What I needed was something delicate. Something that would leave no trace and cast no doubt on my innocence.

I turned the problem over in my mind. I considered all the angles and discarded reasonable plots with a cold, calculated detachment. It was the only way. Nothing less than a faultless solution was demanded to win him back.

These two girls were not worthy of Jack. They never were and never would be, no matter how much they fooled themselves or each other. Frankly, I'd be doing them a favor.

The solution would come to me. And when it did, it would be seamless in its simplicity and its ability to absolve me of any direct involvement. Such a thought would take time to form. Fortunately, I could wait for Jack for as long as it took.

Whatever the idea would be, I couldn't help but be haunted by the possible consequences. I still couldn't silence the tiny voice inside my head that knew what I wanted was wrong. I just needed to push through the discomfort and focus on what would become a sound resolution. If I found the right path forward, I would not be the hand that tipped the scales, but the architect of a scenario for each girl that was so fraught with potential misfortune its eventual outcome seemed inevitable. The world would see their individual ends as a tragic twist of fate rather than deliberate acts.

"I can do this," I whispered.

To protect myself, I would need to weave an alibi as tight and intricate as each plan itself. I would need to be visible and surrounded by the usual loudmouths on campus. I preferred to exist in the dark, but it was a sacrifice I was willing to make.

As I lay in bed that night, I imagined what the world would be like once the two girls were gone. The sureness of it all gave me an eerie sense of calm. I should have been full of adrenaline and incapable of such a meditative state. But this path, as malevolent as it would become, felt like it was the only way to cleanse Jack of his sins. It was the only way to erase his stains of betrayal and start anew.

I drifted into a powerful sleep and dreamed of what would be. What would our children look like? What house would we live in? It was all a picture of sublimity. And when my deeds were said and done, I would tell Jack everything. He would understand and thank me for freeing him from the prison he had built around himself.

Those two girls would soon be gone like they never existed. The countdown to their end had begun. There was no stopping what was in motion.

I traced the scar on my hand and exhaled.

CHAPTER THIRTY-FIVE

Present day

I stare at the screwdriver set Jack left in the kitchen. He's off in the living room, watching TV. All the while, I'm stuck in here, desperate to learn why the Wihas are suddenly back from the void.

In my distraction, I screw up the sauce I've been stirring and overcook it. A bubble of the red liquid bursts and splatters the backsplash, creating yet another mess I need to clean. I squeeze the bridge of my nose and exhale.

As much as I'm dying to find out why Jack had his screwdriver set with him, I decide not to ask about it. He probably took it to school for some reason and I just didn't notice. If I question him about the set, I won't be able to get through the conversation without sounding weird or awkward. Jack will think something is wrong and press me for more. I already lied to him about the situation at number six. I'll just have to put this mystery to the back of my mind alongside the hidden storage in his study.

Once I have dinner ready, I call the family in to eat at the table. Jack comes in first, phone in hand. The kids barrel past him in a rush of energy and squeal.

"Damn it, slow down," he calls in a voice that's too firm. He's brought his bad day home with him. This happened one day last week as well. I should say something, but I know what will happen if I make a comment right now. We'll fight. Despite needing to hold a united front on this Nicole situation, Jack is already drifting away from me. We had amazing sex last night, but his day seems to have deleted the memory from his brain. This has to be more than some bad news from school.

As dinner gets underway, Jack's phone buzzes on the table, prompting him to lift it to his face. I hate when he uses his cell phone during a meal, and he knows it. Just as I'm about to ask him to ignore the distraction, I notice something. There's a flicker in his eye as he looks at his phone. He quickly masks it when he sees me looking at him. He then locks the device and pockets it. "Nice spaghetti, honey," he says, forcing a smile. He hasn't had a single bite.

I nod, offering a tight-lipped grin in return. The second Jack glances away, I scowl at him and shake my head. What is he up to?

While I stare at my husband, the kids eat dinner. Noah drops half of his meal on the table. The rest is smeared across his face. I attempt to distract myself and eat, but every few bites, I look up from my meal and glance at Jack. Each time I do, I catch him staring at me. It's like he's waiting for an opportunity to check his phone again. Who was texting him?

The kids are oblivious to the silence between Jack and me and are chattering away about every random thought that comes into their innocent little brains. I try my best to talk to them the way a mom is supposed to, but I can't concentrate on their words.

Jack's cell phone emerges from his pocket with a fresh text notification. He holds the device up and stares at the screen. A scowl forms on his brow. Whoever is texting Jack is upsetting him. Why? Whatever this is, it's not helping. I need to pull his focus in the right direction.

"I didn't have time to clean the house today, sorry," I say. "I got called into work."

"Okay," Jack says, half listening.

"They needed help with a problem," I add.

"A problem?"

"Yeah. Nothing major, but something only I could solve, apparently."

"Did they pay you for this?" he asks.

"Well, no," I say. There's no way for me to be paid for my fake visit to work, so it might as well have been for free. "But it doesn't matter."

"It kind of does, honey," he says, concerned.

"It's fine. Don't worry about it."

He continues to scowl as he mutters to himself.

"Is something wrong?" I ask.

"You shouldn't work for free."

"It was only for a few hours."

"That doesn't matter. They're taking advantage of you."

"You do extra work at school all the time."

"That's different."

I go to respond, but Jack gets yet another text. He cuts off our conversation as if we aren't talking and stares at his phone again. This time, he replies to the text with furious fingers. There's a sense of urgency in the way he types. Who is he responding to that's more important to him than his own wife?

Jack mutters something inaudible while shaking his head. I see my opportunity and take it.

"Who are you texting?"

He locks his cell phone and places it face down on the table. "No one. Just my brother."

"Uncle Andy?" Dot asks.

"What about?" I ask.

"Just the usual. Nothing important."

Before I can follow up on the 'nothing', Jack picks up his fork and gets back to eating. He stabs at the food and

147

glowers at the meal. Why is he so upset? This must be more than what's going on at work. I highly doubt he's texting his brother. They never chat about anything serious. There's something he isn't telling me, and the answer is in the texts he's being secretive about.

Determined to find out what's pulling my husband away from me, I come up with an idea that is as stupid as it is desperate.

"Can I get you another beer?" I ask Jack in a casual tone. With his current mood, it's an offer he's unlikely to refuse.

"That'd be good, thanks," he responds with a mouth full of food and a hint of relief in his voice.

As I head to the refrigerator to fetch Jack a beer, my mind races. Is getting my husband drunk so I can snoop through his phone a good idea? It sounds awful when I think about it, but what else can I do? He's not the sharing type when he gets like this. He never used to be so closed off to me. We used to tell each other everything and kept no secrets. But time changes the best of people. It even lets them think it's okay to stray.

Once dinner wraps up, I get the kids bathed and into their pajamas. Jack always helps with this when he's around, but I told him to take it easy and have another drink in front of the TV. He didn't protest. Usually, he deals with Noah, who was less than impressed that Mommy instead of Daddy was the one who helped him tonight.

A few bedtime stories later, the kids are asleep. I head down to the living room to make sure Jack's still drinking. If I can get him drunk and sleepy, I'll just have to wait for him to put his phone down and forget about it. Then I can take the device the second he falls asleep on the sofa.

I don't enjoy spying on my husband. The cameras I placed in the house are weighing on my mind, but we have too many unknowns surrounding our relationship at the moment to take any chances. And with Nicole next door, I have to do my best to stay in control. She's already got me frazzled with her whole innocent, forgiving act.

Returning to the living room, I place another beer beside Jack with a smile, noting that he has set his phone face down on the coffee table, out of reach. He's watching some violent show on Netflix I would never watch on my own. He doesn't offer to change it to something we might both enjoy. I guess everything he said last night about not wanting to lose me was only drunk talk.

Jack's phone buzzes several times during the next few hours. The second it does, he hoists himself up from his slouch and checks the notification, answering long texts with just as many words. Who the hell is he speaking to? I doubt it's Dave.

The night drags on, and it's now past ten. We hardly speak, and Jack declines his fifth beer. "I shouldn't. I have to work tomorrow. Thank you, though."

My useless plan seems like a wash until Noah inadvertently gets things back on track.

"Daddy," he calls from upstairs.

"Crap," Jack mutters. My moment to strike is at hand. Jack gets up to help Noah, leaving his phone behind. Jackpot.

My heart thuds in my ears as I wait for him to be halfway up the stairs before I make my move, my hands trembling as I reach for his cell phone. Just a quick look through his texts will do. Then I'll figure out what's going on.

But as my fingers brush against the cool surface of the phone, I hesitate. Am I ready for what I might find? I can't honestly say. Either way, I need to know. The truth has to be better than any lie I can tell myself.

I enter Jack's pin into his cell phone. It's been the same one for a while now: 030388, Kara's birthday. But instead of the phone unlocking the way it's supposed to, the screen shakes and vibrates. I must have entered a wrong digit, so I try again.

It doesn't work. "No, no, no," I mutter. This is his code. 030388. The numbers have been embedded in my brain. Why would he change his pin and not tell me? The last time he did this was when . . . Oh God. When he cheated on me.

149

Footsteps from the kitchen make me freeze. It's Jack. He's done with Noah. I slap his cell phone down where I found it, right as he enters the room. I stare forward at the TV, but my eyes don't take in the images. All I can think about is the fact that Jack has changed his code. I can't access his phone. And now, he is standing in the room behind me, not saying a word.

CHAPTER THIRTY-SIX

"What are you doing?" Jack asks me from behind the sofa. I don't know if he saw me trying to unlock his phone, but I need to avoid his eyes.

I stare ahead at the commercial that's running on the TV and focus on my breathing. If Jack hears me sucking in a lungful of air right now, he might think I've been up to something.

"Bianca?" Jack asks as he steps farther into the living room. I turn to face him. "Pardon?"

"I asked you a question."

"You did? Sorry. I must have zoned out. It's been a long day. What was your question?"

He stares into my eyes with a wrinkled brow, then shakes his head. "Nothing." He walks to the sofa and sits down beside me. He leans forward and snatches up his cell phone from the coffee table. I pretend not to notice the odd way he's picked up his phone and continue to gaze at a commercial for a luxury car. In an instant, I'm reminded of the black Audi A3 that was in Nicole's driveway when she first arrived. I still have no clue who it belongs to. It couldn't have been her car. She couldn't honestly have thought I'd forget the make and model of that damn vehicle. Not after Kara died.

151

We sit in silence. I avoided Jack's question, but now I'm stuck in the living room with him in an awkward standoff. I stare at the TV while he clutches his cell phone and glances at me every so often. Is he watching me? He must be. It's like he's trying to decide if he should follow up on his question.

Jack must have heard me place his phone back down on the coffee table in a hurry. It made a loud clang. If I'd taken half a second more to be careful, we wouldn't be trapped in the living room, wary of each other. I need to break the tension and give him something else to think about. The perfect thing comes to mind.

"Are you okay with tomorrow?" I ask.

"Tomorrow?"

Of course, he's forgotten. "Our session."

"Oh, right. Marriage counseling. Yeah. Okay as I can be, I suppose."

I give him a second to breathe, then hit him with the hard stuff. "Do you think we should bring up this thing with Nicole?"

Jack runs a hand through his hair and lets out a long breath. "I don't know. I mean, just explaining it all will take up half the session."

"It will, but it's important. Her moving in next door is going to put stress on our relationship no matter what. Especially considering what memories she's going to drag out."

Jack's nostrils flare as he stares at me with a scowl. "What memories?"

He knows what I'm talking about. Or more importantly, whom I'm talking about. It's almost as if he's testing me. After inhaling and exhaling, I push forward.

"Kara."

"Don't say her name," he grunts.

My goal was to force him to storm off to bed, but then I'm hit with an overwhelming desire to understand why he won't ever talk about his sister. It's a topic that should be left well enough alone, but a question spills from me on autopilot.

"Why?"

"Because," he says, raising his voice. "Just don't, okay?"

I shake my head. Not at him, but at myself. I need to stop and quit while I'm ahead. Nothing good will come of this. I close my eyes and attempt to let it go, but I have to know.

"Why won't you talk about your dead sister?"

"Because."

"Because? What the hell is that supposed to mean?"

Jack huffs. "You sure you wanna do this?"

He's giving me an out, but I refuse to take it. "Yes."

"Fine. You wanna know why we never talk about Kara? It's simple, Bianca. She died because of you." Jack holds a dark glare for a long while until his eyes go wide. He seems to realize what he has said a moment too late. I stare at him as my hands tighten into fists. I feel an anger course through me that sets off a tremble. "Excuse me?" I say, doing what I can not to scream.

"Bianca, I'm sorry. I didn't mean anything by—"

"You knew exactly what you were saying. I always suspected this was what you thought. I guess I never imagined you would be dumb enough to say it." Rushing to my feet, I stomp to the kitchen.

"Honey Bee, wait," he calls after me, as if his nickname for me will fix everything. I don't know where I'm going, but I need to be anywhere but here. I collect my phone and keys and rush to the garage.

"Where are you going?"

"Out," I snap.

"Out? What does that mean?"

I turn and face him with bared teeth. "It means I'm getting out of this house to give myself some time to consider the future of this marriage. Understand?"

Jack nods with a gulp. He knows I'm serious, and so do I. What started as a way to get him to leave the room has backfired worse than I could ever have imagined.

I spin away from Jack and head through the garage to my car. When I reach my Subaru, I unlock it with a trembling hand and climb in, slamming the door a second later. I hope the kids wake up, so Jack has to deal with them. Before any guilt can run through me at the thought, I start the engine and hit the garage door remote. The damn thing refuses to open.

"Fuck you," I shout at the remote as I smack the button again and again. Eventually, the stupid remote signals the sensor on the ceiling and kicks the motor into action. The garage door opens as I back my car out. I come close to hitting the rising panels with my impatience.

Once I'm clear of the garage, I hit the gas and speed out of our driveway in reverse, not bothering to go slow in case anyone is there. Maybe Nicole is standing in my driveway. With any luck, I could run her down and call it an accident.

My Forester bounces into the street. I shove it into drive and go. Jack runs from the house as I speed off. I don't look back as I fly out of Maple Court and drive in a random direction. I don't know where I'm going or when I will be back.

CHAPTER THIRTY-SEVEN

I can't believe what Jack said to me. Even if it was just the four beers he drank this evening doing the talking, it's no excuse. Despite being a terrible idea, I have spent years trying to drag so much as a full sentence out of him about the death of his sister, and the first thing he says about the topic is that it was my fault she died.

I should have slapped him for those words. We both know the blame he has been funneling toward me is nothing but guilt. Kara was driving my car when she died. But I wouldn't have needed her there with me if it wasn't for him.

I drive through the streets of Cedarwood Rock and see people through their windows, enjoying their evenings. Some people in the town have their lights off and are probably in bed, asleep. It must be easy to drift off when you haven't been accused of something heinous by the person who is supposed to have your back above all others.

I find my way to the Cedarwood Rock Mall and park far away from the entrance. The mall closes at nine each night, so the parking lot has emptied with only a handful of cars around. I don't know why I'm here, but it's as good a place as any to stop and calm myself down. I just need a moment to breathe. Plus, doing some deep thinking while driving is not the best idea after I got that speeding ticket today.

I kill the engine and lights on my Subaru and lean back in my seat with a sigh. This week has been absolute misery, and it's far from over. What else do the fates have in store for me? I already can't shake off what's happened, but tomorrow I'm supposed to wake up and do it all again. Except at the end of the day, I have a therapy session with Jack.

"God," I whisper. I'd give anything to take a week off from my life. No husband. No kids. No manipulative exes from the past emerging from the depths to ruin my fragile little world. Sadly, my problems can't be wished away.

With my phone connected to my car's Bluetooth, I see the option on the central screen to make calls. I'm extremely tempted to contact Ellie. Not to tell her what Jack said to me, but to hear her voice and talk to her about anything other than my husband or his damn ex.

I'll have to wait until morning, though. I can't bother Ellie this late at night. Not after her mother-in-law has visited. Ellie was putting on a brave face for me earlier today. I know Georgia's drop-ins affect her more than she lets on.

Down the far end of the parking lot, there are a few cars parked close together. Some young people have gathered around and are drinking and smoking what I'm certain aren't cigarettes. There's loud music with a deep bass line thudding away. The sound of it takes me back to my younger days. More specifically, to college.

It was the week before everything changed. A week before the crash. Jack had taken me to a house party outside of town. One where we hardly knew anyone. We had a few beers and found somewhere private to make out like a pair of horny teens as a droning bass line rattled the walls of the home. He whispered into my ear that he loved me. It was one of the first times he'd ever said those words to me.

I didn't know if he meant them or if he was simply trying to get laid. Either way, his confession burrowed its way down into my brain like a tick and refused to leave. I told him I loved him, too, and I meant it. Without question. What happened over the next week both challenged and cemented our relationship, for better or worse.

One of the young people smashes a bottle of something on the hard surface of the parking lot, pulling me from my memories. The sight of it reminds me I've left my husband at home with our two children. The same man who's had four beers this evening. After I stormed out, that number may have increased.

"Oh, God," I mutter. I have to go back home. I don't have a choice. Jack may be more than capable of looking after the kids, but not if he's been drinking. What was I thinking charging out of the house like this?

With a heavy sigh, I start my car and put it in gear, knowing I have to make the short drive back home, back to my problems. But right as I'm about to leave the parking lot, I notice a set of headlights flash on in the distance. They are pointed at me. They weren't there when I arrived.

Ignoring the light, I get underway and crawl through the parking lot. But a few seconds later, the other car drives toward me.

Figuring it's probably a mall worker leaving after a long day, I try to put any paranoid thoughts out of my mind. I can't let the last couple of days creep inside my head.

I fail to take my own advice as I question why a mall worker would still be here in the first place. It doesn't take hours to close up a store and balance the till.

Picking up the pace, I put my foot down a little on the gas and rush for the nearest exit. The car, with its powerful and bright headlamps, does the same, bypassing a closer exit to drive toward mine. Or to me. Maybe the driver needs to go in the same direction as I'm traveling. It's possible, but my rational thinking goes out the window the second the trailing car gets close enough for me to make out its details.

It's a black Audi. And without a doubt, I'm positive it's an old A3. It's the car I saw in Nicole's driveway.

I hit the gas harder and speed out of the parking lot, making a rushed left into the street. The Audi follows and matches my pace.

"Are you serious?" I yell, questioning my sanity. Why is this person following me? And in a damn black Audi A3? My eyes dart between the road ahead and my rearview mirror as I swerve all over the place. If a police officer sees me, I'll be pulled over for sure. But then again, at least I'd be safe from whoever this is.

My brain shifts to my number one suspect, Nicole. Has she really gone to the effort of following me in the same car she once stalked me in? The same car she hoped to kill me with? If she wants there to be peace between us, if she wants to be friends with me, this is not the way to go about it.

The Audi catches up to my Forester without a struggle. I won't be able to outrun it through these winding streets.

As it closes the gap, I try to make out who is driving, but I can't see through the dark tinted windows of the A3. It's just like the one Nicole drove in college. The one her father had bought her. It looks to be the same year and model. This is no coincidence. I'm being stalked.

I'm unsure if I should call the police or try to make a run for home. I could call 911 and have them send out a cop to chase off my pursuer, but part of me wants to find out what would happen if I return home. Maybe I could drive straight to number six and park in Nicole's driveway. I could blare my horn and see if anyone comes out. If no one does, it would confirm what I already know. It would tell me exactly who is chasing me through the streets of Cedarwood Rock late at night.

With a calming breath in, I steady my resolve and focus on staying ahead of the Audi. Its headlamps flood the interior of my car as the driver tails me close enough that we are almost trading paint. If I were to tap my brakes too hard right now, it would cause a crash. It's like someone is trying to recreate that night from eighteen years ago.

158

I may not have been driving, but I'll never forget that long, secluded road or the uncontrolled spin my Honda Civic fell into. The last thing I remembered was the shift of gravity as my car flipped and rolled three crunching times on its side.

When I came to and crawled out of the wreck, no matter how hard I try, I will never forget what came next.

CHAPTER THIRTY-EIGHT

Eighteen years ago

I sat hunched over in the driver's seat of my car, my eyes glued to the entrance of Jack's café across the street. The aroma of coffee filled the air, but it wasn't coming from the establishment I was staking out — it was from the thermos of coffee I'd brought along with me. I needed to stay vigilant.

Every so often, I glanced at my watch to count how much time had passed since Jack's girlfriend had gone inside. It had been fifty-two minutes since she'd ventured through those doors, carrying her favorite handbag and a stack of books. She was studying at Jack's place of work, The Artful Bean, but Jack wasn't there.

From my vantage point in the parking lot across the way, I saw everyone who entered and exited the café. The barista on shift was a lanky guy with a man bun and unkempt facial hair — a U-Dub student for sure. He kept glancing at her table, no doubt hoping for a smile or an opportunity to get her phone number. But he could stare all he wanted. She wouldn't give him anything. She belonged to Jack. I understood her loyalty all too well.

She sat alone with her head buried in a textbook. Her long hair cascaded over her shoulders like a waterfall. There was no doubting her beauty. It was easy enough to see what Jack saw in her physically, but there was something about her that bothered me more than anything else. She came across so normal. So boring.

Around campus, everyone knew her as Jack's girl. The official one, anyway. He paraded her about like the naïve accessory that she was. Her ignorance was nauseating. I often sat awake at night, wondering how he had pulled the wool over her eyes so well. Maybe she just had too much faith in humanity. Jack's innocent angel.

I shifted in my seat, pulling my hoodie tighter around my head. If anyone spotted me, I wasn't sure what the implications would be. I wasn't friends with Jack's two women, so I had no business watching either one of them in such a way.

The late afternoon air was chilly that day. The sun was fast on its approach to setting and would soon dip below the horizon. Within the hour, the café would close. Not being a restaurant that catered to much more than coffee and scones, it wasn't open at night.

Once again, I was running out of time. The reason for my presence was simple: I needed to find a weakness. A flaw to exploit. Something that would help move my plans along and remove her from Jack's life. It had to happen for both girls, but I could only manage one of them at a time. To eliminate both of them from the chessboard at the same time without casting any suspicion upon me would take good timing and a hell of a lot of luck. For now, I was targeting the weaker of Jack's two distractions.

I had my notebook with me. It was filled with unsent letters to Jack, poems about our interactions, and my inner thoughts about each girl. There were also a lot of random scratchings. I couldn't help but write my favorite words on the page, over and over: *J + N forever*.

A group of students exited the café. They laughed and made noise as they went down the street, oblivious to the real world. They were the typical college students I'd come to know: a mix of unnerving confidence and arrogance.

But she remained at her table, not glancing up from her studies. The coffee in front of her had hardly been touched and would be long cold. I smirked as a realization hit me. Had she been waiting for Jack? Was he supposed to join her? The poor thing. He wouldn't be coming. Not today. He was with his secret shame. The girl I knew he cared about the most. She would be the bigger hurdle to overcome.

As fast as any satisfaction came to me, it melted away. I clenched my teeth at the familiar surge of anger that bubbled up inside when I thought about Jack being alone with anyone other than me. How could he keep doing this? Why had he stooped so low and been with these unworthy harpies? The way he kept one so unaware of the other left a permanent knot in my shoulders. But I wouldn't let it bring me down. I had a mission to complete. And the war was far from over.

Twenty minutes passed by. Finally, she gathered her things to leave. With her handbag slung over her shoulder and her books in hand, she stood up and waved at the barista. Man Bun almost looked shocked, but he beamed back at her with a glint of hope. I rolled my eyes and sighed as she approached the exit. I would be forced to slouch lower in my seat the second she walked out the door.

She stepped outside and scanned the street. For a moment, I thought she'd noticed me, but then she turned left and headed down the sidewalk.

"Okay," I breathed, unsure if I should follow or call it a day. I had discovered nothing new. Nothing I didn't already know about her. I could have left and gone home. God knew I was tired of the stake-outs. But, I couldn't leave. The thing I needed might present itself when I least suspected it.

I waited a few heartbeats longer before slipping out of my car to follow on foot. I couldn't stalk her while driving as much as I wanted to.

Keeping a safe distance, I followed her with my hoodie up. The hum of the local traffic muffled the sound of my footsteps. No one would look twice at me.

She turned a corner, but I didn't quicken my pace to catch up. I knew where she was going. As I continued to move around the corner, I glanced ahead and regarded her confident steps. Not once did she glance over her shoulder. She was caught in an ignorant bliss. It was as if she believed nothing bad would ever happen to her. Stupid girl.

She soon reached a nearby parking lot and pulled out her keys. She hadn't parked closer to the café because she had stopped off at a bookstore earlier.

A second later, the faint beep of a car unlocking echoed in the half-empty parking lot. I ducked behind a parked SUV, peeking out just enough to keep watching her while she opened the trunk of her car. There were other people around, but none of them noticed me. No one ever did.

She finished offloading her books and climbed into her car, ready to leave. I hadn't learned a single thing about the girl I didn't already know. My time had once again been spent observing a boring person going about her pathetic life.

"Dammit," I muttered as she started her car. But then a thought came to me. One I should have come up with sooner. I stared at her vehicle as the perfect idea came to me. Could it really be so simple?

She drove off without noticing me, oblivious to the fact that her world was about to come crashing down. I stepped out from my impromptu hiding spot as a smile crept across my face.

I was no longer going to remove Jack's whores one at a time. In the space of one night, I would destroy them both.

CHAPTER THIRTY-NINE

Present day

The Audi that is chasing me doesn't let up, but I manage to put some distance between us. Enough to significantly reduce the chances of me crashing. As a test, I ease up on the gas and watch as the car behind me does the same thing. She's following me, not trying to run me off the road. Why?

With some breathing room, I don't know what to do. Should I go home or drive to the nearest police station? Both options have their downsides. Before I can make a decision, I'm pulled back to the aftermath of the crash eighteen years ago.

After Kara died, I was told to spend the night in the hospital for observations. I wasn't badly injured. I only had a cut on my eyebrow and a few bruises on my body and arms. The seatbelt had saved my life. At that point in time, I still didn't understand why Kara had been flung from my car.

While I was in the hospital, I had a visit from the police. I told them what had happened — about Nicole's car and the person I had seen driving it. When it came time to talk about Kara, I broke down. Everything became real and was too much to bear.

With Jack at my side, the police confirmed what we already knew. They had spoken to Nicole that morning and had uncovered some critical details. Ones that couldn't be ignored. The police also said that the seatbelt in the driver's seat of my car had been tampered with. Someone had sliced partway through it with a sharp knife prior to the crash. They asked if I had any knowledge of the pre-existing damage. I didn't and was certain the seatbelt had been fine before the accident.

Nicole called Jack to explain her version of events, but he refused to talk to her. He didn't want to hear her lies and hung up. She told him where she would be once he had calmed down. But something inside him snapped. He got so upset that he left my room and the hospital. With bloodlust in his eyes, he made a beeline to where Nicole said she'd be. I had no choice but to discharge myself and rush after him. When I arrived only minutes later, Jack was trying to attack Nicole. He threatened to kill her multiple times. Fortunately, there were police officers with her. They stopped Jack from doing anything stupid and didn't arrest him. They understood he was grieving.

The A3 behind keeps its distance, but the driver doesn't give up following me. When I make the unconscious decision to head home, the car charges right up behind again, forcing me to speed up. The next few streets pass by in a blur. As I travel around a long bend in our estate, I realize I'm going way faster than I know is safe. Thankfully, it's late at night. There won't be any kids crossing the road or sudden traffic to contend with. Plus, I'm only a few streets away from home. The second I arrive, I'm going to go through with my plan. It will be disruptive as hell, but disruption is what's needed if I'm going to best Nicole.

After going around another long bend, I'm almost at the entry to Maple Court. The Audi doesn't show any signs of giving up. "Good. Follow me home, Nicole," I say to the rear-view mirror. If she's dumb enough to do this, everyone will see that she's not in her house when I arrive. I'll make plenty of noise to bring them all outdoors. It won't prove much, but it might prove that she is the one screwing with my life. With the way things have been going, the truth is more important to me than my pride.

I rush into Maple Court, screeching around the corner as the engine of my Subaru whines in protest No one is in the way in the cul-de-sac, so I go straight down the middle toward number six. I see Nicole's driveway empty and smile as I aggressively brake out front of her home and roll into her parking space. As soon as I come to a complete stop, I press down hard on the horn and don't let up.

The honking sets off the Rodriguez's dog and some on the next street over. In response to the chaos, multiple internal lights come on in every house on Maple Court. Even my own. But number six stays dark. Only my headlamps illuminate her home.

Considering the racket I'm making out front of Nicole's house, she doesn't respond. And that's because she isn't home. She's in the idling black Audi A3 that's sitting at the end of Maple Court.

"Got you," I say as people appear from their homes in bathrobes and sweatpants. They all squint at me with furrowed brows and angry glares. I've woken them all up. I let off the horn and climb out of my car, stumbling as I go.

"What the hell are you doing?" Dave calls out to me, wearing his old college shirt. He's not alone. Renato and Bonita Rodriguez arrive at his side, looking equally perplexed. I glance to my right and find Jack doing the same as he stands close to the Morrises.

"Bianca?" Jack asks. "Are you hurt?"

"No, look there," I point down the court, taking a few steps with a wild sneer. My finger stabs at the Audi that still hasn't left. Its headlamps are filling the street with a bright light, making it near impossible to see anything else. "That's her. She's been stalking me in that car. Look at it, Jack. It's the same one from eighteen years ago." I approach him with wide eyes and too much enthusiasm. He backs up a step as if I'm the unhinged one chasing people through the streets. As I do this, the Audi reverses. It's already too far away and is hidden by its headlamps.

"No, wait," I call out. Then I face Jack and usher for him to follow. "She's getting away."

"Who is?" he asks, keeping his voice down.

"Nicole," I shout, loud enough that everyone will have heard me. "She almost ran me off the road. She's trying to kill me."

Jack squints at the bright light as the car continues to back out of Maple Court in a hurry. Before he can take a decent look at it, the driver rolls backward around the corner and vanishes. I run out into the court after it, but I hear the car pulling away.

"She's gone," I mutter, coming to a stop. Then I raise my voice in the relative quiet. "That was Nicole," I repeat. "She just tried to kill me." When I turn around, everyone is staring at me. I don't care, though. It's worth it for them all to see what Nicole has been doing to me.

Right as I feel like I'm getting on top of this entire week, Nicole walks out from her front door in her pajamas, hugging herself in the cold. "What's going on?" she asks Dave.

"That's a great question," he replies, rubbing the back of his neck.

I stand frozen, gawking at Nicole and am lost for words. The entire cul-de-sac stares at me, Darell Vargas included. Even Ellie is looking at me like everyone else.

Please tell me this isn't happening.

I face Jack and rush to his side. "Take me inside. Please," I beg him with pleading eyes.

"Uh, yeah," he says as he guides me away from the mob. "Come with me."

"Thank you," I mutter to him as I stare at the ground, embarrassed. I take one last glance back over my shoulder and catch sight of Nicole. She glares straight at me with a clear smirk, and I know then and there that I have been played. She isn't working alone. She hasn't been since she got here. Someone is helping her.

CHAPTER FORTY

Jack takes me inside and closes our front door, locking out the hateful stares of the disappointed neighbors. I walk like a lost puppy as Jack guides me by the elbow. My mind is running with too many possibilities at once. So much so, my hands shake.

"Are you okay?" Jack asks me as I release myself from his light grip and stumble into the kitchen. When I reach the island bench, I plant my palms flat on the granite surface to steady the jitters that are running through me.

"Bianca?" he asks again.

My mouth falls open to speak, but nothing comes out. Instead, I shake my head and stare at the bench. I'm afraid to say the wrong thing.

"Come on, honey. You've got to talk to me. Say something."

I move away from the bench and Jack, needing a second to declutter my foggy brain. How did Nicole pull this off? How was she able to be in two places at once? There was no way for her to have been driving that car and be in her home at the same time. Someone has to be helping her. But I don't know who or why.

"Bianca?" Jack asks, the annoyance in his voice increasing.

I go to answer but am saved by the patter of small feet.

"Daddy?" Noah asks at the bottom of the stairs through the open door to the kitchen. He can go up and down the steps on his own quite well, given his age. The sight of him distracts me from what is going on. At least for a second.

"Hey, buddy. Did we wake you?" Jack asks.

He nods. "Car went beep beep."

"It did," Jack chuckles as he walks toward our son.

Noah closes the distance first and steps into the kitchen doorway. Jack scoops him up as Noah says, "So noisy."

"Sorry, buddy. Let me take you back to bed, huh?"

Noah sees me and gives me the saddest face I've seen from him in a while. The kind I only ever receive when he's distressed. I did this to him. All in my pursuit to oust Nicole. I acted without taking the time to consider the consequences. This must be so easy for Nicole. Especially given how quick I am to overreact to things.

I rush over to Noah and give him a cuddle, slipping him from Jack's arms.

"No, I want Daddy," he says, sending a dagger through my heart.

"Okay, baby. You stay with Daddy."

"Sorry," Jack mutters. Then he carries Noah upstairs in the dark, leaving me all alone in the kitchen. A sigh leaves my body as I close my eyes and try to shake off the awful thoughts that are coursing through my mind. Before I have time to clear a single one of them, I realize my car is still in Nicole's driveway with my keys and cell phone inside. I can't leave them there. But I also don't want to face anyone.

I can picture them all now, chatting to each other with arms crossed over their chests as they speak openly about my behavior. "I've never liked her," Renato might say. "She yelled at me at In-N-Out Burger," Darell could add. Then Gabrielle would weigh in with what happened earlier with the knife. Before the night is through, my name will be ruined. They will all think the worst of me.

When Jack comes back down, I ask if he can do me a favor and move my car into the garage. Then I can retrieve my things from it.

"Okay, but then you and I are going to have a talk about what happened out there. Got it?"

I nod, avoiding his eyes the way one of his students might do when they are in trouble. The tone in his voice makes me feel about half my size.

As Jack heads out the front door, I rub my hands over my face in rhythmic circles, thinking I can somehow push away all my guilt and stress. It doesn't help and only leaves me feeling dizzier than I already do. What a day.

I exhale while leaning on the island bench in the kitchen and hear a familiar sound coming from the living room. It's Jack's cell phone buzzing with a notification.

My heart rate picks up as I feel a tingling sensation run over my skin. He's left his phone on the coffee table. He must have continued to watch TV when I stormed off. I could check his screen while he's busy. I won't be able to unlock his phone, but I can at least see what the notification was. He has pretty standard security and allows his lock screen to show the contents of his text messages. Well, the last time I checked, it was like that. He has changed his code to unlock the screen and may have made some other changes

Before I lose my nerve, I rush to the living room and find Jack's cell phone on the coffee table. The screen is face down again. I lean over to pick it up right as Dot calls out.

"Mom? Are you there?"

"What's wrong, honey?" I shout back. I'm so close to Jack's phone I could flip it over and take a peek. But I don't want Dot catching me in the act. Not that there would be anything suspicious about me touching her father's cell phone.

"I heard lots of noise," she says as she walks into the kitchen. I rush to meet her and hear my Subaru's engine ticking over. Jack is in my car and will have it returned to the garage in less than a minute.

"There's nothing to worry about," I say to Dot. "You go back to bed, okay?"

"But there was a long beep. Like a car crash. Is someone hurt outside?"

"No, baby. I promise. Now head up to bed, and I'll come tuck you in soon."

"Okay," she says with a crinkled forehead. Dot has always had this uncanny ability to sense when I'm lying or not telling her the complete story about a situation. I wish I possessed the same insight.

With two gentle hands, I assist Dot out of the kitchen toward the stairs. At the same time, I hear the garage door rattle open. Jack is almost done moving my car, so I charge to the living room, back to his cell phone. Right as I'm about to scoop it up, it buzzes again, frightening the hell out of me.

Jack pulls my Forester into the garage and kills the engine. I'm out of time, but I pick up the damn phone anyway. On the screen, I see a stack of texts layered on top of one another. They are readable from the lock screen. Fortunately, he hasn't changed the security level just yet. The texts are all from a contact with the name 'N.' I read as many as I can, starting with the newest one.

N: *Is everything alright?*
N: *I hope you are okay!*
N: *That was weird . . .*

Jack opens the garage door that leads into the kitchen, and I place his cell phone back where I found it. I get the job done without a clang this time and rush out of the living room. I circle around through the formal dining room we hardly ever use and make my way back to the kitchen.

As I reach the kitchen, short on breath, Jack sees me and places my car keys down on the bench. He even thought to bring my cell phone inside, too. He places it down on the bench beside my keys and gives me a smile. "Done," he says.

I force a grin and stare at him as the texts run through my brain. I only have one question for him, and I can't ask it.

Who the hell is N?

CHAPTER FORTY-ONE

My eyes are locked on Jack's as he speaks to me. I have no idea what he's saying. All I can think about is what I saw on his phone. As he continues to talk, the same question rolls around in my head, over and over: who is N? I am confident I know who this N person might be, and the answer is as screwed up as the question.

Nicole.

How can it be possible? Not the technical aspects. She texted him after the barbecue, as well as me, asking if we could all be friends and act like the past never happened. I understand the how, but not the why. Why would Jack be in contact with Nicole?

"Did you hear what I said?" Jack asks me.

"Sorry?" I blurt.

"I said, do you want to tell me what all that was about outside?"

My eyes dart left and right as I search for an answer. He's stumped me with a question I should have been preparing for. Instead, it feels like I've been hit over the head with a hammer.

"Bianca?" he presses.

"I don't know," I say. "I guess I wasn't thinking straight. I saw a car that reminded me of Nicole's Audi and freaked out.

I'm sorry." I stare at him for a second, then look away. From that glimpse, I observe one clear thing: he doesn't believe me.

Dammit.

I take a step back and hold my head. This is all backward. I should be the one asking the questions. Jack should be the one getting flustered as he's backed into a corner. Why do I feel like I'm the guilty one?

Jack steps closer to me and whispers, "Why did you say Nicole was trying to kill you? Has something happened? Did she do something to you?"

I keep my body half-turned from Jack and wonder if Dot is going to call out for me to come upstairs to tuck her in. For once, I need her to interrupt us.

"If she's threatened you, I want to hear about it," he says.

I shake my head. If he is texting Nicole, and I tell him about the mailbox, the knife, and the screwdriver set, what will he do with that information? Help me, or tell her about it so she can plot her next move against me? Nicole can't have Jack on her side. Not after everything that happened back then.

"She hasn't done a thing," I blurt. I can't trust Jack. Not while he is texting Nicole or whoever this N person is. Maybe N is the one that's helping Nicole screw with my head. Or maybe N is no one. Just a co-worker. A co-worker who is texting Jack with ultra-specific questions about things happening on our street late at night. Not likely.

"God," I whisper to myself.

"What's that?" Jack asks, leaning toward me.

"Nothing." I face him with my hands out wide. "I need to go tuck Dot in. I woke her up before with my car, so I should go." I start to leave the kitchen.

"Where are you going?"

"I just said—"

"I know what you said, but do you honestly think you can walk away from this conversation?"

I blink rapidly in response. "Yes. I can. Are you saying I can't?"

"No, but I think we should talk about everything. There's something going on, and you're shutting me out."

"Are you serious?" I spit out. "Do you really want to get into a conversation about shutting people out?"

He narrows his gaze, crossing his arms over his chest. "Maybe it's time we lay it all out."

My mouth hangs open as I stare at my husband and try to see if he is being genuine. Does he really want to do this? And now? Is this just an attempt to deflect any attention away from himself and throw it onto me? Because if it is, it's a terrible idea.

Jack moves closer to me again and grabs me gently by the wrists. "Bianca, please. I know I've been a crappy husband in the past, and that I'm still a lousy one now, but if there's something going on with Nicole, you have to tell me."

I stare into his piercing gaze and think about the stream of texts he received at dinner and the ones I just saw now. Is this all an act? Is he pretending to be concerned? I need to ask him the question I can no longer avoid. "Who is—?"

"Mom!" Dot calls out, cutting me off from asking who N is. I glance over my shoulder toward the doorway that leads to the stairs. I break away from Jack's grip and rush to leave.

Jack mutters something inaudible as I go. I ignore him and thank God that Dot yelled out. I wasn't prepared for the fallout that would follow if I had completed my question. If I had spoken that extra letter, Jack would have known I was snooping on his phone. The ensuing argument would have woken up the cul-de-sac for the second time tonight.

As I exit the kitchen, Jack gets in his last words. "This conversation isn't over. You know what? I'm looking forward to our session tomorrow. Should be an interesting one."

"Crap," I mutter to myself. I almost forget that we're booked in for our marriage counseling session after he finishes school. Again, I give him no response and try to keep my composure.

I walk away in silence, all the while knowing that I'm no closer to finding out the truth about Jack or Nicole or the person who chased me down in the Audi tonight.

As I climb our stairs and make my ascent to Dot, each step feels heavier than the last. I don't know how much more of this chaos I can take. Whoever is doing this to me is winning.

The image of the knife buried in the bloody note rushes into my brain.

"Lies breed chaos," I whisper.

CHAPTER FORTY-TWO

Eighteen years ago

My plan to eliminate Jack's two girlfriends was impeccable. Unfortunately, though, pulling off what I wanted to achieve was going to require perfect timing. Two weeks ago, I bugged each of Jack's girlfriend's dorm rooms with listening devices. I needed the ability to listen in on anything they had to say regarding their schedules or general plans. Plus, it gave me a few opportunities to listen in when Jack graced them with his company. There was one major downside, though.

I hated hearing them have sex. Knowing Jack was being intimate with someone else only ruined the moments we had together and cheapened the experience. Still, for the sake of my plan, I had to listen in. Whenever it happened, the only way I coped with the torment was by remembering the times Jack and I were together in such a way. Besides, both of his pathetic women sounded vanilla by comparison.

His girlfriend still didn't know about the one he was seeing on the side. She was still his dirty little secret. For months, he'd slept with her behind the back of his supposed girlfriend. No one else knew about them. All except for one person: Jack's sister. But she had kept their secret so far. From what I could tell, she didn't want any part of the affair, but her loyalty to her brother stopped her from revealing anything.

One evening, when Jack was alone with his secret shame, the one I had almost attacked, the two lovebirds got into a heated discussion. I listened to the conversation with my earphones in. To be a fly on the wall in their private space, I needed to be close by, down the hall. The argument was predictable. One I'd seen coming for weeks. She was sick of being kept in the shadows.

"You said that you loved me," she yelled, barely containing herself within the walls of her dorm room.

"I do love you," Jack replied, defense lining his voice.

"Then why the hell are we still running around like this? Why are you still hiding me away?"

"I'm not hiding you away, babe," Jack said.

"Yes, you are. Apart from your sister, no one knows about us."

I chuckled at the very idea that she thought they were being so careful, that no one else knew about them.

"I thought this was what you wanted," Jack said. "I thought you liked the sneaking around."

"I did. We've had a lot of fun. But it's not enough anymore. I want us to take this relationship to the next level. You know what that means."

Jack didn't respond straight away. I imagined he was pacing her dorm room with his hands on his head as his little world was crumbling. He thought he could have it all and keep them both happy. All when he should have been with me instead. If we were together, he wouldn't have needed to find someone else to have fun with. I would have shown him what a real woman was capable of.

"What are you saying?" Jack asked.

"Don't act like any of this is a surprise. I want you to end things with her. And not in a few months or sometime in the future, like you keep promising. End it now."

More silence followed. Then Jack said the dumbest thing he could have possibly uttered. "I'll think about it."

"You'll think about it? What is there to think about? If you love me like you claim, then you know what needs to happen. You need to break up with her. You need to end it tonight."

If Jack went through with what was being asked of him, his public girlfriend wouldn't take it well. She may have come across as cool, calm, and collected to everyone else, but I saw the real her that existed below the surface. She was as wound tight as the rest of us and ready to unravel.

"Tonight? Are you serious? I can't do that."

"Why?" she asked. "Give me one good reason why you can't call her right now and end things?"

The next words out of Jack's mouth would be crucial. With any luck, I wouldn't need to go through with my current plan. The couple was on the verge of splitting up. I'd only have one whore left to deal with. That would be simple enough. If that was how things turned out, part of me would be disappointed. I had psyched myself up with the perfect end for them both and was ready to do what was necessary.

Jack gave his answer. "It's complicated."

She huffed. "Get out."

"Please, just listen."

"No, I don't want to hear it. You either love me, or you don't."

"I love you. You know I do. It's just—"

"What?" she roared, loud enough that I had to pull my earphones out for a second.

"I'm afraid of her father," Jack said.

Her voice dropped to a normal level. "You're what?"

"Afraid of him. I'm worried if I break things off with her, she'll go running to her dad and ask him to ruin my life."

"Why would he do that?" she asked. She still sounded annoyed, but her voice was calming down.

"I don't know, but he seems like the kind of dad that would do something like that. The few times I've met him,

179

he's given me this look that is very threatening. I really don't want to push him."

A sigh filled the room. Without being there, I knew it belonged to her. I'd listened enough to her annoying habit. She also loved to talk to herself when she was doing her make-up and clicked her tongue when she was studying. Every sound she made was like fingernails down a chalkboard to me. I wasn't sure how much more of it I could take.

"So, what's the plan then, Jack? Marry her? Have children? Stay with her until her father dies?"

"No. I'm just saying that if I break it off with her, it needs to be her idea. And it can't end badly. I need her to get bored with me or something."

"God," she muttered. I couldn't see, but her voice told me she wasn't going to dump Jack. She would not walk away. Of course not. Someone as pathetic as her wasn't capable of growing a spine and doing what was right. That was going to cost her. More than she could ever comprehend.

I listened for a while longer and heard them kiss and make up. There would be no break-up. Jack didn't have what it took to end both relationships. I pulled my earbuds free and let my head lean back against the icy wall, closing my eyes.

It was one last test. Jack was seeing if I had what it took for us to be together again.

I opened my eyes and stared down at the scar in my palm. I traced the carving, feeling the J + N against the tip of my finger. A tingle ran along the veins in my wrist and traveled on until it settled in my heart. "Soon, my love."

CHAPTER FORTY-THREE

Present day

After tucking Dot in, I go to bed and pray that Jack doesn't ask me any more questions. As I pass by the stairs on the way to our bedroom, I glance down the steps and realize Jack must still be up. The lights in the kitchen are still on. What the hell is he doing now? I'm about to dismiss the thought when I remember my cell phone is downstairs, sitting on the kitchen bench.

I sigh, filling the corridor with my frustrations. This entire night has me so frazzled. I keep making one mistake after another.

Deciding I can't go to bed without my phone, I trudge back downstairs and hope that Jack is no longer in the kitchen. With any luck, he's stewing in the living room or somewhere else. I don't care. I just need my damn phone and to go to bed. Maybe a few hours of sleep will help me. If I can get any.

When I reach the bottom of the stairs, I tiptoe toward the kitchen. The flooring in there is tiled, so I slip off my shoes and peek into the open doorway. He isn't here.

Not screwing around, I rush into the kitchen and find my cell phone and keys where Jack left them. I move with purpose and swipe my phone up from the bench. As I do, I hear Jack in the living room clear his throat. I don't know what he's doing in there. The TV isn't on anymore. For all I know, he could be on his cell phone, texting Nicole back.

As I head back to the stairs to go to bed, I remember something important. In all the fuss today, I forgot I installed three cameras around our house. I also forgot to re-enable notifications on the app after I turned them off when Ellie was here.

"Idiot," I mutter to myself as I slip my shoes back on. With a glance over my shoulder, I make sure Jack isn't following me and rush back upstairs. The steps are also carpeted, so I can do so without making much noise. I want to be alone so I can look at the cameras and find out what Jack has been up to and what he is doing now. Hopefully, the limited camera angles have captured something.

As I make my way to my bedroom for a little privacy, I can't help but think about the therapy session we have booked in for tomorrow after work. We've been going once a week for some time now. It costs a damn fortune. Plus, the kids have to be watched while we attend. Fortunately, Ellie takes them. It's been a tremendous help. If we had to pay for a babysitter on top of the session, we wouldn't be able to go.

I'm usually all for the session, but given how things have fallen apart this week, it's the last stress I want to deal with. Jack has also promised to use the visit to his advantage. He's normally so closed off when we attend. It's ironic that he is desperate to talk about us for a change. Well, not us. Me.

In case Jack comes to bed, I don't bother getting changed or brushing my teeth. Instead, I drop onto my side of the mattress and open the camera app. There are a million notifications.

I take a second to absorb what it is I'm about to do. Jack has no idea I've set these cameras up. If he were to find out about this, I don't know what the consequences would be. I could delete the app now and remove the cameras, but my brain won't let me. I need to know what is going on with my husband.

I scrub through several recordings, seeing Jack and me arguing in the kitchen. I watch myself sneaking back in there too. Before I go through the rest, I open the live view in the living room. I have the camera pointed right where Jack likes to sit on the sofa. I find him still there, staring at his phone in the dark. The glow of his screen lights up his features. He has a scowl on his face as he scrolls through something I can't make out on his cell phone. It doesn't look like he's texting anyone. Most likely he's on YouTube or X.

I breathe a sigh of relief that he isn't texting anyone. But the calm that has entered my head soon vanishes when I go through previous recordings — specifically, ones from earlier when I stormed off in my car.

I find multiple recordings of Jack on his cell phone in the living room, texting frantically. Each video is a fragment of the time I was away and doesn't give me much. But I can tell from the stress in his eyes that he is in a heated discussion with whomever it is he is texting. Is this N, or someone else? Maybe David? Andy even? The three of them have a habit of texting stupid things to one another at random times. But Jack isn't laughing.

In one recording, I watch Jack stand in a hurry and walk to the kitchen. I check the kitchen camera for a corresponding angle. Jack passes through the room without stopping. I can't see where he goes next because of the limited range, but I can guess he has either gone upstairs or to the guest bathroom. The only other camera I can check for around this time is the one I placed in his study.

"The study," I whisper. I should have looked at it first. I was so hung up on seeing what Jack was doing in the living room that I forgot all about it. I switch to the study camera and find two recordings during the time I was away. He wasn't in the room for long, from what I can tell, but he did indeed go in there. Why would he need to venture into that space so late on a weeknight? And right after we had a fight?

I exhale, slowly letting my unsteady breath out as my finger hovers over the play button for the first recording in Jack's study. I don't want to do this, but I'm well beyond the point of using ignorance as a coping mechanism. I have to find out why Jack is being so secretive.

I tap the damn button and prepare for the worst. The camera angle is from a vent in the wall that stares down at Jack. It starts with him walking across the small room with haste in his step. When he reaches his desk, he doesn't sit down. He does the one thing I was hoping not to see. He rolls his chair out of the way, then does the same with the plastic square and extra piece of carpet. I can't see it well, but he's going into the hidden storage compartment. The one I found empty.

"What to the hell?" I let out. I might not be able to see behind the desk, but I can hear on the audio that he is opening the trapdoor. He knows what he is doing. It's like he's done this before.

Once the trapdoor is open, Jack pulls out the same box I caught him staring into the other night and places it on the desk. I see the word "college" written on the side.

"You son of a bitch," I mutter as I tap the pause button on the recording. My eyes flick away from my phone to the hallway to make sure Jack isn't coming to bed. I'm clear for the moment.

Before I tap play again, I take a second to settle my rapid breathing. I can feel a pounding in my chest as a familiar fear rushes through me. My hand shakes again. I place my cell phone down and clasp my hands together to steady myself. It takes a few seconds, but the gesture removes most of my jitters.

I think about this damn box that is frozen on my screen. Where did he move it to before returning it to its hiding place? And how did he know I would go looking for it the next day? He must have heard me sneak away from his study the other night and had gotten paranoid. Maybe that's why he had his screwdriver set out. He's probably got another hidden compartment in this house that is only accessible with those tools. Maybe.

"Okay," I tell myself. I've messed around long enough. It's time to find out what this damn husband of mine has been up to. I hit play and watch as Jack spins absently in his desk chair and rummages through the college box. The resolution on my hidden camera isn't high enough to make out any details, but I see a pile of photos in the box. It's the Polaroids again. I roll my eyes. Didn't he get his fill with these things the other night? Am I that awful to be married to that he has to stare at the memories of another woman and pine for a different time with a better person? I guess so.

The recording ends with Jack trawling through the box of Polaroids. "Dammit," I whisper. The one disadvantage of these cheap cameras is the brief recording time after motion has been detected. It wasn't like I could fit a fancy, continuous recording security camera into the vent in such a short amount of time on a limited budget. I worked with what I had. And for what it's worth, I'm glad I did.

Hoping there's more to watch, I go to the second recording and hit play. My jaw drops when I view the file. So much so I have to scrub to the start and watch it again three more times. I can't believe it. Just as I thought I was getting somewhere, I see Jack putting the carpet and plastic square back into position along with the chair. Then I stare at my screen as he walks out of the room with the college box tucked under his arm.

He moved it again while I was away, and I have no idea to where or why.

CHAPTER FORTY-FOUR

I rewatch the two recordings four more times. I want to be sure what I saw was real. I still can't wrap my head around the fact that Jack is moving a secret box all around the house. Does that mean he knows I'm suspicious of him? If so, why is he on the offense, coming after me for my behavior? Is it all a deflection?

I hear the creak of the stairs as Jack ascends the steps. He must finally be coming to bed. I close the app and lock my phone. Shoving it into my pocket, I rush to the bathroom, flick on the light inside, then close the door. Feeling like I'm trying to hide from a serial killer, I step back farther into the small room to avoid casting a shadow over the gap at the bottom of the door. I want Jack to think I'm in here for a reason.

Closing my eyes, I realize I need to pull myself together. Jack is coming to bed and will see that I'm still awake. He might use the opportunity to push me further into a corner and ask me more questions about Nicole. Maybe I should tell him everything. Then he might understand what I've been going through. These past few days, I've been afraid to tell him about the things Nicole has been doing, all to prevent him from flying off the handle and attacking her. But my fears have changed. The college box and Jack's secretive texting are screwing with my head.

One minute, he's pouring out his feelings, saying he doesn't want to lose me. The next, he is relocating that box from his study to somewhere else and back again. I'm ninety-nine per cent certain the person with Jack in all those Polaroids is Nicole. But if he hates her so much, why the hell would he be going to great lengths to keep old photos from their time together hidden from me?

A knock comes at the door. "Bianca?" It's Jack.

"Uh, yeah?" I ask, my voice cracking a little.

"Is everything okay?"

"Yes," I reply, keeping my answer as short as possible. A pause floats between us, and it feels like it lasts forever. I stare at the door and don't know how to feel. Part of me wonders if Jack is asking because he cares, while the other voice in my head is convinced he might kick the door down.

"Are you sure?" he asks. "Because we never close this door. Even when we use the toilet."

I curse under my breath. I should have known he'd say this. To keep him at bay, I blurt out the first thought that comes to mind. "I didn't want to bother you with the light in case you came to bed." I shake my head and question the nonsense that just spilled from my mouth.

"It's no bother, honey. Can I come in? I need to brush my teeth."

I stare wide-eyed at the door and pace on the spot. He doesn't want to brush his teeth. He wants to talk to me again. If I let him in here, he will get it all from me. I won't be able to hold back any longer.

"I'll just be a minute," I say. "Then it's all yours." I fumble to turn on the tap in the sink on the vanity, hoping the running water gives the impression I'm doing something.

"Okay," Jack says.

I don't know if he is still standing there, but it doesn't matter. I've bought myself a minute at best. It's not like I can jump out the window and run away. There's no reason to. Jack doesn't want to hurt me. He only wants to understand what is going on. And I can't tell him.

With few options left, I brush my teeth to make it sound like I'm in the bathroom for a reason. I don't have time to remove my make-up or much else, so as soon as I'm finished, I open the door to leave. Jack is standing right there and hasn't moved. I let out a startled gasp. "Jesus, you scared me."

"Sorry," he replies as I pass by him, avoiding his gaze. He stares at me and seems to track me as I go. I feel his eyes on my skin as I rush to our walk-in closet to change for bed. He stops his staring and heads into the bathroom, keeping the door open the way he normally would.

I finish changing into my pajamas — the boring, long-sleeved, button-down ones with a fading floral pattern I usually wear. They are pajamas that send an obvious message that I want to go to sleep and do nothing else.

While Jack enjoys the perks of marriage, using the toilet with the door open, I rush to my side of the bed, cell phone in hand. The thought of my camera app stirs inside me. I can't let Jack see it. Ever. With that in mind, I need to change my lock screen code. I've had the same one since I got my first smartphone. It's my grandmother's birthday. Growing up, she was one of the few adults in my life I could stand. Jack knows the code, so I should change it to something he would never guess.

As Jack brushes his teeth ten feet away from me, I fumble through my cell phone's settings to figure out how to update the code. After going down several dead ends, I figure it out. I choose a code Jack has no hope of working out: Ellie's birthday. He can barely remember mine, so it's the perfect idea. The thought of my friend reminds me of the babysitting duties she will need to do tomorrow unless I can get out of that damn therapy session with Jack.

Before he comes to bed, I plug in my cell phone and slide under the covers. I close my eyes and roll away from his side of the bed. That way, when he climbs in, he might think I'm falling asleep and am in no mood to talk. It is late, and he has work in the morning. I also have to work at the library after taking the kids to school.

Jack hops into bed a minute later after turning off all the lights. The mattress rocks a little with his movements as he settles in. He hasn't said another word to me. I might be in the clear.

A breath escapes me as I feel the weight of the day sink me further down into the bed.

"Honey?" Jack says.

My eyes flick open. I pretend not to hear him and try to imitate the sound of someone sleeping peacefully.

"Bianca?" he says, trying again. This time, he shakes my shoulder. I can't fake being asleep now.

"Yeah?" I ask, feigning a touch of confusion.

"I just want you to know that whatever is going on, I'm here for you."

"Okay," I reply, unsure what else I'm supposed to say. Jack either means what he is saying, or he is screwing with my head as much as Nicole is.

"Goodnight," he says, not following up his statement with questions or an explanation.

I stare into the dark with darting pupils and mutter back, "Night." Whatever happens tomorrow, I need to find a way to cancel that therapy session.

CHAPTER FORTY-FIVE

I lie awake in our bed while Jack is sound asleep, snoring. I've put thoughts of our pending therapy session to rest for the time being. My focus for the last restless hour has been the college box.

Jack hasn't moved an inch. No doubt his fatigue has combined with the amount of alcohol he's consumed over the past few days. Because of this, a single idea fills me. One I wish I could forget. While Jack is fast asleep, I could search for the college box. It's a terrible plan, but I have to try.

I've checked my cameras to see if there were any recordings I missed besides the two in the study. All the app could show me was Jack coming back to the kitchen and living room without the box in hand. From his study upstairs, he could have gone into the attic or downstairs to any other room — even to the backyard. The only place he couldn't have taken the box was to the garage.

I have no way of tracking this box down short of asking Jack what he did with it. I'm not at that stage yet, but if things continue like this, I will. He won't be able to deny it, either. Not when I have video evidence.

Deciding I can't lie in bed for another minute, I get up. As quietly as I can, I leave our bedroom with nothing but my pajamas and cell phone like a teenager sneaking out to go to a party.

As I amble down the corridor, I let my feet take me where they want to go. I have no clue where Jack has hidden the box.

My weary bones carry me around the house to every room that doesn't have someone sleeping in it. I don't find a thing. Nothing jumps out at me as a place to hide a small box within our home. Needing some air, I head out to the backyard. It's cold outside but not freezing. I hug my chest and think about turning around. The last thing I want is to catch a cold. The breeze is refreshing and keeps me there. Plus, the open space is calming my frantic mind.

I've never felt more alone than I do right now. Especially after the incident in the street. Even Ellie stared at me in dismay. She probably thinks I stuck the knife in Nicole's door. And why wouldn't she?

I sit down on the deck and sigh into the night air. I close my eyes and feel the cool breeze ebb and flow like I'm sitting by the ocean, listening to the crashing of waves. It's a nice escape, if only for a moment.

The wind picks up and blows something toward me. A scrap of black flutters past my face. "What the?" I blurt. The piece of trash disappears before I can make sense of what it is, but I soon discover where it came from.

Standing, I tuck my cell phone into my pocket and walk toward the source of the debris — Jack's smoker. He rarely uses it anymore. We don't need it with the number of barbecues Bradley and Gabrielle host in the cul-de-sac.

As I get closer, I'm overwhelmed by a burning odor. I'm surprised I couldn't smell it before at the step and figure the breeze must have been carrying it in different directions. The stench smells like something chemical and plastic has been set ablaze and extinguished. And from what I can tell, the burned item has been left in Jack's smoker.

I edge closer to the round shape of the grill with caution. The lid is shut, but I can see more scraps of debris hanging from the gap fluttering in the wind.

The breeze shifts direction again and frees more charred scraps from the smoker. I find pieces scattered across the backyard in all directions. Someone has been out here burning things.

"Jack," I utter. It must have been him. And I don't need to guess what it was that he was burning. I can't see the college box nearby, but I bet it's now empty.

I yank open the lid on the grill and confirm my suspicions. Inside are the blackened remains of burned Polaroids. There's hardly anything left apart from ashes. Only traces of photos here and there. Nothing solid. Below the grill is a puddle of water. Jack must have needed to put the flames out in a hurry. Maybe this happened as I came home. I don't know. Either way, something sped him through the process.

I dip a hand into the pile and lift out a fistful of smelly ashes. The move unleashes more stench — enough to make me cough in response. I let the remains fall from my fingers, then wipe the grit on the pants of my pajamas.

"Great," I mutter when I think about the stain the ashes will leave on my clothing. But any concerns I have for my aging sleepwear soon evaporate when I find something poking through the pile. There's a single Polaroid that has partially survived the fire. The water Jack dumped into the smoker must have saved it. I remove the Polaroid from the ruins like it's a phoenix rising from the ashes.

"Oh my God," I whisper as I hold up the photo in the moonlight. Half of the image has been burned, but on one side is a clear picture of Jack. He's wearing his Seattle Mariners baseball hat and is smiling. The photo looks old, and I know by the sight of him that this was taken in college.

He doesn't look much older than he does now. He's one of those men who seems to age slowly. Apart from a few wisps of gray hair and crow's feet around his eyes, he hasn't changed.

The sight of my husband isn't the thing freaking me out, though. It's the person in the photo he has his face pressed against. It's another woman. Not me. Most of her side of the photo has been destroyed by the fire, but the small section I can see confirms this isn't a photo Jack and I took together. This is him and someone else.

I stare closer at the damaged photo and try to determine if it's Nicole. Is she the woman that was in Jack's hidden box? I guess she isn't anymore. He's destroyed her. My only question is why now? Why hold on to these memories for eighteen years and dispose of them when Nicole appears in our lives again?

I take one last look through the pile of ashes to see if there are any other Polaroids that have survived the fire. None appear, so I place the half-ruined photo in my pocket, then return the lid to the smoker.

As I step away from the grill, I bombard myself with questions. I don't have an answer to any of them, but a final one hits me as I reach the back door. It's a question I don't want to answer. Because now I have to decide if I should take what I've found to Jack and ask him why the hell he's been burning old photos from a hidden box in our backyard.

Great.

I head back inside. With my back to the door, I feel my eyes go wide as the reality of what I have found hits me. I pull out the half-destroyed photo and stare at it again. Unconsciously, I slide to the floor.

I glare at the Polaroid, into Jack's eyes, and realize I know when this photo was taken. I didn't think anything of it at first, but like I had already noticed, Jack is wearing his Seattle Mariners baseball hat. It looks brand new. And with good reason.

I try not to think about the hours that led up to the crash, but the Polaroid in my hands is making the task impossible. Two days before everything happened, I gave Jack that damn hat. It was one of the best gifts I had ever given him, and according to this photo, he wore it while he was with another woman.

"You son of a bitch," I mutter. I grip the Polaroid tight and think about Nicole. Jack has kept this memory of her and a whole box full of them from their time together. Why? With the hell that came over the next few days after this photo was taken, it makes little sense. Had he regretted what he'd done after the crash? If so, it means he's held onto their relationship for eighteen years.

But something changed. He's destroyed Nicole and their history. And all moments after blaming me for Kara's death. I've never been more confused in my life.

I let my hand holding the photo fall to my side as a wave of exhaustion presses into my skull. I need to go to bed. But how am I supposed to sleep next to a man who has been lying to me for eighteen years? Has our relationship been built upon the death of his sister and nothing else? Does he even love me?

Only Jack can tell me the whole truth. I should go to him right now and show him the photo. I should demand that he tell me who is in the picture with him and why he kept the box for so long. But what will I be unleashing upon myself if I do this?

I don't think Jack would ever lay a hand on me for asking a hard question, but I don't want him to explode when the kids are around. I need to wait for the right time.

As I push myself up to my feet, the perfect thought comes to me. I was dreading the idea of going to our therapy session tomorrow afternoon. Jack plans on hitting me with some tough questions. Well, maybe I'll have a few of my own.

I hide the photo and go to bed, making sure to wash the ashes and grit from my hands and fingers as best I can.

Exhaustion pulls me into a deep sleep. It doesn't take long for my dreams to seize control. They rip and tear at my soul, attacking my every sense. And no matter how hard I try, I can't escape them. I can't escape her. I can't escape Nicole. She hunts me in her Audi until she has me cornered.

"Confess," she roars as she revs her engine. "Lies breed chaos."

I snap upright in my bed. Ragged breaths rush in and out of me as I scan the room with frantic urgency. I blink rapidly and feel a severe pounding in my chest.

"It's okay," I whisper. "You're safe."

My eyes adjust to the room, and I realize it's early morning. I check my phone and see 5:15 a.m. on my lock screen.

"God," I let out as I drop back down to my pillow with a sigh. I've had hardly any good sleep and won't get an ounce more. Not after a nightmare like this. Parts of it fade from my mind, but the finer details linger. I know exactly what the dream was about.

Therapy should be fun.

I roll over in bed and find Jack gone. With my phone in hand, I open my camera app to locate Jack. The study is empty. I check the living room and find the same, but notice a light is on in the kitchen. I switch to the kitchen camera and see him there, sipping a coffee. It seems innocent enough until I realize where he is standing in the kitchen.

Jack is by the window that faces Nicole's house. The curtain is drawn, and he is staring straight into her home.

CHAPTER FORTY-SIX

Eighteen years ago

Not much happened over the next week. My plan to free Jack heavily relied on certain things falling into place. Until those opportunities arose, there wasn't much I could do but watch and wait.

I had followed her to the library — Jack's shame. The girl he hoped to retain for that little while longer until he could think of a way to keep them both. Did he realize he was dooming them by doing so? I wondered.

I kept my distance and wore a hoodie over my head. I didn't want her or anyone else seeing me in the library. The gap between us wasn't a problem, thanks to the listening device I had planted under her table. She always sat at the one by the window. Every damn time.

I had my earbuds in again. To the casual observer, I was another student in the library, listening to music and studying — a nobody in the background. No one would ever suspect what I was really up to.

Jack's secret shame had been using the library a lot in the past week. I had found her there several times, always when

Jack's girlfriend was studying. Was she watching her from afar like I was? Was she waiting for an opportunity to present itself? Part of me wondered why I had placed myself in the middle of these two girls. Whatever the reason, I was going to come out on top.

Jack's girlfriend wasn't around on this occasion. His secret whore may have actually been in the library to learn for a change.

Before long, a certain someone showed up, unannounced.

"What are you doing here?" she asked Kara.

Kara sat down in the opposite chair. "I could ask you the same question."

"I'm here to study. What does it look like?"

Kara took a few glances around, then leaned forward. "You know what this looks like, don't you? You're trying to spy on her."

Jack's side piece shook her head. "I don't know what you're talking about, Kara. Like I said, I'm here to—"

"Don't lie to me," Kara snapped. She was doing her best to keep her voice down. A library wasn't the ideal place for them to have this conversation. I stared straight at them both and couldn't help the grin that formed on my lips. Seeing Jack's skeleton in the closet squirm sent a flurry of happiness through my insides. She fired back at Kara.

"What is your problem?" she asked her. I let the tiniest chuckle slip free. She had just asked Kara the worst possible question.

"You want to know what my problem is? Are you serious?"

"Yes," she said, crossing her arms over her chest.

"Okay. It's you and what you've done to Jack."

"I haven't done anything to him."

"Bullshit. You're letting him screw you behind his girlfriend's back. You're letting him get away with this affair. Why?"

She didn't answer. At first, I thought my listening device was malfunctioning, but when I stared at her, her lips were trembling. For an instant, I actually felt sorry for the girl. But

197

my weakness soon subsided when I remembered what was at stake.

She spoke again. "I don't want things to be this way. I tried giving him an ultimatum, but he talked his way out of it."

"Then what happened?" Kara asked.

She gazed down at the table. "We had sex."

"Come on," Kara said. "You're stronger than this. I know you have it in you to do what's right."

She sniffed as her sobbing started and stopped. "Wait, what are you saying?"

Kara sighed. "You need to dump him. End it. I don't care how. Just get it done."

She shook her head. "Why?"

"Because it's the right thing to—"

"No," she said, cutting Kara off. "I don't want to hear about some moral reasoning. I want you to tell me why you care so much about this. Why do you want me to end things with Jack?"

Kara chuckled. I watched as a transition in her demeanor shifted like the wind. Her lips parted to speak. "I'm only going to say this once: end things with Jack. Otherwise, I'll do it for you."

"What do you mean?" she asked.

Kara stood and pushed her chair back in as if their little chat was nothing but a friendly passing by. "Tell Jack it's over, or I'll go to his girlfriend and let her hear all about everything you and Jack have been up to. You've got one day."

And like that, Kara went away. She didn't glance back or say another word. She left her there alone with nothing but a threat hanging over her head. All the while, I wondered if Kara was serious. Would she expose the secret romance to Jack's girlfriend? I doubted it. Not with the consequences that would follow. Jack would never trust her again.

I leaned back in my seat and soaked in the possibilities. In one day, Jack's side girl was going to end things with Jack or force me to step in and intervene. I could easily guess how it was going to play out. For the time being, my plan remained the same.

I knew her well. I had observed her for some time and understood what went on in that head of hers. I knew her better than she knew herself. She tried to convince the world she was strong and free-willed, but the truth was she was weak. There was no way in hell she was going to dump Jack. She wasn't capable of surviving on her own. She was going to continue sleeping with Jack while his girlfriend remained blissfully unaware. Pathetic.

I left the library, knowing there was still much to be done.

CHAPTER FORTY-SEVEN

Present day

I stay in bed and periodically check on Jack's movements throughout the house. By six, he departs without so much as a goodbye. He doesn't leave a note or send me a text. It's unlike him to do this.

I want to send him a text or call him to check if he is okay, but the same reasons as before stop me from striking up a conversation. Despite what's been happening, I still care about my husband. If he's in any sort of trouble, I want to know so I can help him.

The kids stir from their rooms at the same time as if they had synced up their schedules. Dot immediately asks me where Daddy is. I tell her he had to go to work early. Noah doesn't take the news well and bursts into tears.

"It's okay, baby. You'll see Daddy later. I promise." Noah goes on for a few more minutes, upsetting Dot. Their combined sadness forces me to turn the TV on and give them both sugary cereal for breakfast.

I sit in the living room with the kids, eating some toast as I scroll through social media to hopefully forget everything. After only a minute, I lock my phone, realizing I'm too preoccupied.

The burned photo stirs in my pocket. I hid it in the empty suitcase I keep above my clothing in our walk-in closet. I went to the effort of locking the suitcase with a small padlock that has only one key and kept the key under my pillow. It stayed locked up overnight until I retrieved it this morning.

Every so often, I pull the Polaroid from my pocket and study it again as if something new will pop out. Nothing does.

"That Daddy?" Noah asks when he catches sight of the photo.

"No, sweetie," I say as I stuff it away. He gives me a quizzical look but is soon distracted by a cartoon animal on the TV. Thankfully, it wasn't Dot spying on me.

I get the kids ready for school. Before we leave, I ask Dot to watch her brother for a minute and tell her I will be right back. I just need to drop in at Ellie's place and make sure she's okay to watch the kids this afternoon. I know I shouldn't leave the kids alone like this, but I need to see Ellie. Given the embarrassment I went through last night in front of everyone in the cul-de-sac, I'd be lying if I said I wasn't nervous about seeing her. But she's an old friend. Surely each of us is entitled to the occasional meltdown now and then?

I lock the front door on the way out to be safe. I would do it under normal circumstances to stop Noah from escaping, but my reason now is to prevent anyone from coming in. The safer option would be to make a phone call to Ellie instead, but I think talking to her in person is the better choice.

As I walk up my driveway toward my friend's home, I'm ever aware I will need to pass by number six to reach number four. It's like walking by the old creepy place I passed on my way to school when I was a kid. Is this what it's going to be like with Nicole living here? Am I forever going to be on edge when I leave my house?

I make sure not to dawdle and keep my eyes forward. The last thing I want is for Nicole to notice me and stare through her uncovered windows. I'm not playing her games anymore.

I pass by number six without incident and exhale the breath I'd been holding. My skin tingles and makes me shudder the second I'm clear. This isn't right. I shouldn't have to feel so unsafe in my own neighborhood. Unable to resist, I take a glance at Nicole's place. I don't find anyone there, and there's no car in the driveway. Definitely not a black Audi A3. I don't find any signs of her being home and figure she isn't there. She's probably out somewhere planning her next move.

In the back of my head, a little voice asks me a stupid question. It wants to know if I think Jack left the house early to meet with Nicole somewhere private. Away from prying eyes. It makes no damn sense, but then again, this week makes no sense. I ignore the question and continue to Ellie's house.

When I reach her front door, I see Ellie arriving home in her car. She gives me a wave once she kills the engine and climbs out of her minivan.

"Hey," I say.

"Is everything okay?" she asks.

The front door opens. Dave says hello and walks by me. He grabs the grocery bags from Ellie as she collects them from the trunk, then rushes away from the two of us into the house as if he is trying to avoid a conversation with me. I get it.

"Thanks," Ellie calls after him. "I've never seen him so eager to help," she says with a chuckle.

"My fault," I offer. "After last night, I understand why no one would want to be around me."

"Hey, don't talk like that. I'm sure you had your reasons."

"I did, but still. I made a total ass of myself. I'm sorry."

Ellie places her handbag down at her feet. "You don't need to apologize. You didn't do a thing to me."

"I'm sure I woke you up, at the very least."

"I was still awake."

I shake my head. "You're supposed to be upset with me, not let me off the hook."

Ellie chuckles. "We're friends. Simple as that."

"Thank you," I say, giving her a hug. "You're the best."

"I am, aren't I?"

We share a laugh and get to chatting like the incident never happened. Out of everyone I annoyed in the cul-de-sac last night, Ellie is the only person whose feelings I care about — apart from Jack, of course. The rest of them are just neighbors.

"So, I suppose you want to know if I'm free to watch the kids this afternoon," she says.

"Yeah," I reply with a hint of caution. "You can say no if it's a problem."

"It's not a problem. I was going to call you and tell you nothing has changed."

"Thank you," I say, placing a hand on her forearm. "You have no idea how happy I am to hear you say those words. I thought that—"

"Bee, it's fine. We all make mistakes. Don't worry."

I let relief wash over me and unclench my body, wondering if I can put the car chase behind me. At least for now. I still need to find out who was driving that damn A3 for Nicole.

"So, what happened?" Ellie asks. "What made you think Nicole was trying to . . . you know?"

"Kill me?"

"Yeah, that."

I sigh, knowing I shouldn't tell Ellie much else. I don't want to drag her into my world of problems more than I already have.

"If you don't want to talk about it, that's fine," she says.

"No, it's okay. I do. I just need a second to think."

Ellie stares at me with her concerned face. I've seen it many times before. We share most of our problems with one another. Apart from what happened in college, there isn't much she doesn't know about me.

"Take your time," she says.

I touch the burned Polaroid stirring in my pocket. I don't know why I brought it with me. Well, in reality, I do. I want to show it to Ellie and ask her what the hell it all means. She won't have an answer for me, but that's not the point. I just want someone else to see it so I can convince myself I'm not going crazy.

I take out the Polaroid. "There's something I need to show you."

203

CHAPTER FORTY-EIGHT

I hold the half-burned Polaroid in a shaky hand and lift it to Ellie's gaze.

"What the heck is that?" she asks me with a scowl across her brow.

"It's what I want to show you. Please, look." I hand her the photo. She slowly takes it and squints at the picture. "Is that . . . Jack?"

"Yeah. From when he was in college."

"Oh, wow. I thought it was old. Not old, but you know what I mean."

"It's okay, Ellie," I say. I'd be a touch awkward too if someone had handed me a photo of their husband from eighteen years ago that had been set on fire.

"What happened to it? Why is it burned?"

I exhale through my nostrils. "That's a good question." I continue and explain to Ellie where I found it and lie that it was by pure chance alone. I tell her there were dozens of other destroyed photos with it, but this one had survived the fire. She hears how it was left there accidentally by Jack, but I leave out any details about me spying on him or my suspicions about Nicole.

One step at a time.

"Wow," is all Ellie can manage.

"I know. This is a lot to take in."

"Yeah, no kidding. I gotta ask you something, Bee. And please don't take this the wrong way."

"What is it?"

Ellie's eyes avoid mine for a moment. She's got something bad to say.

"It's okay," I say again. "You can ask me anything."

Ellie takes in a breath. "Is that Nicole in the other half of the photo?"

It's my turn to scowl now. "What made you say that?" I snatch the photo out of Ellie's hand and study it again. I know there's another woman in the picture, but it's almost impossible to identify her. "What makes you think this is Nicole?"

Ellie reaches out a hand. "Bee, look." She flips the Polaroid over in my hand. On the back of the picture, there's a single piece of scrawled handwriting. There are no words. Only a couple of letters. I take them each in and say out loud, "J + N." It's written in the bottom corner. I was so focused on the photo itself that I never looked at the back.

"Oh my God," I let out. "J + N. Jack and Nicole."

Ellie stares at me with nothing but pity. "Are you okay?"

I shake my head and can't help the sobbing that escapes me. Without meaning to, I break down in front of Ellie.

"Oh, hey, hey. It's okay, Bee," Ellie says, pulling me in tight. "Everything's going to be all right."

"It won't be," I say through a mess of tears. "She's going to ruin everything. I think she's here to win him back or something."

Ellie pats me on the back. "How? You told me he hates her."

"Maybe he's just been telling me he hates her. Maybe he wished they had been together all these years."

"Shh, shh," Ellie whispers. "You know that's not true. Jack loves you. Sure, you've had your trials like the rest of us, but do you really think he would ditch the mother of his children for some crazy ex from college? I mean, isn't she the one who . . . you know, caused Kara's death?"

I pull back, realizing I had told Ellie all about Kara. I shouldn't have done that.

"Isn't that what you said?" Ellie asks.

"I'm sorry. I shouldn't have told you."

Ellie places a hand on my forearm. "It's okay. I haven't mentioned it to anyone. I mean, I didn't even understand what you meant when you said Nicole caused Kara's death. I guess I still don't."

I stare at the floor and think about what most people know about Kara. We've only ever said that she died young in a car accident. We've never let out any more details. Jack never wanted to talk about it, and I guess neither did I.

"What did Nicole do?" Ellie whispers.

I study her eyes and see her warmth. There's no reason for me not to tell her everything. She's the one person on this street I can trust with this kind of thing.

With closed eyes, I focus on my breathing and steady my heart. When I open my eyes, I lock on to Ellie and tell her the truth. "She tried to kill me." I fill Ellie in on the night in college that ended with Kara's death. At least as much as I can stomach.

Ellie stares at me with her mouth hung open.

The rest of it follows. The note I found in the mailbox. Jack's weird behavior. The damn college box. Jack leaving early this morning without an explanation. All of it. Every word I let out eases the swirling delirium that has been building in my mind. By the time I finish, I almost feel like my old self again.

"Holy crap," Ellie says. "That's just . . . I don't know what to say."

"I'm sorry for putting this on you. I should be strong enough to handle it on my own, but I had to tell someone."

"It's okay. I'm just trying to process everything." There's anxiety in her features and it's all my fault.

"I'm sorry," I repeat.

"No, Bee. Don't apologize. No one should have to go through this kind of hell on their own. You were right to tell someone."

"Not someone. You, Ellie. Like I said, you're the only person I trust anymore."

"That kinda sucks when you think about it. You should be able to tell Jack some of these things. I guess he's in the middle of it all, huh?"

"Yeah," I say. "And the worst part is, I don't know what to do next. If you have any suggestions, I'm all ears."

Ellie shakes her head. "I have no idea, sorry. I wish I could tell you what to do to fix everything, but I've never been through anything like this. I'm just a boring working mom."

"You're not boring," I say. "I would kill for your life."

"Really? You'd take on Georgia for me?"

We both laugh.

"Well, maybe not Georgia," I say, continuing to chuckle. Just as we are about to continue to chat, I remember I've left the kids alone for far too long.

"I gotta run," I say, rushing to leave.

"What's wrong?" Ellie asks, following.

"Just running late, sorry." I don't tell her I've left the kids on their own. I already feel like the worst mother in the world. No doubt she will have figured it out after hearing Jack had left super early.

"Bye," Ellie says. "Try to take it easy. And if you need anything, call me. Send a text if you want. I'm here for you, got it?"

I pull Ellie in for a hug and whisper, "Thank you." I fight back the emotions tugging at my throat and rush back home before I break down again.

I walk past number six as fast as I can and make my way to the kids. When I unlock the front door and go inside, I find my babies where I left them staring at the TV. I release my held breath and close my eyes. They're safe.

"Mommy," Dot says.

"Yeah, honey?" I ask as I move over toward her.

"Where did you go?"

"Oh, just over at Aunt Ellie's place."

"Are we going there again today?"

"Yeah, baby." The last few times I've asked Ellie to watch the kids, I could sense Dot's unease. She enjoys going over to number four and loves playing with Ethan and Olivia, but the little detective within her knew something was up.

"Where will you and Daddy be?"

How do I explain marriage counseling to a five-year-old? And should I bother to? I pull Dot closer and try to think of something to say, but a thump at the back door startles me.

"What's that?" Noah asks first.

I rush through the kitchen and make my way to the back door. Dot follows. "Stay with Noah," I say, rougher than I mean to.

"Okay," she replies with a crack in her tiny voice.

When I get to the back door, I grip the handle and suck in a breath. What the hell else is going to happen on this cursed street?

CHAPTER FORTY-NINE

I feel my heartbeat in my ear as I hold on tight to the door handle that leads to our backyard. Should I even be opening this door? Am I playing right into Nicole's hand? It could be as simple as a bird crashing into the house. I guess I'm still on edge after unloading everything onto Ellie.

I bring my spare hand up to the lock and twist the bolt open. Ignoring the noise isn't an option. I have to protect my home and especially my children. I can't believe I left them alone before. That was stupid. It won't happen ever again. Not until Nicole is gone from Maple Court.

I yank the door open, hopeful my abruptness will startle whatever might be waiting for me on the other side. Nothing is out of the ordinary. Apart from the scattering of ash around Jack's smoker, it's business as usual. Then I glance down.

I find two items at my feet: a rock and a small box. The rock is pretty self-explanatory. I scan the fence line and wonder if Nicole has done this. Could she have hopped her own fence, left the package on my back step, then thrown a rock against the door so I would find her special delivery?

It's not impossible. The fence between our houses is a standard size. Nicole could manage it. Hell, even I could. And

209

it wouldn't have taken her long to get the job done. Ridiculous theories aside, I still have an unknown package on my back doorstep left potentially by Jack's unstable ex. I can't just leave it here and pretend it doesn't exist. The way I see it, I have two options: trash it or open it. For now, I need to take the box inside and hide it. I can deal with its contents later.

As I turn to go in, I find Dot standing in the doorway, staring straight at me with curiosity on her brow. "Mommy?" she asks.

"I said to go back to your brother. What are you doing here?"

Her eyes go wide as a worry line rips across her face. "I'm sorry. I just—"

"Go!" I shout, stabbing my index finger into the air. Dot cowers away from me, barely holding back her tears. She doesn't go back to the living room. Instead, she runs to the stairs and charges up them, crying as she goes.

"God," I let out, squeezing my eyes shut. When I have a second to think, I realize I've yelled at Dot for no reason. What the hell is wrong with me? She didn't deserve my anger. But as much as I should rush after my little girl to make things right, I first need to find somewhere to stash this goddamn box.

I huff as I walk through to the kitchen and collect my car keys. I can hide the thing in my Subaru in the garage for now. I'll have to wait to open it. The kids still have to be taken to where they need to be, and I have to go to work for six hours. Normally, I would be working from ten until six today, leaving Jack to pick up the kids and sort out dinner, but I've arranged to finish at three on Wednesdays to have time to pick up the kids and drop them off at Ellie's. All so Jack and I can go to our therapy session.

As I walk into the garage, making sure there are no little children behind me, my cell phone rings.

"What now?" I moan. I'm close to breaking. Fumbling with the box and my car keys, I pull out my phone and realize it's Ellie calling.

210

"Hi," I say.

"Sorry to call you. I know we usually text. I forgot to ask what time you'll be dropping off Dot and Noah today."

"Oh, right," I say. Sometimes the time can vary. "We should be back by four at the latest. Will that be okay?"

"It will," Ellie says with a hint of disappointment in her voice.

"Is something wrong? If you can't take them, I understand."

"No, it's not that. It's Georgia. She just called. She's pestering me to take the kids to her place for dinner tonight. Apparently, I promised her I would do that today of all days. But with Dot and Noah over, it won't be possible."

"Could they come with you?" I ask, squinting a forced smile. It's inconsiderate of me to put such a burden on her like this.

"You know what? Why the hell not? She loves to cook and clean and show off how good she is at it. I'll take them along. This way everybody wins."

"Except you," I say, unable to quash my guilt.

"No, that's just it. Dot and Noah will be great distractions. They're tiny and cute and will pull more attention away from me. As long as you're okay with it."

"Trust me," I say, "I am. This visit to our therapist is going to be tough enough as it is given everything that's happened this week. Jack and I will need a few hours to chat after. Wish me luck."

"I'll be thinking of you, Bee. Bye."

"Bye." I end the call and feel a weight ease off my shoulders. Ellie can look after the kids while I deal with the fallout of today. That is, if I even make it through until the session. With mom guilt and another 'special' box giving me hell, I'm about ready to climb into my car and drive away.

I lock the box in my trunk and check in on Noah. He's happy watching TV while playing with his toys. I take the fading window of time I have left and pace upstairs to Dot's room, where I know she will be sulking. Her favorite place to do so is behind her bed in the gap next to her window. Sure enough, I find her there with her head buried in her knees, sobbing.

"Dot," I say with a gentle voice as I enter. She curls tighter into herself, trying to shrink away from me. I continue into her space and sit on her bed. I reach a hand to pat her shoulder. Again, she retreats from me and murmurs something inaudible.

"Dot," I repeat. "I'm so sorry. Mommy shouldn't have yelled at you like that."

"Yeah, you shoulda."

"No. You didn't do a thing wrong."

"I did. You said to look after Noah, but I didn't."

"I know that's what I said, but Mommy wasn't thinking. She was stressed out from—" I stop myself from saying more. There's no way I can explain away my problems to a young child.

"I'm sorry," is all I say. Then I drop down and scoop Dot up into a hug. At first, she tries to scramble away from me, but it doesn't take her long to give in and curl into my arms, then continue to sob like she's two years old again. I forget that she's only five. She's still so little.

We stay like this for several minutes and burn through time I don't have. Fortunately, Dot comes out of her shell in time for me to get her and Noah ready and into the car. A traffic alert buzzes on my phone, adding more anxiety to my brain. There's been an accident on the route I usually take to drop the kids off at preschool and kindergarten. I attempt to find an alternative, but it's a waste of time. The best option is to drive through the crash.

For obvious reasons, I hate having to drive past a car accident. Unfortunately, sometimes they just can't be avoided. Whenever I am forced to be close to one, I focus on my breathing and the road ahead of me. On a typical day, it does the trick. But not today.

Before we reach Dot's school, I come across the crash site. It's a bad one. Two cars collided head-on, leaving crumpled glass, broken fenders, and twisted metal in all directions. Fluids have leaked from both vehicles, but luckily, I don't see any of the people involved in the accident. They've probably been rushed to the hospital already.

I tell Dot not to look, but I know she won't be able to resist and will have a dozen questions for me once we are clear of the area.

I can never erase what happened that night. Every gory detail from the burning smell to the crunchy sounds of the shattered glass I stepped on when I crawled out of the wreck. But most of all, it was Kara's face I will never forget. Her eyes will haunt me forever.

Jack had rushed to the crash as soon as he could. I was sitting in the back of an ambulance when he arrived. He didn't come running to me to see if I was okay. Instead, Jack broke through the police line and scrambled over to Kara's body. He fell to his knees and ripped off the white sheet they had placed over her. From there, it was nothing but screaming and yelling as Jack tried in vain to wake Kara up. But there was no saving her. She was dead.

A horn blares behind me, pulling me from my daze. The traffic in front has cleared enough that I can get moving. I drive away from the destructive site as fast as I can.

"Was anybody hurt?" Dot wastes no time asking.

"Hopefully not," I say.

"What happened? Why did the cars crash?"

"I don't know, baby. Sometimes it happens. That's why we have to be careful when we drive."

"And always wear your seatbelt," she says.

"Yeah . . ." I say, trailing off. "Always wear a seatbelt." My hand lowers to my own and unconsciously checks for a cut that isn't there.

"I hope they're okay," Dot says in her tiny voice.

"Me too," I whisper.

We put the crash behind us and get back to a normal speed on the road. The traffic is its typical self ahead. When we reach Dot's school, she hits me with a question I've been waiting to come from her mouth. I had hoped the crash would have made her forget, but of course, she hasn't.

"Mommy, what was in the box you found?"

CHAPTER FIFTY

Eighteen years ago

Moonlight bathed the street in a pearly glow, casting harsh shadows across the pathways. The modern brick buildings stood silent as I wandered along an empty sidewalk. My footsteps echoed in the stillness while the scattered trees whispered in the gentle breeze.

It was late. Only a few students could be seen wandering along Northeast 41st Street as I made my way to the Cedar Apartments where she lived: Jack's secret girl. I was finally ready to go through with my plan. Everything had fallen into place. I just needed to follow through.

I crept along the sidewalk with my head down and my hoodie up. It was cold outside, so the necessity for a hooded sweatshirt wasn't an uncommon sight. I felt invincible under its protective layer, like I could see the world, but no one could see me.

In my pocket, I toyed with the thick handle of the knife I was gripping in a gloved hand. Sweat from my palm soaked into the material as I kept the sharp blade pointed down. I was ready to do whatever it took to go through with my plan.

I was ready to cut and stab and slice anything or anyone who got in my way.

Jack's shame would be fast asleep in her dorm room. The apartment building was a decent walk from the main campus. I had watched her make the trip many times as she strolled, jovially unaware of who was behind her, studying her every step.

I'd given her several chances to do the right thing and so had Kara. But it's been more than twenty-four hours, and she hadn't broken things off with Jack. She had come close. I heard her talk it over with herself, alone in her dorm room. The conversation always ended the same way: "I won't do it."

I'd heard nothing on Jack's end, either. He'd been busy with class as usual and had even seen his public girlfriend in the middle of it all. He'd been texting in class a touch more than normal, but apart from that, it was business as usual.

His side piece was calling Kara's bluff. It was a bold move. She was risking everything to stay with a man who kept her a secret from the world.

"So be it," I whispered.

As I predicted, Kara wouldn't reveal their private affair, either. She had played her hand and laid it all on the line, but her bluff wasn't enough. Her threat had failed. Jack's secret girl was stronger than I had first thought. Her pride, though, was going to be her end.

As I played with the knife, a single thought ran through my mind. Was this what Jack wanted? I understood deep down that he loved me more than his two girlfriends and that this was all a test, but did he really want me to go through with this? Was it a case of him being too weak to end things, or was it all part of the trial I'd been made to suffer through to prove my worth?

It didn't matter. Either way, I was going to go through with it. There was no turning back. For once, I wasn't making my way into her apartment building to listen in on one of her pathetic chats with her roommate. I was looking for her car. I knew the license plate number and the make and model. Even the color. She never used the thing, but soon she was going to rush to her Honda Civic and speed out of the campus on her way to an emergency. Bianca had no idea what she was in for.

I'd watched her for months. I knew where she worked, what she liked to eat, and who she was friends with. I'd even attended her classes and understood her schedule down to the minute. And now, all that information was going to aid me in bringing about her destruction. She thought she was worthy of Jack, that she could one day take the place of his girlfriend and be center stage for all to see. What a joke. She barely deserved to be his hidden shame.

I found her Honda Civic in the parking spot she paid a lot of money for. Her parents, no doubt, were covering some of her expenses on campus. She only worked a few nights per week at a nearby restaurant and did a lousy job serving customers. She rarely got a decent tip. And why would she? She didn't have the same charm his girlfriend possessed. From what I had observed, she came across to most as abrasive. But beneath her rougher layers, she was weak.

She was Jack's backup and nothing more. I had thought he loved her more out of the two of them, but I was confusing love with lust. She excited him more, purely because of the circumstances in which their relationship was built. Without the sneaking around, it was meaningless.

I strolled up to the Honda Civic and made quick work of the lock. It was an older model that had a major flaw. I'd learned how to break into the car without causing any damage via some information online. It was easier than I expected and only took me a few minutes to achieve.

Once I'd broken into Bianca's car, I sat in the driver's seat and ran my gloved hands over the steering wheel, imagining what was going to happen to her. I would have given anything to see her face when she realized her life was about to end. That split second between life and death would have told me everything about her.

217

Exhaling, I pulled the seatbelt out with my left hand and brought it across my lap. I then produced the knife from my pocket and regarded its sharp edge and stabbing point. It glinted in the slate gray of the moonlight like a thing of beauty — an instrument of inevitability.

The weight of the knife felt heavy, enough to make my hand shake. It jittered more as I brought the blade closer to the seatbelt.

If I did this, there was no turning back. I would have to go through with every step of my plan from start to finish. I exhaled and steadied my grip, killing the tremble in my wrist. It was time.

Halfway across the sash of the seatbelt, I used the blade to make a single slice. I ran the knife three-quarters of the way through the sash and removed it, satisfied with my work. The first step was now completed. Bianca's seatbelt had been sabotaged.

I was tempted to carve a J + N into the material before I left, but I couldn't leave any evidence of what I had done behind.

With the seatbelt ready, I left Bianca's car and locked the door. She would never know I had been inside her Honda. Not until it was too late.

I returned the knife to my pocket and moved to the side of her car. I had one last thing to do before I left. The tracking device slipped into my hand, then under the rear wheel well of Bianca's car. It was going to be vital to execute my plan.

With my tasks completed, I made my way back down the street, away from Bianca's dorm. My hoodie stayed over my head as I avoided the gaze of the occasional student who was walking along Northeast 41st Street. I just needed to get to where I had parked my car and avoid running into anyone who recognized me along the way.

Then I saw him. I saw Jack.

He was across the road, heading in the opposite direction. He must have been walking to Bianca's dorm. I couldn't help but stop and stare. He wasn't supposed to be there. Jack was supposed to be in his own dorm room, studying. That's what my schedule had told me. He was complicating things with this impromptu visit to Bianca.

Had he found out about the ultimatum? Was he rushing to his side-action girlfriend out of desperation? Heaven forbid Jack would have to exist with only one partner.

Whatever he was doing, I had to follow him.

CHAPTER FIFTY-ONE

Present Day

I tell Dot the box was left on our back doorstep by mistake and that I am going to take it to the post office as soon as I finish dropping off Noah.

"Why was it at the back of our house?" she asks, following up my lie with sharp logic.

"I'm not sure. Maybe the person who delivered it got confused."

Dot laughs. "What a Silly Billy."

I force a chuckle to help sell my lie and absorb another shot of guilt. How many times am I going to deceive my daughter today?

We leave the house in a rush. Once Dot has been dropped off, I take Noah to preschool, then drive to work. My shift doesn't start until ten, but there's a task that needs completing before I can get my day underway.

In the parking lot of the library, I sit with the box in my lap. I'd retrieved it from my trunk when I arrived and rushed to take it into my car. It felt like I was doing something illegal. For all I know, there might be something illegal inside this thing. Or it might be nothing. Just some box left on our back step by mistake.

"Doubt it," I mutter.

The box was meant for me. That much I'm sure of. No amount of lying to myself will change that fact.

With no one around, I take a breath in and out. The box feels light in my hands. Whatever is inside can't weigh much. I don't know if that's a good thing or not. There's only one way to find out, and I've delayed the inevitable long enough.

"Here goes," I say as I take the sharp edge of one of my house keys and run it over the taped middle of the box. The lids part and spring half open. I place my keys down and lift the flaps the rest of the way. When I look in the box, I find a thin layer of brown paper. Whatever is in this package is beneath the sheet.

I could still walk away and not play into this game I'm being drawn into. I could throw this stupid thing in the nearest dumpster and go to work instead. I'd be starting my shift early, but it would also mean I wouldn't have to face the contents of the box. If only it were that easy.

As I pull the paper aside, my heart rate picks up its pace. I find another note. It's the third one I've seen this week, but this time it's not covered in blood. That's an improvement, I guess.

All three notes have been for me. Even the one that was left in Nicole's front door. I found it before anyone else. That can't have been a coincidence.

The current note I'm holding is folded, meaning I will need to pull it out of the box with my fingers to read it. It's only a piece of paper, but I have an overwhelming sensation that I'm putting my hand into a box of cobras. I pinch at the note and slide it out, unfolding it straight away.

A lump catches in my throat when I see the words within. I read them aloud. "What could have been . . ."

Confused, I don't know what to make of the note. It's not as direct as the others. It seems vague at best. I'm about ready to toss it in the library's dumpster when I realize what is sitting beneath the note.

"Oh, God," I yell, throwing the box. It collides with the steering wheel and falls to the floor of my car. My breath flows in and out of me as I stare in all directions, snapping my head left and right to find Nicole. The psycho must be watching me through a pair of binoculars, enjoying the show.

Once my breathing settles, I take a second to think straight and calm myself down.

"It's okay," I say. "You can handle this. It's just a game." I repeat the advice again and again until I find the strength to reach down and collect the box. When I have it in my lap again, I take another look at what made me freak out.

The silver K charm looks the same as it did when I spotted it in Jack's study, all except for one crucial difference. The K has been dipped in blood. Or something resembling blood. Nicole saved that little detail for now. She's trying to break me, and I'm afraid it's working. Kara's bracelet stares at me and penetrates my soul. I remove the tape holding it to the box and hold the light piece of jewelry in my hand.

I read the note again.

What could have been . . .

I close my eyes, sealing them tight. This isn't happening. I'm not holding Kara's bracelet. The K isn't covered in blood. But when I open my eyes again, nothing has changed. The bracelet is still firm in my grip.

How did she do this? How did Nicole enter my home and take the bracelet from Jack's study? It was there when I first went looking for the college box. Since then, I've been extra cautious by making sure the doors are locked and the alarm is set. I've even installed cameras.

"The cameras," I let out. How do I keep forgetting about them?

Chiding myself, I fumble to pull out my cell phone and attempt to unlock it with my face. There must be an awful expression coating my features because the damn thing won't unlock.

It asks me for a code instead, so I type in the numbers but make multiple mistakes. By the time I unlock my cell phone, sweat is slick on my palms and forehead. My hands quiver as I open the security camera app and navigate to Jack's study. I go through the history and find nothing out of the ordinary. I see the recordings of Jack that I have already watched and nothing new. How is this possible? How has Nicole gone into Jack's study and taken the bracelet without my hidden camera recording it? And more importantly, how did she get into our home without breaking a thing?

Too many thoughts rattle around in my head, and they all point to one possibility: Jack. Did he take the bracelet out during the gap in the recordings? Then what? Nicole stole it from him and shoved it in a box for me to find? Why go through so much effort to punish me? Why not get it all over with and end what she started eighteen years ago?

I give up on the app and bring my mind back to the driver's seat of my Subaru. The box is sitting in my lap with its damn note and Kara's bracelet. I seal it back up and tuck it down under my seat. I should return the bracelet to Jack's study and destroy the note. Or maybe I could show it to him. I was already planning on hitting him with the half-ruined Polaroid. Why not throw this bit of crazy on top?

"No," I say, speaking to myself again. I couldn't do that to him. No matter how bad things become, he doesn't deserve such a cruel punishment.

Needing to calm myself down, I lean back in my seat and close my eyes. My head feels like it weighs a ton as I meld into the cushion of the driver's seat. Exhaustion finds me and beats the noise and chaos that is roaming my insides. Without meaning to, I fall asleep.

CHAPTER FIFTY-TWO

I snap awake in my car from a fresh nightmare. This time, it was as clear as day and was less of a bad dream and more a memory. A painful one I've spent years trying to forget. The experience leaves me coated in sweat and panic as I take in my surroundings.

"What the hell?" I say, panting. As if I'm not going through enough torture, I had to relive that night. Sadly, it makes complete sense with everything that has been thrown in my face over the past three days. Nevertheless, I shouldn't have to go through this misery again.

With trembling hands, I fumble to find my cell phone and raise it to my eyes. The time stares back and mocks me. I'm one hour late for my shift. There are three missed calls from my supervisor, Susan. "Dammit," I mutter, wondering why I thought it would be a great idea to shut my eyes. I guess I figured I wouldn't fall asleep under the circumstances.

Maybe the stress of this week is getting to me and I shut down. Whatever the reason, it doesn't matter. I need to rush to work.

I charge inside and start my shift, apologizing a dozen times for my screw-up. My supervisor is less than pleased, but she lets me off with a warning and docks me for the time I missed. I thank her for her leniency. I love this job and need it. If things don't pan out well with Jack, we could be looking at an expensive divorce. This job might be my saving grace if that happens.

My shift passes by in slow motion as my mind stays focused on everything else but the library. Several times I have to ask people to repeat themselves when they are talking to me. It's like I can't comprehend a word they have to say. Eventually, the day goes by and it's time for me to leave.

"Thanks again for letting me take off early today," I say to Susan.

"You're welcome," she says. "Just try to be on time tomorrow."

"You know what? I'll be in early to make up for today."

"That would be appreciated, Bianca. I know you are going through some personal issues at the moment but try to stay on top of the rest of your life. Trust me, it's the only way to survive what might come of it."

Susan went through a challenging divorce a year ago. She and her ex-husband are in their sixties and parted ways once all the kids were grown. Apparently, they had never been happy, but thought they could stay together until the end. It was not to be, though.

Things got ugly when they didn't need to be. Her ex was vindictive and didn't want their assets split fifty-fifty. He wanted the lion's share because he claimed he had worked more hours than her. The court took into consideration the fact that she had raised their two children while he was working and argued against his demands.

"I'll see you tomorrow," I say. "Bright and early."

Susan gives me a brief smile and focuses on her work as I rush out the door. I need to collect the kids and bring them home. Well, not home — to Ellie's place so she can mind them. I can't be late, either. She needs to head off to Georgia's. She's going to have a busy evening.

As I drive to pick up Noah then Dot, Jack contacts me. His call comes through my car's Bluetooth. I haven't heard from him all day and have been too afraid to ask why he left so early.

"Hi," I say, reservation lining my voice.

"Hey," he replies. "About the session today . . ."

"What about it?"

"I'm running behind at school and might be late."

"How late?" I ask, resisting the urge to find out where he was this morning. The temptation is killing me.

"Maybe ten to fifteen minutes by the time I arrive. Should we reschedule?"

I take a second to think about what he is saying. Out of the hour, only fifty minutes is spent with us. He's going to miss up to a third of the session. It seems like a waste of time and money. But then again, maybe something has changed and he's just trying to get out of it. "Let's not cancel. Just get there when you can."

"Are you sure? We kind of left things a little heated last night."

"Exactly why we can't miss a session. I'll get things started and fill in Dr. Carabello on what's been happening this week."

"Is that a good idea? Shouldn't we both be there for that?"

"That would be ideal, but I don't think we can wait a whole week to see her again. Anyway, I promise to be honest with my side of things. I won't try to paint you in a terrible light, if that's what you're worried about."

"I'm not," he says, sounding less than convinced. "I'm just worried about you. After last night—"

"I'm fine," I say, forcing the words. "Just hurry to the session as soon as you can. Bye." I end the call before I ask him where he was or about the Polaroid I plan to show to him and Dr. Carabello. So much has happened since I found that damn photo. I now have Kara's bracelet to consider too. As awful as it is to lay eyes on it again, it will hurt Jack even more. I still remember Kara wearing it that night. The way the blood-stained K caught the moonlight will never leave my mind.

I shake the thought free before more comes back. It's not safe to do so while I'm driving. I just hope I can keep it all inside me when we have our session.

CHAPTER FIFTY-THREE

After picking up Dot, we go to Noah's preschool and collect him. He looks exhausted, as always, but I know he will brighten up the instant we arrive home. I remind him that he and Dot will be at Aunt Ellie and Uncle Dave's house until after dinner and that they need to be on their best behavior. I then throw in that Ellie will be taking them to Ethan and Olivia's grandmother's home for dinner, so it's not some major surprise. Noah doesn't understand what I'm saying, but Dot looks stressed out about the entire outing.

"You'll be okay," I say. "Just listen to Aunt Ellie, and you'll be fine."

"Okay," she says with worry smudging her forehead. Dot doesn't seem to cope all that well with change. It's most likely a trait I've passed on to her. The multiple times I've snapped at her this week hasn't helped either.

"You'll have fun," I tell Dot in the rearview mirror. She nods while staring out her window.

I focus on driving, doing my best to ignore the pangs of guilt Dot is sending my way on top of everything else. She doesn't mean it. She wants to be in her own space with her family.

When we reach Maple Court, Noah declares we are home. I don't correct him. Instead, I rush him and Dot inside and get Noah changed. After the usual chaos, they are both ready to go.

We get underway and leave the house. With my handbag over my shoulder, I carry Noah with one arm while holding hands with Dot. We walk past my Subaru and bypass number six. Again, I hate having to go by Nicole's home to reach my friend's place. It's like crossing a minefield.

We survive the trek to number four unscathed, giving me a moment to breathe before I'm required to put on a cheerful face for Ellie. I don't want her to think there's anything wrong. More than what she already knows. She'll stress about it. She already has enough on her plate watching my kids tonight while she deals with Georgia.

Dot knocks on the door for me but continues to hold my hand. I remember when she was three. She would hold my hand like this and always hide behind my legs whenever we spoke to other people. She's not as shy these days, but I can still see that side of her.

Ellie opens the door and greets us with what comes across as a rushed smile. "Come in, come in," she says.

"Is everything okay?" I ask. I can hear the stress in her voice.

"Yeah, fine, thanks."

"Are you sure?" I ask as we step inside. "Because if you can't—"

"It's nothing like that, Bee. I'm just . . . dealing with some moody children. You know how it goes."

"I do," I say with a chuckle. Something is up with Ellie, though, and I don't have time to find out.

We head into Ellie's kitchen. I try to place Noah down, but he clings on tight like I'm dropping him off at preschool. He does this every time we come here as if Ellie is a stranger.

"Come on, Noah," I mutter. "I don't have time for this." I pry his arms free and listen as he cries. From his perspective,

I've left him at preschool all day, and now I'm abandoning him again. It's understandable that he doesn't want to do this, but the kid needs to get it through his head that life isn't all sunshine and rainbows. In fact, most of my time is spent doing things that are boring, painful or lonesome.

"Come on, Noah," Dot says. Noah listens and leaves the room with Dot to go play with Ethan and Olivia. A heavy sigh escapes me once they go.

"Bad day?" Ellie asks.

"The worst. If I had time, I'd stay for a coffee and tell you all about it. Is everything okay with you?"

"Can't complain," she says, holding back. I can tell Ellie has a problem she would love to drop on me, but she knows me well enough to spare me the extra stress. She's a good friend. One I don't deserve.

"Thank you again for this," I say as I rummage through my handbag for my car keys.

"It's no problem. I'm happy to help you and Jack. God knows marriage isn't easy."

Ellie walks me to the front door, brushing her side-swept bangs the way she always does. She opens the door for me and says, "Before you go."

"What's up?" I ask with my car keys ready.

Ellie takes a breath in and lets it out. "I don't know if I should be telling you this, but . . ." she trails off and glances away from me.

"What is it? Is something wrong?"

"It's nothing to do with me. It's about . . . Jack."

"What about him?" I spit out, eyes wide. Ellie is avoiding my gaze at all costs, so I move closer to her and lean sideways. "Ellie?"

"Yeah?" she asks.

"What about Jack? Please?"

She squints for a moment, then finally speaks. "Okay. I saw him at lunchtime today."

"You saw him at lunchtime? What does that mean?"

"I was in the garden watering my hydrangeas. They've been struggling, lately. Anyway, the point is I saw Jack next door at number six. He was standing in front of Nicole's house talking to her. I thought little of it until . . ."

"Until what?" I ask, moving closer to Ellie.

Ellie closes her eyes like she can't bear the thought of seeing my face with what she has to tell me.

"Ellie, please," I say, almost begging.

She opens her eyes and stares right at me. "Okay . . . here goes."

CHAPTER FIFTY-FOUR

Eighteen years ago

I followed Jack back to Bianca's dorm, making sure to stay out of sight. Despite the late hour, the occasional student from U-Dub continued to roam the streets. But I wasn't there for a casual stroll.

Jack kept his eyes forward and didn't glance back once as I trailed behind him on the other side of the road. He seemed determined to get to where he was going. Part of me hoped he just needed to pass through Bianca's street and nothing more, but I knew I was wrong. He was rushing to visit his secret girl.

How many times had he taken that path? How many late-night visits had he made to her after spending several hours at his girlfriend's dorm? On more than one occasion, I had heard him on the audio monitors having sex with his girlfriend, only to then head over to Bianca's two hours later to do the same with her. Was that all it was? Sex? Or did he love them both as he so flagrantly claimed to each girl in private? Soon, I was going to find out where his loyalty stood.

Jack reached Bianca's dorm and hit the intercom buzzer at the secured door. "Bianca. It's me," he said.

She took a short while to respond. "Jack? What are you doing here?"

His visit was unplanned. Interesting. I stayed in the shadows as best I could. Jack didn't notice me. He was focused on seeing Bianca. He had a certain determined look in his eye I'd seen a few times before. Something had happened.

"We need to talk," he said.

I held my hand over my mouth. No conversation that started in such a way ever ended well, especially with young love. If I didn't know better, it sounded like Jack was about to give Bianca the bad news.

"Now isn't a good time, Jack," Bianca replied. Had she not caught the tone in his voice? Was she not curious as to why he was there, late at night, demanding to see her?

"Come on, Bianca. This is serious. We need to talk."

Silence filled the air. Jack ran a hand through his hair and glanced around, prompting me to slink back deeper into the void. He didn't spot me.

"Jack, I can't see you right now, okay?"

"Are you serious?"

A grin formed on my lips as I realized what was happening. Bianca knew why Jack was there. She knew he was trying to dump her. But instead of facing facts, she thought she could avoid him, so he couldn't do the inevitable.

Bianca didn't answer his question, so he buzzed her again. "Bianca, please. I'm not joking. We need to talk. Right now. I'm not leaving until you let me in."

More silence came through the intercom. All I heard was the gentle breeze and a car alarm fading in the distance. Then, "Okay. I'll be down in a minute."

"Thank you," Jack said. He took a step away from the entry and sighed. His sudden movement forced me to slink back yet again. To where I was going to be too far away to hear anything. And the second Bianca came down, I would need to be even farther back to avoid detection.

"Dammit," I whispered as I stole around a corner, out of sight. I would need to either move away before someone saw me or circle up to the other side of the apartment building and try my luck there.

With no time to think, I bolted down the street to circle the block and shuffle as close to Jack as possible before Bianca arrived. I ran most of the way and slowed up when I got near enough that my footfalls would be heard. Hopefully, no one in the area had noticed me and thought something suspicious was up. The last thing I needed was the campus police arriving to spoil the conversation.

With my lungs struggling for air, I did what I could to slow down my rapid heartbeat and held an arm over my mouth to conceal the sound. I was closer to Jack than I was before. But all it would take for him to spot me was for him to poke his head around the corner. He would recognize me in an instant and would have a lot of unpleasant questions.

Bianca arrived and stepped out into the night with Jack. I listened to her footsteps. I crept a little closer but kept my back toward their conversation in case something made them walk in my direction. If they saw me, they would only find my hoodie. As a last resort, I could run away into the night.

"Kara? What are you doing here?" Jack asked this time.

It wasn't Bianca meeting him outside. What was his sister doing there?

"Stopping you from making a mistake."

"What do you mean? I thought you wanted me to end things with Bianca."

Kara sighed. "I did. And part of me still does, but I realized what I was doing was wrong. It wasn't my place to tell you both what to do."

"So you're not going to tell my girlfriend about Bianca?"

"No. Your secret is safe with me. At least for now. But if you piss me off enough, I might change my mind."

"I won't," Jack said. "Thank you."

She sighed.

I took a moment to think. Kara must have gone to Jack with the same threat she gave Bianca. She must have done it via text or email. Otherwise, I would have known about it.

233

And now she was trying to undo the wonderful thing she had almost made happen. With clenched fists, I listened in and did what I could to suppress the rage I had in my gut. Jack was going to do it. He was going to end things with Bianca. But Kara stopped him out of some kind of misplaced guilt. Why? Did she not feel bad for his actual girlfriend?

I listened in some more to the pointless conversation, knowing how it would play out. Jack's attitude shifted the moment he got the news. The joy had returned to his voice. He could continue screwing both girls.

Inevitably, Bianca buzzed Kara and Jack back inside the building, leaving me in the cold. Leaving me to deal with the loss of hope that I had in the palm of my hands for a fleeting minute. What did it take for things to go my way? How much pain did I have to swallow before Jack would see what he was doing to me?

As the door to the building closed, I drifted back into the shadows as a burning lined my lungs. Kara's incompetence didn't matter. My plan could still work. I would simply need to escalate what I already had in place and risk not having a solid alibi to cover my tracks. Given the way things had all transpired, it was a chance worth taking.

I lowered my head and got underway, running down the street.

Time was my greatest enemy. Whether destiny was making me wait or working against me, I could never seem to have things line up at the right moment. But that night, I was going to achieve my goals no matter the cost. I was sick to death of the waiting. Once morning came, Jack would be mine.

I hustled across campus toward her. Toward Jack's precious girlfriend. She would be alone tonight. No roommate to keep her company as she studied long into the wee hours. I still had the stolen key that could grant me access to her room. I just had to walk into her building without being seen. That wouldn't be hard. What would come after would be the true challenge. But I would not hesitate. I would not back out and let them all win. Jack belonged to me.

As I rushed through the cool air of the night, I traced the J + N that was scarred on the palm of my hand and embraced the tingle that shot along my veins. Soon, I would no longer need to watch him from a distance or listen to him in private spaces. We would be one. The equation would be solved.

Once I got to his girlfriend's building, I spotted another student approaching the entry. I just needed to wait for him to go in first, so no one saw me there at that moment. The security cameras wouldn't be able to identify me. Not if I kept my head down and my hood up as planned. I would dispose of my clothing once it was all said and done.

I watched the student. He was some guy. No doubt a student on his way back from a social event I wasn't part of. He was only ten feet from the building's entrance when he stopped and turned around. I swiveled away from him and continued to walk as if I wasn't headed into his dorm. He wouldn't regard me as a threat. I would come across as nothing but a quiet student on her way back to her dorm.

He continued. When he reached the door, he entered a code I already knew. An electromagnetic bolt unlocked. He made his way inside and let the door swing itself shut. Calmly, I walked to the door and entered the same code that hadn't changed in six months.

I moved inside Jack's girlfriend's dorm building. All I had to do was walk up the stairwell to her floor, then to her room. The whole time, I needed to keep my head down and focus on the path ahead.

The bottom floor of the building was empty. Up in the room's corner would be a dome security camera. I wondered if it even worked or if it was there for show. Even if it did record, the footage would be grainy at best.

When I made my ascent to her floor, thoughts of the future flooded my mind again. These images kept me awake at night. Where would Jack and I go once we left college? What life would we live together? Again, I imagined our children and the perfect combination of us they would be. I would stay at home and raise them while Jack went out and changed

235

the world. He would be more than a teacher. He would rise through the ranks and become an important figure in the education field. And when he had reached the top, he would thank and honor me for my support and love.

I snapped out of the daydream and realized I was still climbing the stairwell. I had stopped on a landing between floors and was gripping the handrail for dear life. That was a mistake. I wasn't supposed to touch a thing. Fortunately, I still had my gloves on. Not that I imagined there would be a forensics team sweeping the building for fingerprints and DNA.

The guy who had entered the building before me came back down the stairwell. I lowered my gaze and continued upward, acting as if he didn't exist. If I were to turn around and go back down, it would have looked suspicious. All I had to do was pass him by and not make eye contact.

We passed each other like two ships in the night, but then he came to a stop and turned toward me. I felt my pulse race, but I didn't slow. I continued my climb and kept my focus. He grunted as if he were about to say something but then seemed to think better of it. He carried on with his descent, allowing me to breathe again.

My plan was going to work. I was going to reach her room and make my way inside without her knowing it. Then, she would pay the price. She would suffer the consequences of getting between Jack and me. It was nothing personal. You could call it unfortunate if you had to put a label on the situation. I didn't feel sorry for what had to be done. She was a problem. One that would be dealt with swiftly.

I came to her door and drew the key from my pocket with a gloved hand. I hovered it at the lock and closed my eyes. As my breath flowed out of me, I found my purpose. I channeled the energy I would need in the coming minutes and hours. In my jacket, I held the tools that would bring Jack and me together.

His girlfriend's life was in my hands, and she would never see me coming.

CHAPTER FIFTY-FIVE

Present Day

Ellie takes another breath in before she speaks. "I can't believe I'm saying this. And I could be wrong. It was sunny at lunchtime, and I was tired from a bad night of sleep."

"What are you saying?" I huff. I don't mean to be rude, but it's obvious Ellie has something awful to tell me.

She squints again, looking away from me. "It looked like they were kissing."

"Who?" I ask with a lump in my throat.

"Jack and Nicole."

I take a step back from my friend and feel the world close in on me. I'm outside, but suddenly it feels like there's no air for me to breathe. Shaking my head, I say, "Are you sure it was them?"

She nods with a certainty I can't ignore. "If it wasn't, then they could pass as twins. I'm so sorry, Bee. I don't know what else to tell you."

"There's nothing to say," I mutter.

I stare at Ellie's front garden and listen to the birds chirping away without a care in the world. I'd give anything to live their simple existence right now.

"What are you going to do about today?" Ellie asks.

The question pulls me from my daze. I stare at her with an intensity that makes Ellie take a step back toward her own house. "I'm going to meet him at our therapy session."

"Is that a good idea?"

"Yes. No. I don't know. I can't answer that question. You want to know why? Because ever since that psycho at number six showed up, things have gone to hell."

"I'm sorry," Ellie says, shrinking back. "I shouldn't have said anything."

"No, you did the right thing, Ellie. Trust me."

She nods, keeping her eyes low. "Can you do me a favor?" she asks.

I squint. "A favor?"

"Yeah. Can you leave my name out of this? I know it's selfish of me to ask, but I don't want anything getting back to Dave. He'll hate me if he thinks I've done anything to cause trouble between you and Jack, even though I was right to tell you."

Clutching at the strap on my handbag, I give Ellie a nod. "I can do that. I'll just tell Jack that I saw him myself. What difference does it make?"

Ellie smiles at me with pity in her eyes. "I'm so sorry, Bee. I can still watch the kids tonight. Take as long as you need. They can even stay over, if you want."

I hear Ellie's words but don't seem to process them. The image of Jack and Nicole together floods my mind instead. It fills me with a burning rage that won't be extinguished until I see Jack pay the price for what he's done to me.

"Bee?" Ellie asks. "The kids?"

"Uh, yeah. That would be amazing. I'll call you later. Thank you."

"Anytime. I'm always here for you. And remember, no matter what happens, you'll get through this, okay?"

"Maybe," I say as I drift away from Ellie. I walk along the sidewalk toward my house. As I go by number six again, Nicole's home no longer comes across as something to fear.

All I want to do is throw a brick through every window and set the place on fire. I want to watch it burn to the ground with Nicole inside it while she screams for mercy.

Eighteen years ago, she tried to kill me. She tried to take me out of the picture so she could keep Jack all to herself. I should be the one seeking revenge.

As backward as things have become, what I don't understand is why Jack is having an affair with Nicole. Kara might not have been her target the night of the crash, but in the end, she was the one who paid the price.

Whatever happens to my marriage in the coming hours and days is no longer important. I only need to find out one thing: what lies has Nicole told Jack?

CHAPTER FIFTY-SIX

I reach my car and rush to climb inside. I have an appointment to keep and a husband to kill. Not literally, of course. But it might come to that if he admits to what Ellie saw. I don't doubt what she witnessed, either. Jack has a history of being unfaithful, and I'm now convinced he's done it to me more than once. When I think about us and our past, our relationship was founded on a pile of secrets and lies. What hope did we have?

As I drive to our therapy session, the three notes run through my head until I say them out loud. "Confess. Lies breed chaos. What could have been." I whisper them to myself, repeating the words like a mantra. They all point to the same thing. The one thing that changed everything. I've tried to ignore the obvious. I've tried to convince myself that this has all been a cruel coincidence, but I can only live in the dark for so long.

The truth is about to break free.

When I reach the parking lot of our therapist's office, I notice Jack's car is already there. He isn't running late. In fact, he's on time and is sitting in the waiting area inside with his hands clasped together.

I don't know what Nicole has told him. But if he has been spotted kissing Nicole, then I can assume she has filled his head with enough poison to get him on her side.

Until I find out what Jack has been up to, I have to continue to act dumb. I'm just the clueless wife who believes her husband is a decent, faithful man. I can play the part for now, but it won't be long before my restless anger boils to the surface and explodes.

I reach over to my handbag on the passenger seat and check for the Polaroid. It almost seems pointless bringing it with me. I know who that burned woman is. Still, I'll need it. Having it with the box containing Kara's bracelet and its ominous note will help me show Jack who he has sided with over his wife.

I stow the box in my handbag along with the Polaroid and take a deep breath in. As much as I want to start my car and drive in the opposite direction, I need to do this. I need to see things through and find the truth at the bottom of the well.

This session won't be easy, but it will be the last one we ever attend.

When I open the door to the waiting room, I'm greeted by Jack with an icy reception. He can barely make eye contact with me.

"You made it on time," I say, doing what I can to keep the anger from my voice. I have to play my role for now. At least until we are in the session. I want everything to come out in the safety of the room and not when we are at home. I'm not saying Jack would hurt me. He's never laid a hand on me in our entire relationship, but I've seen him at his limit before. I know what he is capable of, and today is going to put him to the test.

"I got my work done," Jack says, half-muttering. There are other people in the waiting room with us. Other couples. You can almost feel the divide between some of them. It makes me wonder if they are throwing good money after bad, attempting to fix something that is beyond repair.

Are we one of these couples?

"Did you get the kids to Ellie, okay?" he asks.

"Yes. She was more than happy to help. She's taking them to Georgia's for dinner. It'll give us some time alone. Once we're done here, of course."

"That's nice," he says while staring into the distance. I study his reaction as best I can. From what I can tell, he doesn't know Ellie saw him kissing Nicole. If he did, there's no way he would be happy for her to watch the kids.

"Maybe we could go out for dinner," I say, testing the waters.

"Oh," he says. "Sure." He projects a smile at me, but it lacks any warmth and fades in an instant. Something has changed. And it's prompted him to sneak around and kiss his ex.

After I'm done with him, he'll wish we had never been married. If he's lucky, I'll let him back in the house to retrieve his suitcase and some clothing.

Thoughts of the months ahead hit me hard. I'm already imagining the devastation a divorce will bring to the kids. We'll have to sell the house and divide our assets. And once the lawyers are finished picking over our remains, we'll each walk away with a bit of money, joint custody of the kids, and a world of problems.

I exhale and try to remind myself that Jack hasn't even confessed to anything yet. There's still a chance that this is all some giant misunderstanding. Maybe I don't have to ask him about the kiss. I could sweep it all under the rug and pretend that everything is fine. But would I be happy to live such an existence?

"Mr. & Mrs. Anderson?" calls Dr. Carabello's administrative assistant. "You can go in now. She's ready for you."

"Thank you," Jack replies, his voice quiet. If I didn't know better, I'd swear he was nervous. This isn't what I was expecting. Now that I think about it, he seems defeated more than anything else. He was like this on the phone earlier, too. What am I missing here?

When we enter our session, I suddenly lose the edge I had bolstering me along. What if I'm wrong? What if I'm about to accuse Jack of something he hasn't done? I'm not saying Ellie was lying, but her view of number six is farther away than it looks. Maybe it seemed like he was kissing Nicole from where she was standing. Then again, what was he doing there in the first place?

"God," I let out. I hate being crippled with indecision. It's like there's a virus in my brain telling me to have two opposing thoughts at once. Each voice is convincing and confident, but I don't know which one to believe.

"Take a seat, Bianca," Dr. Carabello tells me. Our therapist is in her late forties with dark hair and thin glasses. That's about as much as I know about her.

"Thank you," I reply, settling in beside Jack on the sofa that is opposite Dr. Carabello's desk. Dr. Carabello adjusts her glasses and opens a folder in front of her, wearing her standard expression: an uneven mix of professionalism and empathy.

Our folder isn't very thick. We haven't been doing this long enough to build up much of a file. Still, she knows plenty about us. I'm sure she could pinpoint each of our weaknesses in a heartbeat and break us down. If things go the way I think they might today, her small folder will double in size.

"Let's pick up where we left off," the doctor says. She goes over some bullet points from our last session. The problems we discussed last week seem so minuscule given what's happened since then. So much has changed in such a short amount of time. My brain hasn't had time to process most of it.

I study Jack as we go through the early details of the session. I don't want to hit him with the big stuff straight away. I need to build up to it. He shifts in his seat as Dr. Carabello asks us the same old questions. We each give basic non-committal answers as always, but I notice Jack's eyes darting around the room like he's searching for a fire escape.

Dr. Carabello glances between us. She knows something isn't right. Her gaze settles on me. "Bianca, you mentioned last session that you were feeling a lot of uncertainty about your marriage. Can you tell me how this doubt has been this week?"

I swallow hard. My mouth is drier than I expected. She's hit me with something major. I should have been better prepared. "Well, to be frank, this week has been tough."

"Why?"

Jack glances at me with telling eyes. We never discussed it, but I think he doesn't want me to mention Nicole's name. It's coming out, though, one way or another.

"Something strange happened last weekend," I say.

"Oh. Could you elaborate?"

"Yes," I say, letting the word hang in the air. The week floods my mind and clenches up my entire being. The room feels smaller than it should. When the walls close in, I hide my face in my hands and stare through the gaps in my fingers at the floor. For a moment, the reality of airing our dirty laundry seems to get under my skin.

"Bianca?" Dr. Carabello asks. "If you need a moment to—"

"I'm fine," I say, cutting her off. "I just have a lot to get out."

"That's fine. Start at the beginning."

"Okay," I say, exhaling. Then I tell the doctor about our week. As much as I can without revealing anything to Jack. It's hard enough telling Dr. Carabello about Nicole moving in next door, let alone the rest of it.

Dr. Carabello's brow tightens with every word I release. She makes copious notes in her folder as I spill one detail after another until I reach a line I'm not ready to cross. The entire time, Jack stares at the floor like he's not listening to a word I'm saying. He should be stressed out right now.

I guess this confirms the worst. Jack no longer cares about me. That talk we had the other night after having sex was just that — talk. He didn't mean a word of it. Why did he even bother to show up today?

"That's quite a week," Dr. Carabello says.

"Uh, yeah," I say, looking away from Jack.

"No doubt it has placed some added pressure on your marriage."

I nod. If only she knew the half of it. Dr. Carabello recites some lines we've heard a few times before about remembering not to let external stresses impact the way we view one another, but it's like telling someone to ignore a lion when they've fallen into its cage.

I try to listen and give the impression that I'm taking in what the doctor has to say, but the entire time, I can't take my eyes off Jack. He is still staring at nothing. It's like he isn't in the room.

As if reading my mind, Dr. Carabello shifts her focus to my husband. "Jack," she says softly, "You've been rather quiet today. How do you feel about what Bianca has shared?"

He lifts his head. His eyes meet mine for a second, then dart away. "I don't know," he mutters. "It's been a strange week."

"Can you be more specific?"

Jack sighs and runs a hand through his hair. "This whole thing with Nicole moving in next door has been messing with me."

"In what way?"

He leans back on the sofa and stares up at the ceiling as if eye contact is too much to handle. "Just the sight of Nicole has stirred up a lot of memories."

"Memories like your sister?" the doctor asks.

Jack closes his eyes for a second and grits his teeth. "Yeah."

"Would you like to talk about Kara?"

I shift in my seat and feel like I'm a fly on the wall in Jack's own personal session. He leans forward and rests an elbow on his knee and props his head up with the same arm.

"Jack?" Dr. Carabello asks.

"I don't know if I can do it," he says. And as he does, my mind snaps to the box in my handbag. Maybe bringing Kara's bracelet along with me was the worst idea possible.

"Death can be a difficult subject," the doctor says. "Especially when the person we loved died in such a horrible way. If you're not ready to talk about Kara, we can move on to—"

"I hate the way she died," Jack says, cutting her off. "It was so meaningless."

Dr. Carabello nods. "That factor can make death much harder to deal with. Did you receive counseling after the crash?"

The night that changed our lives enters my mind, creeping in without permission. It tugs at my reality and threatens to take over.

Jack continues. "Yeah. Some therapist like yourself tried to get me to open up about the whole thing."

"And did you?"

"No. What was the point? It wouldn't bring her back."

"It's not about bringing someone back. It's about closure. It's about accepting the terrible thing that happened to your sister so you can move on with your life as best you can."

He shakes his head as his eyes water. "Why should I move on? Why do I deserve to live, but she died? She was a better person than I could ever hope to be, and she died for nothing."

Without wanting to, I place an arm on Jack's shoulder. I expect him to shrug me off, but he doesn't. I've never seen him open up like this before. He never talks about Kara. His words send a pang of anxiety to my stomach as I think about the bracelet.

"It's okay, Jack," Dr. Carabello says. "Speak your mind. Whatever you feel comfortable saying."

Jack sobs into his hands and sniffs. "No. I don't want to talk about it anymore. My sister was an angel. I won't ruin her memory with this conversation for a second longer."

I remove my hand from his shoulder as he turns away from the doctor and shuts down. He cries some more and she offers him a handful of tissues. He takes them without a word and buries his face in them.

Once I have some time to process what I'm seeing, a cold thought enters my mind. I should feel ashamed and sickened for it, but I can't stop what's running through my head. With Jack shutting down, I won't be able to get to the truth. I won't be able to flash the burned Polaroid at him without feeling like the worst human being on the planet.

I can't ask Jack if he kissed Nicole today.

CHAPTER FIFTY-SEVEN

I know I'm being selfish, but I couldn't be more disappointed if I tried. I have Jack in our therapy session, vulnerable as hell, while I sit here with the damning knowledge that he has been cheating on me with Nicole. He has broken down and is refusing to talk to me or Dr. Carabello, all because this week has dredged up too many memories of his dead sister.

"Perhaps we should take a break," Dr. Carabello suggests to Jack. He waves her off. It's like watching a small child with anxiety problems being overwhelmed by a large crowd. I've never seen Jack like this. Sure, his sister's death has always been a sensitive topic, but I didn't know things were this bad.

"Jack?" Dr. Carabello says. "Are you sure you don't want to take a moment? This is a delicate issue."

Jack sniffs and turns back toward our therapist. "Sorry. I didn't . . ."

"It's okay. You've just released something that has been brewing inside you for quite a while. It can be intimidating."

Jack keeps his gaze on the floor. When he finally lifts his head, he gives me a sideways glance and then faces Dr. Carabello. "Can we talk about something else?"

"Sure. We can come back to it later. When you're ready."

"Thank you," he mutters.

Dr. Carabello checks over her notes and runs a finger over the writing. From her expression, she seems to be contemplating the best way to steer the conversation. I suppose she needs to keep Jack engaged in the session while not pushing him too hard. With any luck, she can make him stay on track. Then I can hit him with what I know. I won't bring out the bracelet, but the Polaroid is still an option.

"Jack," Dr. Carabello starts with her soft voice, "let's shift gears for a bit. We've touched on some painful memories today. How about we talk about something a little more current? Maybe something from your day-to-day life that's been on your mind? Can you think of anything that's been bothering you?"

My eyes go wide when I hear Dr. Carabello's question. It's damn near perfect. He can't sit there and ignore the things he's been up to. He can't hide behind Kara's death.

Jack nods, still looking drained. "Yes," he says.

Dr. Carabello gives him a reassuring smile. "Okay. You mentioned last time that work has been quite stressful. Do you want to share more about that?"

Jack sighs, rubbing his temples as if trying to ward off a migraine. "Yeah, work has been a real pain. As I told Bianca, the district is considering cutting our history department down. I've only been at the school for three years, so there's a good chance I'll be the first one put through the firing process."

I watch Jack closely. When he mentioned the budget cuts, he wasn't saying he would be the one fired or put on leave. What happened at school today?

"What's been the most challenging part about this news?" Dr. Carabello asks.

Jack frowns. "The pressure. I now feel like I have to perform perfectly. Every little mistake feels like it could be magnified a thousand times. And the principal . . . she's not the most understanding person. We don't see eye to eye very often."

I nod, trying to present myself to the room as a reassuring wife. "I noticed you left early this morning. You must be exhausted."

"I'm okay," he says quicker than he should, without glancing in my direction.

"Are you sure? It's not good for you to take on any extra stress on your own. Is there anything I can do to help?"

"No."

The room falls silent for a moment. Dr. Carabello shifts in her chair as her gaze shifts between Jack and me. Does she see it? Can she recognize Jack is hiding something? He's avoiding our eyes again.

"Jack, it sounds like you're carrying a heavy load," Dr. Carabello says. "It's important to lighten that burden, even a small amount. Allowing Bianca to ease some of that pressure is a great start. How do you usually cope with stress?"

Jack hesitates and takes a moment to answer. "I suppose I try to keep busy. You know, stay focused on the task at hand."

"And how's that working out for you?" she asks.

He shrugs. "Okay, I guess."

Dr. Carabello nods, jotting something down in her notes. "With everything that's going on at work, have you considered talking to someone at the school about your concerns? Maybe they can offer you some support or reassurance about your job security."

Jack's face hardens. "There's no one to talk to. The principal has made it clear that everyone is on their own. She wants to build up her other departments."

Jack goes on about the school and the principal some more. All the while, I sit there and try to keep my rage from shining through. How can he act like this is the biggest issue he's facing? He's been sneaking around and kissing Nicole behind my back. Only God knows what other secrets he's keeping. Is he really going to hide behind Kara and his supposed pressures at school for this entire session? He must be on to me in some capacity. He's not asking me questions about my behavior like he promised he would.

I take a deep breath, trying to keep my emotions in check, but I don't know how much longer I can contain them. "Jack," I breathe, "maybe there's more going on than just work. You've been distant lately, not only with me, but with everything."

He looks at me, lifting his eyes from the floor. "What are you saying?"

I raise an eyebrow. "You know what I'm talking about."

He doesn't respond, but he also doesn't look away.

Dr. Carabello leans forward and cuts in with her soothing voice. "Keeping everything bottled up always makes things worse. Have you thought about what might help you feel more grounded or supported?"

Jack runs a hand through his hair again, looking more agitated now. "God, I don't know. Maybe I need some time away. From everything. From everyone."

"What do you mean, time away?" I snap, trying to keep my voice steady.

He shrugs. "Maybe I need to step back for a while. Clear my head. Figure things out."

Dr. Carabello steps in again, stopping me from exploding. "We all need it now and then, Jack, but it's also important to communicate with Bianca. You can't shut her out and hope for the best. Relationships thrive on open and honest communication. Wouldn't it be better to navigate this together?"

Jack stands up in a flash. "I'm done with this."

A surge of panic runs through me. He's trying to escape. I have to stop him. "Jack, please. Sit down. We can work through this."

He shakes his head, looking trapped. "I can't, Bianca. I'm sorry." Without another word, he moves toward the door, leaving me sitting there with Dr. Carabello. It even catches her off guard.

"Jack?" she calls. But he doesn't stop for her either. With a slack jaw, she watches him leave, then turns to me. "Uh, Bianca. I'm sorry, but it seems like Jack is—"

"Just bill us for the hour," I say as I rush out of the room. Dr. Carabello struggles to respond, and I don't wait around for her to find her voice and hit me with another one of her canned responses.

When I reach the reception area, I find Jack outside, heading straight for his car. If the bastard thinks he's outsmarted me, he's got another thing coming. I'm not letting this go.

"Is everything okay?" Dr. Carabello's administrative assistant asks me. We haven't even completed half of the session. I ignore her and charge out the door before Jack drives off on me. Where is he going? Is he meeting up with Nicole somewhere? Nothing would surprise me at this point.

"Jack," I call out as he climbs into his car. He pretends not to notice me and starts the engine.

I jog over to him and stand in front of his car. "Where the hell are you going?" I ask with outstretched arms.

Jack lowers his window a few inches. "Get out of my way."

"Not a chance. Not until you tell me what you're doing." Without looking, I realize there's a waiting room full of people watching me make a dramatic fool of myself. I don't care. They can film me and put it online if they want. Jack is not leaving this parking lot until he answers my questions.

My husband stares at me through the windshield with a thick scowl. I can almost hear him sigh as he turns the engine off and crosses his arms over his chest.

I walk around to the driver's side of his car and lean down close enough for Jack to hear my heavy breathing. "Where are you going?" I repeat.

"Anywhere but here. I need some space."

I scoff. "Space? We both know where you are heading. Why don't you save us some embarrassment and come clean?"

"Come clean? What are you talking about?"

With both my hands planted on Jack's car, I glower at him and cannot for the life of me understand what he is holding on to. Have we not reached a point where he feels comfortable enough to drop the act?

"You're going to make me do this, aren't you?" I ask.

"Do what?" he asks like a gambler going all in on a bad hand. He commits to his play, choosing to do things the hard way.

"So be it," I say. And I pull out the Polaroid that has been plaguing my mind since the second I laid eyes on it. I hold the photo up to the glass and ask, "Who is she, Jack?"

Jack squints at the Polaroid for less than a second until a worry line takes over his features. "Where did you find that?" he asks, his voice just above a whisper.

"In the backyard, in your smoker, buried amongst a pile of other destroyed photos. But it survived your little fire. So, I'm asking you again, who is she?"

Jack grabs the steering wheel of his car with both hands as if he's about to fall over. "You're telling me you found it in the backyard in my smoker?"

"Stop playing games," I shout. "Just tell me who she is. It's Nicole, isn't it?" I flip the Polaroid over and tap the small writing. "J + N. Jack and Nicole. Admit it."

He shakes his head. "Bianca, you don't understand."

I almost leap inside the car. "I saw you kissing her today at lunchtime when you thought no one was watching, but I was watching, Jack." It's a lie, but only to protect Ellie. She doesn't deserve to be caught up in this mess.

Jack's jaw drops open. "You saw me?" he asks. "With Nicole?"

"Don't deny it."

He shakes his head like I'm the crazy one. "What you're saying is impossible. Why don't we head home, huh? We can talk about this some more."

"No! Not until you see what kind of psycho she is. I pull my handbag around and dig my fingers inside it. I don't give a damn what this might do to Jack. He needs to see what Nicole has done. I find the box with the bloody bracelet inside and pull it out.

"What are you doing?" he asks.

253

"Showing you who Nicole really is." I open the box, ready to pull out the bracelet. But when I lift the flap away, all I find is more cardboard. It's empty.

"What is this?" Jack asks.

"No," I utter. "She must have taken it while I was working." I almost shove the empty box in his face. "She stole it. You have to believe me."

Jack stares at me with a pity in his eyes that shouldn't exist. "Bianca, this has gone on long enough. It's time to go. We can talk about everything at home. I'll answer any question you have for me. I swear."

"I'm not going anywhere with you," I yell, taking a step back. "She's in your head, isn't she? She's got you wrapped around her little finger. What did she tell you to do to me when we're alone next? Are you going to murder me in my own house?" I throw the empty box at him. It falls short and bounces off his door.

"What the hell?" Jack yells. "Have you lost your mind? Get in the car before someone calls the cops."

I take three more steps back with a wild stare in my eyes. "How stupid do you think I am?"

Jack climbs out of the car like he's going to hit me over the head and throw me in the trunk.

"Stay back," I yell.

He holds his arms out wide. "I'm not going to hurt you. I promise."

"You promise? Like you promised to never cheat on me again? Fuck you, Jack." I look at my car and run. He won't chase after me. Not when there are people around.

"Where are you going?" he shouts after me.

I don't look back. Instead, I rush into my car and fire up its engine. Jack doesn't run after me and watches as I speed out of the parking lot.

I know Ellie is at Georgia's place and is up to her eyeballs with kids and judgmental in-laws, but I need her now more than I've ever needed a friend.

CHAPTER FIFTY-EIGHT

Eighteen years ago

It was done. The next stage of my plan was complete. It wasn't easy, and I wasn't sure if I was going to have it in me to do what was necessary, but in the end, I came through.

Jack's girlfriend had been asleep on her side when I crept into her room with a balaclava on. She was facing the wall and never stood a chance. She never saw me coming. With as much confidence as I could muster, I dropped to her side while she slept and grabbed her by her ponytail. Before she shot up awake, I rammed the syringe into a vein in her neck and depressed the contents into her bloodstream. I'd practiced the trick a hundred times on a doll, marking out where the jugular would be.

I had stolen the contents of the syringe from one of the campus labs. It was almost too easy to sneak in after hours and take what I needed. I just had to pay the right person to look the other way.

She reacted as I expected her to and tried to bolt upright in her bed. Anticipating this, I let the syringe fall to the floor and placed my entire weight on her upper body, putting a gloved hand over her mouth. At first, she thrashed like hell and tried to scream, but the sedative soon kicked in and took over. Within a minute, she gave up her fight and passed out. I was free to do what came next.

My pulse raced as I stood over her helpless body. An overwhelming sense of power flooded my system. I held her life in the palm of my hand. In my pocket was the knife I used to slice Bianca's seatbelt. A tempting opportunity sat beneath me.

I pulled out the blade and held it close to her throat as she lay on her back with her eyes closed and her arms splayed. How easy it would have been to end her existence then and there.

Instead, I brought the knife within a millimeter of her delicate skin and slid the sharpened blade up to her cheek. I ran it over her face and drew some blood. She didn't move an inch.

I repeated the process a few more times for good measure, making sure the cuts appeared to be the minor injuries a person might sustain in a simple accident. One they would survive. Once I'd done enough, I wiped the blood off my knife and returned it to my pocket. I would destroy it later, of course, but I would not relish the task. I had hoped to keep the knife as a trophy of sorts, but the risk was too high.

Next, I took her pillow from under her neck and removed the cover. I then wrapped some of her heavier textbooks from her desk in clothing I found strewn about the room and placed them inside the pillowcase. This part I knew I was going to enjoy. Three times in a row, I swung the filled pillowcase and slammed it into her face. She took each blow without stirring. Every time I struck her, I increased the strength of the hit. After the third bash, I had to stop myself from doing more. Beating her to death wasn't the plan, much as I wanted it to be.

I stood back from my work and nodded. Her face would soon look like it had collided with an airbag. It wasn't noticeable yet, but she would bruise. Anyone who spoke to her in the morning would have questions and suspicions. Especially the police.

I placed her textbooks and clothing where they belonged and returned the cover to her pillow. I slid it under her head and tucked her in for the night.

"Sweet dreams," I said as I left her room with my tools returned to my pockets. I also took her keys with me. I would need to return them before the night was through. I locked the door behind me, making sure she had no way of knowing that someone had entered her private space. The way I understood it, she wouldn't remember my attack. The sedative would have made her believe it was all a bad dream.

No one was in the corridor, so I removed my mask and made my way to the stairwell again. As I did so, I pulled out my burner cell phone and made a call. It rang and rang. The hour was late, so I didn't expect a fast answer. Even so, every ring added another ten beats per minute to my heart rate. If Bianca didn't answer, I would have to think of another way to lure her out.

"Hello," Bianca said. It was showtime. I put on my best doctor's voice and got to work. After a brief conversation, I had her nice and panicked. No doubt she would be in a rush to leave the comfort of her dorm room and scurry off to a hospital over an hour away from campus. She was under the belief that her mother — a woman who lived alone — had been in a terrible accident and was in a bad way in the intensive care unit. The beauty of my lie was Bianca's inability to find out if what I was saying was true or not. Her mother always switched off her cell phone at night. And she didn't have a landline either. She didn't have a partner and was divorced from Bianca's father.

There would be no reason for me to worry about Jack. He would not go with Bianca to the hospital. In about ten minutes, he would also receive a call to lure him away from his secret woman. He wouldn't be able to resist what I had in store for him, either.

When I ended the call, I knew I needed to hurry. I would have to find the car that the stolen keys in my pocket belonged to. Jack's girlfriend didn't know that her car was going to be used to run Bianca off the road to her death. By morning, her keys would have been returned to her room and Nicole would be in a state of confusion, working off the sedative I had given her. The police would be called not long after the "accident" by an anonymous witness who saw the hit-and-run crash take place. This good Samaritan would be clever enough to catch the crazy driver's license plate number, too.

By morning, if everything worked out the way I had planned it, Bianca would be dead, and Nicole would be arrested for Bianca's murder. Jack would be rid of his two problems in one fell swoop, and I would be there to pick up the pieces of his shattered life. It was what he needed. Sometimes, to fix a problem, you had to destroy it first.

I moved with purpose to the stairwell entry again. As I went down, hurrying to her car, familiar footfalls bellowed up the steps. I raised my hood and lowered my gaze. Nothing was going to get in my way now.

As the man climbing the stairs brushed by me, he came to a stop, just as he had before. I didn't let it faze me. I had a singular purpose and didn't have time to worry. He wouldn't be able to identify me with my hoodie pulled tight over my head.

"Nora?" he asked.

At the sound of my name, I came to a stop. I didn't mean to.

"That's you, isn't it? What are you doing here?"

I faced him and smiled. It was Damon. Just some nobody frat boy who had hit on me at a few parties. I gave him an answer. "Visiting a friend. I know it's late, but we were watching a movie."

"It's not that late," he said, giving me that same sly smile I'd seen before. Only this time, he wasn't holding a beer in his hand. "Where are you headed?"

"Back to my dorm. I've got classes in the morning. Anyway, it was nice seeing you."

"Hey, wait, Nora. No need to hurry. Why don't you come party with me?"

A sigh fell from me as I crossed my arms over my chest. "A party? I haven't heard about any parties tonight."

"It's a small one, back in my dorm room. Just you and me."

"Right. That kind of party. I'll pass, thanks." I turned to leave, but he grabbed my wrist. "Hey. Did I say you could take off? You're not going anywhere."

I slammed the knife into his gut. I didn't mean to do it, but it happened. All the lust left his face as I twisted the blade and yanked it free. Blood spilled onto the steps as he collapsed into a heap and writhed around in agony. His precious little world was falling apart and would soon be over.

I dropped beside him and whispered into his ear, "Don't worry, no one will miss you." He made some pathetic attempt to say my name, choking on the N several times until nothing came out. Instead, blood gurgled from his mouth as he took his final breaths.

I left the dorm building in a hurry, with my hoodie held over my head. Without stopping, I made my way to Nicole's car and didn't look up. We were a similar build. With any luck, the police would blame her for Damon's death. Either way, I didn't care. I had a plan to execute, and I could not be stopped.

CHAPTER FIFTY-NINE

Present day

I drive faster than I should to Georgia's place. It's close to where we live. Ellie has always told me the proximity is a huge part of the problem. When we all first moved into Maple Court, I was convinced that Ellie and David would end up moving out given the amount of unscheduled visits Georgia started making to their house every other day.

Thoughts of my friend make me forget my twisted husband for a minute. I still can't believe how the session with Dr. Carabello went. I thought it was all going to go my way. I thought Jack would be backed into a corner, forced to confess everything. Instead, he's making me question my every belief. The look he had on his face when I accused him of being with Nicole stains my mind. Frankly, he seemed shocked. And not in a defensive way. It was like what I was saying was a bad joke. But how could that be? Ellie saw him. I don't doubt that. Plus, his behavior these past three days would suggest that something is not right. This is how he was when I busted him after his one-night stand.

I'll never forget his face when he admitted it. I could have sworn he wanted to get caught. It almost seemed like a great sense of relief had washed over him when I asked the question. Maybe his subconscious could no longer stand the guilt.

I'm forced to slow down when the traffic in front of me builds up. I have zero patience to deal with it and need to reach Georgia's place to see Ellie. I don't know how, but she's going to make things right again. I'll let her in on everything when we speak.

The traffic grinds to a halt. I'm halfway there, but I might as well be a hundred miles away. "Come on," I yell as if it's going to make a difference. I feel so out of control. Everything is falling apart around me, and I can't do a thing to stop it. My life wasn't perfect before Nicole showed up, but for better or worse, it was my life. Why couldn't she leave things in the past?

My cell phone rings. The call comes through on my center display. It's Jack again. He's already called me three times since I ran off. He can go to hell if he thinks I'm going to answer. I've got nothing to say to that gaslighting prick.

I hit reject and half consider turning my cell phone off. It wouldn't be a great idea, though. Ellie might call. Knowing my luck, one of the kids will bump their heads and need to be taken to the emergency room.

"God," I sigh, thinking about the kids. How are they going to handle things if Jack and I get a divorce? I wish there was a way we could pretend to be together, for their sakes. Am I being selfish?

"No," I mutter. Why should I have to live like this? Why should I let Jack have his cake and eat it too? He apparently didn't get enough of that in college. I should have never agreed to be his girl on the side. Everyone thought he and Nicole were exclusive. Only a select few had any clue what he was doing with me right until the end.

I still can't believe Nicole got away with it. The police let her go free. For God's sake, a guy was murdered in her dorm building the same night. She probably had something to do with that too.

A horn honks behind, bringing me back. After another fifteen minutes of torture, I reach Georgia's house. I park in the driveway and notice Ellie's car isn't there. She might still be on her way over. "Dammit," I mutter. With my engine off, I take out my cell phone from my handbag and check the time. If Ellie isn't here yet, she won't be far off. I decide to go inside and wait. Maybe my presence will help take Georgia's focus away from Ellie when she arrives.

Georgia is always nice to me. Especially in front of Ellie. At first, I thought she was being genuine, but I soon realized it was all an act to make Ellie feel inadequate.

I knock on the door three times and take a step back. I look like hell after the commotion at the therapy session, but I don't care. All I want to do is visit my friend and unload. I should head home to face my problems like an adult, but this is a much better idea.

The door opens. "Hello, Bianca," Georgia says with no surprise in her voice. "Come, come." She waves me in.

"Thank you," I reply. I step into Georgia's home and am greeted by the warm scent of freshly baked cookies. She must have been baking for her grandchildren in anticipation of their arrival.

I walk through a cozy living room that is filled with vintage furniture and vibrant artwork. Soft music plays in the background as Georgia leads me to her kitchen. She points me to an oak table where mismatched chairs sit amidst a clutter of baking supplies.

I take a seat and place my handbag down beside me. It feels weird to be here without Ellie, but so far, so good. Georgia seems to treat me fine. Oddly enough, she hasn't asked what I'm doing here.

"Can I get you anything? A coffee? Some water?"

"I'm fine, thanks. I just need to see Ellie. Do you know when she will be getting here?"

Georgia regards me with a narrowed brow. "Eleanor's not coming here today."

"What?" I ask, squinting. I glance around at the baking supplies and the batch of cookies on her kitchen bench. "But I thought the kids were all coming for dinner."

"I'm afraid you're mistaken, dear. The only thing that daughter-in-law told me was that you would be dropping by around this time. You're a touch early, but here you are."

I shake my head as a wave of confusion flows through me. Ellie said she needed to bring the kids over for dinner. That's what she told me. I swear. Maybe I misunderstood her. I stand from the table and grab my handbag. "I'm so sorry to bother you, Georgia. I think maybe I've mixed up my days."

"Nonsense. Eleanor said you were coming by to pick something up. She said you'd be in the area. I didn't understand why I had to be left with this, but then again, I'll never understand the things she does." Georgia paces down the length of her kitchen to her refrigerator. She takes an envelope off the door that had been held there with a cheap magnet. I find my name written in Ellie's handwriting on the envelope. Georgia hands it to me. "There you are."

"Um, thank you," I whisper as I stare at the envelope with a slack jaw.

"What's this all about?" Georgia asks. "I don't mind you stopping in here, but I'm not the U.S. Postal Service. Eleanor wouldn't tell me. She even sealed it with wax, for God's sake."

I continue to gawk at the rectangle in my hand and shake my head. "I should get going," I say.

"Suit yourself," Georgia says. She walks me to the front door and wishes me well. As I walk back to my car, all I can hear in my head is Georgia saying Ellie's full name over and over. Eleanor, Eleanor, Eleanor. Ellie hates it. She always has.

Forgetting the unimportant detail, I break the wax seal and dig a finger into the envelope to tear it open. When I pull out the single piece of paper and read its contents, I almost fall over. Beside my car, I lower myself to the ground and read the words on the page again.

Hello Bee,

How was your therapy session? Did you get Jack to admit everything you wanted him to? Therapy can be quite revealing, can't it? It must be so cathartic to hear him say the things you've been longing to know. That is, if he even said them. He can be rather stubborn, can't he?

I have a confession to make, Bee. It's not Nicole who's been messing with you, leaving you bloody notes, or stealing things from your car while you work. It's me. Sure, Nicole did have a hand in things, but she was simply doing what I told her to do. Surprised? You probably don't even remember me. I was that girl in college, the one you never noticed. The one who was always there. Well, I noticed you, Bee. I watched from the shadows while you and Jack went behind Nicole's back and violated their supposed relationship. You were always so wrapped up in your own precious world. You could never spare a glance for someone like me. I was just another face in the crowd, invisible to the likes of Bianca.

I saw everything, Bee. I saw how you manipulated Jack into staying with you. You always got what you wanted, didn't you? It made me sick. When Jack and I were together, before the likes of you or Nicole, he would never have done such a disgusting thing. But this is what you do to people. You corrupt them.

I vowed back then that one day, Jack would see the real you. The girl who thought she could take whatever she wanted and never pay a price. And guess what? That day has finally come.

Meet me at the crash site tonight. Come alone. No police or anyone else. And especially, no Jack. He is to be kept in the dark about everything. If you think I'm bluffing, Noah and Dot will pay the price. I mean it, Bianca. This is your only warning. I will be watching you.

You always thrived on control. Now it's my turn. By the end of this night, Jack will be mine. I promise you that.

See you soon.

Your old friend,

Eleanor. Better known to Jack as Nora.

CHAPTER SIXTY

I pull myself to my feet and climb into my Subaru. With the letter still in my hand, I fire up the engine. This can't be happening. Ellie can't be the "N" from the "J + N" I found on the Polaroid. She can't be the girl in the other half of the photo.

Nora. Not Nicole. How did I not see this before? She's Jack's ex — the one he had before Nicole. I guess whenever I look at Ellie, I don't see a threat. Just a nice girl who, as she says, blends into the background. She's always been there for me through thick and thin. Maybe there was a reason for it.

Denial aside, I don't have time to waste. I slap the letter down on the passenger seat and type in the crash site's address into my central display. I know the address well and could get to the spot without my GPS, but I don't want to take any chances.

The screen tells me it's less than an hour away, but it feels like it's going to take a week to get there.

As I reverse into the street, I see a flash of Dot and Noah in my mind. What has Ellie done to them? If she's laid a hand on either of my babies, I swear to God I won't be responsible for my actions. She wouldn't hurt them, would she?

I think back to all the times she came over to visit me. How many moments did she spend alone with Jack while I was busy with Noah or something else? Too many to count. She was never there to spend time with me. She was there to be with Jack. Were they having an affair behind my back all this time? Sneaking around in plain sight?

I was that girl. I was Jack's secret. I knew how much he enjoyed the deceitful nature of our relationship. It was the only reason he stayed with me. Then Kara died, and he didn't want to be alone.

Ellie must have been the one who was driving Nicole's car that night. The police had said they could never definitively prove Nicole had been behind the wheel. She had injuries consistent with an airbag exploding in her face, but because of a murder in her dorm building on the same night, the police had knocked on the door of every room in her housing block and spoken to each student present. Nicole had answered. According to the report, she looked to be intoxicated and sleeping off a lot of alcohol, but she was in her room. And given how far away she was from the crash site, it would have been difficult for her to make it all the way back to her dorm before the body was found. They couldn't prove Nicole had been the one driving. And to add further weight to her story, her keys were missing.

I've known this for the last eighteen years, but I saw what I saw the night of the crash with my own two eyes. I thought it was Nicole. Nothing the police or anyone else had to say was going to convince me otherwise.

Even though Jack wasn't involved in the crash, he felt the same way. He thought Nicole was at the center of it all. But instead of Nicole being the jealous psycho, it was someone I thought was a close friend.

As I drive, the weight of Ellie's admission presses down on me. She is threatening to unravel everything I've fought for years to protect. I thought we were safe from the past, but maybe the past has always been lurking nearby, waiting to resurface.

I push my car to the limit and listen as the engine whines while I follow the GPS to the crash site. The closer I get, the more memories come back to me.

On the night of the crash, I'd received a call from a doctor. She told me my mother had been admitted to a nearby hospital after being involved in a major car accident. I was in my dorm room with Kara and Jack at the time. Kara had just told me she would not tell Nicole about Jack and me. I felt so relieved for that short time because I was positive Jack was going to end things between us. He had even come over unannounced to do so.

After I got the call, I tried to contact my mother on her cell phone, but it was switched off, as always. I didn't know why I thought calling her would be a good idea, but I couldn't sit by and do nothing.

"I need to go," I had said to Jack and Kara as panic gripped me.

"But you've been drinking," Kara said. She was right. With Jack on the brink of dumping me, I had found comfort in some vodka mixers before Kara had arrived.

"I'll take you," Jack offered. "We can go in your Honda."

"Thank you," I said, beaming at him with desperation. We scrambled to get ready. I had no idea if I was supposed to bring anything along with me or just show up. I had never been in such a situation before. Jack was amazing, though. He kept me calm. But as we went to leave, while Kara walked out with us, Jack got a call.

"Answer it," I told him.

"No, this is more important."

"It's fine," I said. "We have a bit of a drive on our hands."

"Okay," he replied. Then he took the call. I think about this moment a lot. If Jack had never answered his cell phone like I had suggested, things could have been very different.

"Oh crap," Jack said. "You can't be serious?"

"What is it?" Kara asked.

"That was Dad. He said he got a call from the police about Andy." Andy was forever getting into trouble. "He's been drinking again and has punched someone. Dad wants me to go pick him up from the police station."

We all stood in silence for a beat until Kara spoke first. "You go. I'll take Bianca to the hospital."

"Is that okay?" Jack asked me without hesitation.

I stared at him with an open mouth. Jack could have asked Kara to handle Andy, but he wanted to go. I could see it in his eyes that he preferred to leave me with my problem and help his brother instead. Would he have done the same thing to Nicole?

"Sure," I said. And away he went, leaving Kara to drive me to the hospital near my mother's house in Snohomish. The rest of the night is one I wish I could forget, but Ellie wants me to relive the pain.

I'm more than halfway to the crash site now. After Kara died, her parents made her a roadside memorial in the approximate location where she took her last breath. I was there when she died. I saw the life leave her eyes.

The memorial cross is still at the crash site and is maintained by Kara's parents alone. Jack and I have never returned, but once a year, we are emailed a photo of the spot showing us the fresh flowers Jack's parents have laid at the base of the cross. Their attempt to guilt us into visiting the place where Kara died has never worked.

Not wanting to, I imagine the crash site in my head. It appears exactly as it does in my nightmares: a winding section of road with narrow single lanes on either side. Tall trees and lush greenery surround the bend, casting speckled shadows in the moonlight. I only ever picture it in my mind at nighttime. Never in the day. The asphalt is smooth with only a few cracks, but the shoulders are covered in scattered gravel and mud.

The section of the road feels picturesque, like a slice of rural beauty. It's a far cry from the rowdiness of Seattle and Cedarwood Rock. But any beauty that might be found on the strip of road is lost when I think about Kara and the black Audi A3 I saw all those years ago. I knew it as Nicole's in an instant. I'd taken the time to memorize her schedule and what she wore, what she drove, and where she would be most days of the week. I had to. For Jack and me to remain a secret, I had to spend my time sneaking around. It was so pathetic. I should never have allowed it to happen, but I was too weak and couldn't stop. Jack had a hold on me.

The crash was a violent blur, but it was the events leading up to the chaos that changed everything. After Jack and Kara had spoken outside my dorm, I thought I'd turned a corner in my life. I thought Jack and I would push through the near miss and come out the other side a stronger couple. I had hoped he would end things with Nicole and not me. But nothing ever works out the way it's supposed to.

Jack calls me again. I stab the reject button this time. I can't take his call. I have to take Ellie's threats seriously. She has my babies. She has Dot and Noah. The thought sends a jerk into my throat I've tried my hardest to ignore. I don't care what happens to me, but nothing bad can happen to my children. They don't deserve to be punished for Ellie's derangement. Or Nora's derangement, I should say. Whatever the hell she wants to call herself.

She's the one behind everything. She has to be. Ellie was the one driving Nicole's car that night. She cut the seatbelt on my Honda. Nicole and Ellie are working together.

Jack tries calling another time. I'm so tempted to answer, but again, I'd be risking Dot and Noah's lives. It's not worth it. Plus, if I speak to him, I'll tell him everything. Even though he has a hell of a lot of explaining to do about Ellie, he's not the enemy here. Yes, I'm certain he's been cheating on me with Ellie for some time, but I doubt he's had anything to do with the bloody notes or the rest of this torture I've been dealing with. There's no way he would have dipped his dead sister's bracelet in blood and shoved it in a box for me to find.

As I think back over our relationship, one thing is becoming clearer: Ellie has always been there. She came onto the scene right after college and was David's girlfriend. I never felt like they were a match. They had next to no chemistry between them. Was she with David to be closer to Jack? If she was Jack's ex, then Jack had to have known who she was when we first met. She said in her letter that she went to college with us, but I never knew a girl named Nora, Ellie, or Eleanor. Did her obsession with Jack start then, or did it go farther back than I could ever imagine?

A headache swirls through my brain. This is all too much, and I know there is more pain to come. Ellie wouldn't go to all this trouble for nothing. How am I supposed to endure what comes next?

I travel the rest of the way to the crash site with the past antagonizing my every thought. This is the longest drive of my life. When I'm only a few miles away, Ellie calls my cell phone. With absolute reluctance, I hit the answer button.

"Hello, Bee," she says with a coldness in her voice I've never experienced from her. I reply with the only words I can.

"Hello, Nora."

CHAPTER SIXTY-ONE

"I see you got my letter," Nora says, her voice booming through my car's speaker system.

How does she know where I am? Has she bugged my car with a tracker? My mouth opens to speak, but nothing comes out.

"Lost for words, huh? Well, let me help you out. When I tell you to, you're going to pull your car over to the shoulder and kill the engine. Then, you are going to get out of your Subaru and walk. Bring your cell phone with you but leave everything else behind. Got it?"

"Yes," I utter. I'm still in shock about Ellie being the one behind this madness. It doesn't seem possible, given the woman I've known for all this time. When we first met, she seemed so innocent and incapable of doing a single thing wrong.

"Slow down and pull over. When you start walking, I don't want you to stop until you reach the crash site. Don't turn around or run away from me. You know what will happen if you try anything."

"I'll do what you say," I let out. "Please don't hurt my babies."

"Do what I say, and they will be fine."

"Where are they?" I demand.

"Safe enough. Now hurry up."

"Okay," I whisper.

I ease my foot onto the brake pedal and bring my car to a crawling stop, pushing it over to the shoulder as far as possible. There isn't much space, just as I remember it. When I climb out of my car, I make sure I don't take my keys or my handbag. I have nothing in my pockets and only hold my cell phone. I've told no one about any of this, exactly as Ellie has asked.

I'm doing whatever she tells me, so she has no reason to hurt Dot and Noah. No matter what has gone on between us, no matter her history with Jack, I have to believe she isn't the kind of person who would harm two children she has known since they were only hours old. It's the last hope I've got left to cling to.

As I walk along the road, toward the winding bend where the crash took place, I can't help but feel like she's watching me. Ellie — or Nora — must be staring at me right now. Has she been doing so this entire time? More unanswered questions rush at me. Who was driving the A3 this week when I thought I had lured the driver back to Maple Court? Both Nicole and Ellie came outside. Jack did too. Did Ellie have a sidekick in her efforts to harass me?

The wind stirs the surrounding trees, swaying and thrashing them about as the invisible energy slices through the thickness of the leaves. The sun is getting low and is close to the horizon. Soon, it will be dark, and I will come face to face with the crash site once again. It's the last place in the world I ever expected to find myself.

As I come closer to the bend, I wish I hadn't run off from Jack at our therapy session. Despite the pain he's no doubt caused me, it would have been a hundred times better to handle this situation with him by my side. If I survive whatever it is Ellie has in store for me, our marriage will face its greatest test. I don't know if there's enough love left between us to stave off divorce, but I guess it's the least of my worries.

I'm approaching the bend and am walking past a gravel driveway that has a County Sheriff election sign nearby. I wonder if a police officer or someone who knows a police officer lives in the house that's at the top of the driveway. I could run up to the home and knock on the door. Someone must be inside who could help me. But I can't risk it. Ellie will be watching. Just like she apparently was back in college — as Nora.

I never saw her once. But she saw Jack and me together. We did eventually go public after Kara's death and after Jack broke things off with Nicole. It's possible that Ellie is lying about witnessing Jack and me going behind Nicole's back. Maybe she guessed that's what happened. But something tells me she was watching us. What I don't understand is why she never told Nicole about what we were doing behind her back. Maybe she thought if Nicole found out, she would break it off with Jack and leave him to be mine. I guess Ellie wanted me gone for good. That's why she did what she did.

I reach the bend and walk along the winding turn. The trees are thicker on the corner than the straight section of the road. There are no more driveways for me to consider running up to. I've reached the point of no return. In less than fifty yards, the crash site will appear.

Who was Nora to Jack? Had they been together in college and broken up? If so, did she not take it well? No matter how hard I search my memories, I can never see her there. When I met Ellie, she told us all that she went to Seattle Pacific University. It wasn't far from U-Dub, but I didn't know any-one from the campus and never had a reason to doubt what she had told me. Jack never said a word. If he had already known who she was, then he played his part and kept their past a secret. Why, though? Was he trying to protect me? Did he think I would become jealous?

Partway into the bend, I spot a car up ahead, parked right next to Kara's roadside memorial. My heart skips a beat when I realize who the vehicle belongs to. It's Jack's. He is standing in front of Kara's memorial cross with his back to me. How is he here right now? Did Ellie lure him to the site as well?

My cell phone rings, startling me. I bring the device up to my face and find Ellie on the caller ID. I don't want to answer her call, but I have no choice. "Hello?" I say with a timid voice.

"Jack is waiting for you. Under no circumstances are you to mention my name. Got it?"

"Okay," I whisper.

"I mean it, Bee. One little breath of my name means the end for your babies. I'll start with Noah."

"That won't be necessary," I spit out.

"Good. See that we don't reach such an outcome." The call ends as suddenly as it began.

I shove my cell phone away and pick up the pace, hurrying toward Jack. I don't care about the cheating. We can work through that. But seeing him here fills me with hope. I don't know how, but together we can stop Ellie and beat her at her own game.

I charge toward him with a bounce in my step until I notice something hanging from his hand at his side. It's her bracelet — Kara's. There's no blood staining the K. The letter sways in the breeze and glints. Why the hell does he have it? Ellie must have stolen it from my car while I was working my shift at the library.

The how no longer matters. Only the why. So why has Ellie given Jack Kara's bracelet? And why is he holding it at his side as he stares at her roadside memorial?

A gasp escapes me. I know the answer to these questions.

I halt less than fifty feet from Jack. I don't want to face what comes next. Ellie has orchestrated something so vile, I'm certain there will be no turning back if I continue. She knows I can't run. Not while the kids aren't safe. Ellie is forcing me into a corner I've been avoiding for eighteen years.

With closed eyes, I continue forward and focus on my breathing, taking deep breaths in and out. I clench and release my fists and count my steps as I walk. If I don't do these things, I'm going to have a panic attack.

My technique takes the edge off, but I'm still ready to collapse into a heap and cry. I don't want to do this. I can't.

Jack glances over his shoulder when I am close enough. He probably heard my shoes scuffing over the loose gravel on the edge of the road. He doesn't say a word and returns his focus to Kara's cross as her bracelet continues to hang at his side.

The closer I get to Jack, the stiffer my legs feel. It's like my body doesn't want to keep going, but again, I am no longer in control. All I can do is get this over with and pray we make it out the other side.

"Jack?" I ask as I step beside him. My voice is weak in the flowing breeze as the sun falls lower in the sky.

"Eighteen years," he says without looking at me. "It still feels like she was alive only yesterday." There's no hostility in his voice. Only an eerie calmness. Maybe there's a chance we can talk about the past without things getting emotional.

I don't know what I should say first. I want to ask him why he's here of all places and why he's not surprised to see me, but there's no point. Deep down, I understand why Ellie has lured him here. I decide to stick with silence.

Jack's face softens as he looks at me. "Kara and I used to sneak out of the house late at night when we were kids. Just the two of us. We'd go down to the lake and just sit there, you know? We'd chat about everything and nothing like it was no big deal to be sneaking around behind our parents' backs. It wasn't until we had these conversations that I realized she had a way of seeing the world in an entirely different way than me. One that was so pure. She believed in people, Bianca. She really did. Even when they gave her every reason not to."

Jack pauses and glances down at the bracelet in his hand. "One night, we were sitting there, and she told me about her dreams. She wanted to travel the world and meet lots of people. She wanted to experience different cities and see what was out there. I thought it was a crazy idea. But I was just a protective older brother who spent his time worrying about how she might get hurt. Still, she wasn't afraid to live. She wasn't like me or Andy. Kara embraced life, even if it meant taking a risk. I think that's why losing her was so hard. She had so much life left to live."

I step closer to Jack's side and reach out to hold his hand. He turns all the way around before our fingers touch and glares right at me. His eyebrows furrow as he holds up Kara's bracelet toward my face. He only has one thing to say to me, and I know what it will be.

"Tell me, Bianca, how did she die?"

CHAPTER SIXTY-TWO

Eighteen years ago

The look in Damon's eyes stayed with me as I drove Nicole's car. It was one of shocked recognition. It took him a second, but he soon realized that it was me, a mere nobody in his eyes, who had killed him. Sweet little Eleanor had ended his life. That was the part of the experience I had enjoyed the most. The feeling of raw power sent me over the edge. I never knew such a sensation existed until that night.

Some student would find Damon's body soon enough. The police would be called, and every dorm room would have an officer knocking on it. Nicole wouldn't answer, though. She would be too dosed up from the sedative to be stirred awake. I was sure I'd given her enough to keep her out cold for most of the night. What happened in the stairwell was not part of the plan, but it was a setback I could overcome. Nothing was going to stop me.

I kept my head down and focused on the drive. I was still wearing my gloves and had taken the murder weapon with me, shoving it in Nicole's glove box. I'd spilled some of Damon's blood onto my gloves and hoodie but would burn them the first chance I got. Once I had completed the last task on my list, the police would find Nicole's car. The discovery of the knife would be a nice extra for them to examine. The blade used to sever the seatbelt in Bianca's Honda was also used in a murder. How perfect.

Once I got outside the city, I activated the tracking device I'd brought along with me. I would be too far away from Bianca to get a fix on her location, but I had the added advantage of knowing where she was heading. Once I was close enough, the little screen in my hand would light up and point me in the right direction.

I came to a set of lights at an empty intersection. It was tempting to blaze right through the area, but until I reached Bianca, I had to observe the law. The last thing I needed was to have my face captured on a red-light camera.

As if the world was listening to my thoughts, a police cruiser pulled up in the spare lane beside me.

"Shit," I muttered, doing my best to stare ahead. All I had to do was wait for the light to turn green. Then I'd be free. As subtly as I could, I hid the tracker screen down beside my leg. The police vehicle was a highway patrol car. No doubt the officers inside had already noted my license plate and were running it through their system. Nicole's car would not have been reported stolen yet, but she may have had traffic violations I was not aware of.

"Come on," I said through gritted teeth, willing the light to change. I could feel one of the two officers in the patrol car gawking at me like I was fresh meat. I knew the type well. He was the kind of officer who enjoyed the power trip that came with the job. He was probably hopeful that the license check would return enough for him and his partner to have probable cause to pull me over. If that happened, it would be all over. Bringing a blood-soaked knife along with me was a dumb move. Then again, so was killing Damon.

The patrol car's red and blue lights flashed on, along with its siren. I was screwed. I would be thrown into prison and would never see Jack again. But right when I was about to hit the gas pedal to flee, the police car did a wide U-turn and sped away in the opposite direction. They'd been called off for something else.

The light turned green. I let the burning air in my lungs seep out of me and got underway. Fate was testing my resolve once more.

When my heart rate settled down, I raised the tracker screen back up and placed it on the passenger seat. I needed to hurry if I was going to find Bianca in an ideal location. I couldn't do what I had planned in a busy area. Fortunately, between the college campus and the hospital she was headed to, there were a lot of back roads and small towns. I still had plenty of opportunities to take Bianca out.

After another thirty minutes of rushed travel, my tracker lit up, doing precisely what it was supposed to do. That meant Bianca was less than a few hundred feet away from me. I had taken the time to study the roads along the route, but unfortunately, I was several minutes behind schedule. Still, there was a stretch of road ahead that would suit the task at hand.

My foot stepped harder on the gas. Nicole's tank had plenty left in it. Enough that I wouldn't run out mid-pursuit. She was quite the responsible little college student. Surprising considering her father had bought her the Audi A3 brand new. It was a shame I would need to damage it. I liked the way it handled itself.

My eyes darted between the road ahead and the tracker in my hand as I held it on the steering wheel. In less than a minute, there would be a straight section. It would let me see Bianca's Honda with my own eyes. Then, it would only be a matter of time before I sent her straight to hell where she belonged.

She thought she could get between Jack and me. That their secret scandal was more powerful than our love. She didn't know who she was messing with. Nicole was never an actual threat to me. That's why I left her alive in her dorm.

Jack never loved her. He simply enjoyed the status that came with dating Nicole Stokes.

He liked her rich daddy, too, and saw her family as a stepping stone to success. All that talk about being afraid of her father was a lie. Once the night was over, Nicole would be in prison, arrested for the murder of Jack's secret girlfriend, Bianca. If the police connected Nicole to Damon's murder, it would be a delightful bonus.

"I'm coming, Jack. It will all be over soon."

I found Bianca's taillights ahead. She was driving faster than I anticipated. From my observations of her, she had been a slow driver. One who wasn't confident at night. That fact was supposed to help me with my plan. Ahead, she took the corner, going at least twenty over the limit. The fake news I had dropped on her about her mother had sent the girl into a panic. With any luck, she would crash on her own. All I'd need to do then was stage the scene, so Nicole got the blame. That was the plan either way.

Once I rounded the corner, I pressed the gas pedal to the floor and sped up as fast as the A3 allowed. It didn't take me long to catch up to Bianca. Before I got close enough for her to see me, I slid a balaclava down over my face. It was only a precaution in case I failed. But I would not fail.

With everything in place, I pulled out onto the opposite lane of the two-lane stretch of road and came up beside the Honda. "Got you now," I said, ready to slam my car into the rear quarter panel of her car to perform a PIT maneuver on Bianca's Honda, just like I'd seen the police do in videos on the internet.

But I hesitated when I saw her. It wasn't Bianca driving but Kara. What the hell was Jack's sister doing there? I slowed down without thinking and didn't run the Honda off the road as planned. I couldn't. Not with Kara inside. Jack would never forgive me if I hurt his sister. What I was doing to Nicole and Bianca, he would understand with time, but no harm could come to his sister. They shared a bond I could never break.

I pulled back into the correct lane and stayed behind Kara as she drove. I even slowed down, so I was a normal distance away as we navigated our way through winding roads on narrow lanes. She was driving too fast, and it wasn't to escape me. She didn't even notice me there when I pulled up beside her. Something was wrong.

Kara started to swerve all over the road with sharp, uncontrolled turns. It was like she had lost control of the steering wheel. I had to do something, so I sped up and figured I could blare at Kara with my horn in the hopes that she would slow down and pull over. But I never got the chance.

Through the screech of tires and the puff of smoke, I witnessed Kara lose full control of the Honda and get caught in a spin. The car flipped over on its side and rolled three times before it came to a violent stop. In that process, I saw a body come flying out of the broken glass of the driver's door. It was Kara.

I slammed on my brakes but soon realized my tires were now struggling to find purchase. There was too much scattered gravel around. I overcorrected and spun the A3 straight into a tree. The Audi's airbag exploded in my face and saved my life.

I blacked out for a few seconds before remembering where I was and what I was doing. The plan was never to crash this hard. I was supposed to clip the back of the Honda and run the A3 into a tree at a low speed — enough to deploy the airbag. Then I was going to let the cops find the scene and conclude that Nicole had targeted Bianca with vicious intent and taken off. In all the excitement, I overdid things and became a serious part of the crash. I needed to hurry if I was going to get away.

Practically falling out of the car, my body felt worse for wear. It was like I'd been whacked with a giant pillow. A trickle of blood ran down my forehead, but otherwise, I was fine. A piece of debris must have sliced into me during the destruction. I made a hurried check to see if any of it had landed in the car itself. Nothing stood out to me.

Ignoring the cut, I hurried toward Kara's fallen body. She lay in the middle of the road and was broken. I had to save her. I couldn't give up and walk away. I dropped to her side and assessed the damage. It didn't look good.

"No," I whispered. "You can't be dead." If Jack thought I had anything to do with the accident, he would kill me. He would never want to be with me again. Just as I was ready to give up, I saw Kara stir awake and move. "Thank God," I muttered, short of breath. I could still save her.

But before I called for help or applied first aid, a second figure emerged from the Honda. She coughed and spluttered as she got clear of the wreck. It was Bianca.

"What did you do?" I whispered. The utterance of my voice made her catch sight of me. Fortunately, I was still wearing the balaclava. We stared at one another for a moment with only the moonlight above to guide us. Both sets of headlights on the Audi and Honda had been destroyed.

Bianca didn't move and kept her eyes glued to mine until she twisted to find Nicole's totaled A3. I could see the wheels turning in her brain.

"Nicole?" she asked.

I didn't say a word. She thought I was Nicole.

Bianca screamed and charged right at me. I could have fought her then and there and probably would have won, but with the knowledge that Bianca thought I was Nicole, I ran away, straight into the thickness of trees. Bianca didn't follow. She was in no state to do so.

Once she had given up the chase, I didn't keep going deeper into the woods like I was supposed to. Instead, I doubled back, needing to understand why Bianca was alive and okay while Kara had been seriously injured. Why had Kara been driving when Bianca should have been behind the wheel of the car with the defective seatbelt?

I hid in the trees and watched as Bianca moved over to Kara. It could have been Jack, hurt and lying in the road, but I knew he wouldn't be able to resist the lie I told his father about his brother. He had chosen Andy over Bianca exactly as

I predicted he would. He was always trying to save Andy from himself. For the most part, these people were doing what I expected them to do. But as much as I thought I knew Bianca, nothing had prepared me for what came next.

"Bianca," Kara groaned. "You need to call an ambulance."

Bianca was on her knees beside Kara. "What did I do?" she asked.

"It's okay. It was a mistake. We can fix this."

But Bianca shook her head and sobbed. "We can't. It's worse than it looks. You're not going to make it."

"Yes, I am. You just need to . . . get your cell phone and . . . call—"

Kara coughed. Blood sprayed into the air and coated her bracelet — the one she always wore.

"I'm sorry," Bianca said, brushing Kara's head.

"No," she wheezed. "You need to help me. Why aren't you . . . helping me?"

"Jack can't know what I did," Bianca said. "No one can. I'm so sorry." She took a few glances around the area and brought her hands close to Kara's face. Jack's secret girlfriend covered Kara's mouth and nose and pressed down, making a tight seal. She was going to end her life.

My jaw dropped as my eyes went wide. I had to stop Bianca, but I couldn't. My legs wouldn't move. My voice wouldn't function. Instead, I watched as she starved Kara of oxygen. I didn't look away until Kara stopped resisting and gave in. A siren began to wail in the distance and pulled me from my trance. Only then was I able to move again. A local who lived nearby had probably heard the crash and called the emergency services. It was time to go.

"I'm sorry," Bianca said as she sobbed over Kara. "It's better this way. He won't ever know . . ."

I got up and ran, leaving the A3 behind. When I glanced over my shoulder and risked tripping over a tree root, the last thing I saw was Bianca lying down in the road with her eyes shut. She was pretending to be unconscious, pretending that she hadn't killed Jack's sister.

CHAPTER SIXTY-THREE

Present day

"Well, Bianca?" Jack asks. "How did she die? How did my sister die?"

"I don't know," I lie, shaking my head.

"Bullshit," he yells, grabbing hold of me by the elbow. "You know what happened. You were there."

My lip quivers. "It all happened so fast."

Jack closes his eyes, but he doesn't calm himself down. Instead, he bares his teeth at me and lets out a growling yell. "You're lying." He shoves me hard to the ground. I land on the road and feel pain shoot through my side. Jack glowers down at me like I'm a vile disgrace of a human being. He's not wrong. I deserve this.

Jack stomps toward me and stands over my vulnerable position. "What did you do, Bianca?" he asks, holding Kara's bracelet up. "Huh? Tell me."

I shake my head as the memories all come back to me. When Kara was driving me to the hospital where my mom was supposed to be, we started talking to pass the time. I needed her to distract me from the possibility that my mother was dead. We got onto the topic of Jack after a while and what had almost happened — how Kara had come close to telling Nicole about Jack and me.

"Thank you again," I had said to her.

"For what?" she replied.

"For everything. For driving. For not talking to Nicole. I really appreciate it."

Kara shook her head as she focused on the road. "I know I told Jack that I wouldn't say anything to Nicole, but I still think you should come clean and tell her yourself. Not today, obviously. But soon."

"I can't," I said. "Jack will hate me if I do that. For real, we'd be over in a heartbeat if I told Nicole any of it. You know that."

"Of course I do. But I have to ask: is this what you want for the rest of your life? Do you like being my brother's dirty little secret?"

I didn't mean to, and maybe it was the situation with my mother that was fueling me, but I lost it. "For God's sake, you won't let this go, will you?"

"Calm down, Bianca."

"No, I'm sick to death of you butting your nose into our business. You've done it from day one. The only reason you caught us at the start was because you were spying on us. How about you tell me the real reason you want Jack and me to split up?"

Kara scoffed. "What are you talking about?"

I laughed right back at her lie. "Come on. Do you seriously expect me to believe the innocent act? I know you don't like me, Kara. That's fine. I don't care. But I've figured it out. No one is good enough for your precious Jack, are they?"

"Fuck you," she snapped, showing her true self.

I still had a fair amount of alcohol in my system and was eager for a fight. "There she is. The real you. It's about time."

"You're insane," she yelled. "The second we reach the next town, I'm parking this car and leaving. I don't give a damn how you get to the hospital. It's not my problem."

285

"Screw you," I shouted. Then I made the biggest mistake of my life. I reached for the steering wheel. Kara swatted me away, causing the car to swerve.

"What the hell do you think you're doing?" Kara shouted as the car sped up.

"Taking back control of my car. Get the fuck out." I lunged at the wheel again like a maniac.

"Bianca, stop," she said. But it was too late. I had already taken hold of the steering wheel and had yanked it toward me. What happened next was all my fault. We crashed. The car rolled three times, throwing Kara from the wreck. All because her seatbelt apparently had been tampered with. At that point in time, I had no knowledge of the problem, but I caused the crash.

When I came to, I crawled from my car, noticing I was bleeding from the deep gash on my forehead. I saw a young woman standing by Kara in a balaclava, of all things. I had no idea who she was or what she was doing there, but then I spotted Nicole's crashed Audi.

"Nicole?" I uttered as we stared at one another. I gazed into her eyes, making the connection. I wasn't sure why she had crashed, but she was wearing a mask. That filled me with concern. Without thinking, I charged at who I thought was Nicole until she ran away into the woods.

The masked girl wasn't my biggest problem, though. Not by far. What I had done to Kara was unforgivable. And if Kara survived, she would tell Jack the second she saw him. She would gladly tell her brother how I overreacted and caused us to crash. He'd never forgive me. I had to think of a way out of the problem and keep Kara quiet. With Nicole's crashed car right there, an idea came to me. One I didn't know was possible.

The way I saw it, there was no other way out of the nightmare I had caused. I made sure the masked girl was long gone. Then I did something that crossed every line imaginable.

I killed Kara.

She begged me for help, but I didn't even attempt to stop the bleeding. I told her she was beyond saving. Then I told her I was sorry. Instead of helping Kara, I covered her mouth so she couldn't breathe. She fought back, harder than I expected, but she was weakened from the crash. When she finally stopped moving, I laid down on the road and pretended to be out cold until help arrived. I was hurt, so no one wondered if I had killed her.

The next day, the police came to me in the hospital. They said someone had sabotaged the seatbelt in the driver's seat of my car. When I thought about the fake call I'd received about my mother and the fact that Nicole had crashed her car right next to mine while wearing a balaclava, the tampered seat belt made sense.

Nicole had tried to kill me. That's what was running through my head on repeat. She must have thought I would be driving that night. I assumed she planned on running me off the road, so I'd die in a crash due to a defective seat belt. Little did my stalker know, Kara had offered to drive me to see my mother in the hospital.

The police also had questions for me. They wanted to know what had happened, so I told them a story. I painted a picture about the A3 that ran us off the road and who I saw driving it. I let my rage and pathetic desperation to stay with Jack take hold. I killed Jack's sister and blamed Nicole for it. Kara should have survived the crash and made a full recovery, but I had an opportunity to protect our relationship, so I silenced Jack's sister and framed an innocent girl. Because, in the end, Nicole truly was innocent. She wasn't the girl in the mask at all.

It was Ellie. It was Nora.

Jack squats down and yanks me to my feet. He lifts me to my tippy toes with ease, taking advantage of his strength. Kara's bracelet scratches at my face as he shoves it toward me. "What did you do to Kara?"

"You already know, don't you?" I ask him as I clutch at his grip.

"I do. Nicole told me the truth."

"Nicole?" I let out. I go to question him further. I want to ask him how it could have been possible for Nicole to have told him these things, but I remember Ellie's words about the kids. I can't correct him. I can't tell Jack the truth about Ellie.

"Yeah, Nicole. She finally admitted everything. She called me after you stormed off from our session and told me how the two of you conspired to kill Kara back in college. She said that Kara had stumbled across a dark secret the two of you shared and that she was going to run to the police about it. But when it all happened, you sold her out and pinned everything on her."

"Oh, God," I say. What lies has Ellie filled his head with? And what control does she have over Nicole for her to lie to Jack in such a way?

"That's right, Bianca. I know everything. I know that Nicole was planning on murdering her parents for the inheritance money and that you were going to help her. But Kara found out, didn't she?"

My mouth hangs open at the insanity of the lie Jack has believed so willingly. I want to tell him it's not true, but I can't.

Jack continues. "She also told me where you were going to be tonight. After your outburst at our session, you needed to come to the one place you always go to when you're feeling guilty. And guess what? Here you are."

I close my eyes and try to wake up from this bad dream. But it doesn't work. Jack is still holding me tight with that look of fire in his eyes.

"It's time to come clean," he says. "Tell me what you did, Bianca." He grips me tighter and lifts me off my feet.

"Jack, I don't—"

"The truth," he spits. "Tell me the truth. If one more lie comes out of your mouth . . ." Jack doesn't complete his thought, but it's clear what he was going to say.

I glance around the road, praying for a car to drive by.

"No one is coming," he says. "It's time to confess, Bianca. I'm not messing around here."

"Okay," I say, knowing I need to tell him what he wants to hear. It's the only way to keep Dot and Noah safe. "We did it — Nicole and I — we worked together to kill your sister. We came up with the fake story about my mother and the one about your brother, so Kara would have to drive me to the hospital. Nicole drove the A3 and ran us off the road. And I cut the seat belt, knowing what would happen if we crashed. Then, after Kara died, I blamed it all on Nicole. I wanted you all to myself."

Jack lets go of me. I drop back to my feet and see him fall to his knees. I take a step back and watch as he breaks down and cries. If we get through this and save the kids, I'll tell him the real truth. It's no better than the lies Ellie has been feeding him, but maybe once he calms down, we can talk. I'll go to prison if that's what it takes. What I don't understand is how Ellie has gotten Nicole to admit to things she never did.

Jack lifts his head to me with that same stare he had that day when he went to confront Nicole. But this time, there are no police officers around to stop him.

"Jack, please," I beg, taking another step back.

He doesn't say a word as he rushes to his feet and charges straight at me. Before I can run, his hands are wrapped tight around my neck. He kicks my legs out from under me and slams me into the road. My head collides with the asphalt, sending a bright flash into my eyes. The air in my lungs disappears, and before I can take a replenishing gulp, Jack climbs on top of me and continues what he started. He squeezes my throat tighter and tighter as I stare at him with wide, pleading eyes. I try to speak, to beg for my life, but I can't get a single sound out. I only want to scream out one name: Ellie.

Jack doesn't slow down, and no one drives past to stop him. I'm about to die, but maybe this is what I deserve. I've been living on borrowed time that I stole from Kara.

As my vision fades, I think about my babies and pray that Ellie has enough humanity left inside her to not harm Dot and Noah.

CHAPTER SIXTY-FOUR

It's been two weeks since Jack killed his wife. Two beautiful weeks, and he doesn't suspect a thing. I don't think he will ever find out about the effort I endured to bring us together. And he never will.

We've been meeting up at Nicole's house. I stole one of her spare keys the day she moved in. She didn't notice. It set nicely with the copy I had of Bianca's.

No one questioned Nicole's suicide. Not even Jack. He believed that her supposed guilty conscience drove her to swallow a bottle full of sleeping pills so she could drown herself in an overflowing bathtub, all after 'confessing' everything to him over the phone. With Nicole's history of mental health problems, it was an easy one for the authorities to believe. What happened to Bianca was a challenge to solve.

The official story Jack told the police was that she had left. I planted enough seeds for the narrative to make sense. The big one being the suicide note I made Nicole write before I forced her to take those pills. She detailed how she and Bianca had conspired together to kill Kara, along with the rest of it. In my version of events that Nicole divulged, Bianca had sold Nicole down the river eighteen years ago. Nicole then came out of the woodwork, seeking revenge.

She bought the house at number six all these years later to guilt Bianca into telling her husband the truth about Kara. It wasn't easy finding the right pressure point, but Nicole had a niece she cared deeply about. When I showed her how easily I could get to the niece and end her existence, Nicole did as I asked. She almost seemed grateful for her life to be over.

I've known about her mental state for eighteen years. After the police arrested and released her in college, everyone thought she was guilty of killing Kara and the attempt on Bianca's life. Her life was ruined. Jack dumped her with threats of violence, her friends stopped speaking to her, and her own family cut ties. She left college early and hit rock bottom.

Her parents, the forgiving types they were, eventually absolved Nicole of her sins and left her a decent chunk of their money in the family's will. As if fate were on my side, a few years ago, they died in a freak plane crash. Nicole walked away with two million dollars. I had kept tabs on her in case she ever sought the truth about that night. She never did, of course. A weak girl like Nicole would never do such a thing. That's why it was so easy to convince her to help me bring Bianca to her knees. She believed every lie I told her.

Jack and I have been seeing each other for years. In secret, we've been running around together whenever Bianca wasn't looking. On weeknights when she'd go to bed early, I would sneak in to see Jack while she slept, using my key. It helped that I would often sneak sedatives into her coffees in the afternoons. Jack would also turn the alarm off for me. Anytime Jack claimed he needed to stay back at school, I was with him, screwing his brains out in an empty classroom. He loved the excitement of it all. He always had. It started in college with Nicole and Bianca, so once Nicole was out of the way and Bianca became the girl he kept front and center, I stepped in. I became his dirty little secret. And for a long time, that's how things went.

I had to find ways to stay close to him and to keep our relationship exciting. Dave was an easy opportunity. He was Jack's best friend. Marrying him made it so much easier for me to be close to Jack without raising any suspicion. Jack did feel guilty about betraying his friend, but he seemed to enjoy the thrill of it more. And the two kids Dave and I have are both Jack's. I've never told Jack as much, but I suspect he's always known.

Before I met David, I took the drastic step of burning my J+N scar off with acid. It hurt like hell, but I couldn't risk leaving it there before I started a relationship with David.

Jack and I had dated before all the drama unfolded with the crash that killed his sister. For three months, he was happy to have me be his girlfriend. But one day, we had a bad argument, and Jack decided he was no longer interested in me in that way. Soon, he started dating Nicole like I had never existed. It didn't take him long to get bored with her, though. Then Bianca came along to excite him once more.

I watched them all from a distance. The way those two girls attempted to control Jack was a joke. Nicole thought she had him on a tight leash with promises of a prosperous future, while Bianca kept him interested in her willingness to be his little side piece. I needed to get rid of them both. I tried. I gave it my all and eliminated Nicole from his life, but, unfortunately, in doing so, I only cemented what he had with Bianca. It took me far too long to work my way into his life again only to become his girl on the side.

Bianca and Nicole never had to die. But Jack saw to that when he came to me about three years ago and told me he was done with all the sneaking around. He'd even told Bianca the truth at the time. Well, a version of the truth. He said he'd slept with a random woman one night that he met at a bar. I was the girl, but we'd slept together a thousand times before then. He wanted to get caught. Apparently, his guilt had caught up to him. It didn't take, though. Bianca forgave him. Probably because of the kids or some other stupidity. And he couldn't find it within himself to end his pathetic marriage.

Some time passed, and it became clear Bianca and Jack were in it for the long haul. Jack had ended us. There would be no more late-night visits. No more going around behind our spouses' backs. No more excitement. Just like that, he thought he could cast me aside. But I wouldn't let that happen, so I came up with a plan. One that required the one thing I've always possessed: patience.

What came next was not what I expected, but it was almost too perfect. After some time stewing in the dark, I contacted Nicole and convinced her it was Bianca who had ruined her life. I confessed to her I had also attended U-Dub and had dated Jack for three months before she did. I told her how I watched in a fearful silence while Bianca stole Jack from her. I didn't have proof, but I gave out my greatest performance that I had been too afraid to get involved. But Bianca had done so much more than steal Nicole's man.

In my version of events, Bianca had supposedly slashed the seatbelt of her own car and paid someone to steal Nicole's car to crash it into her Honda while Kara was driving. Bianca supposedly wanted to remove Kara from her and Jack's life. Nicole fell for my story hook, line, and sinker. She actually believed that Bianca had risked her own life to frame her for the death of Jack's sister. Like I said, she was vulnerable and easy to convince. I guess part of my story was true. Bianca did want Kara gone. She murdered the girl.

Nicole was more than willing to help me bring Bianca down. She even came up with the idea of buying the house next door and moving in to psychologically torture Bianca. After all, Nicole had the money. She'd spent several years in and out of therapy, but the idea of making Bianca pay for ruining her life seemed to give the woman focus. It almost helped her.

We worked together and came up with a plan to drive Bianca crazy. I had things lined up for months. Piece by piece, I was going to bring Bianca to her knees, but this time around, I couldn't wait. I was sick of the wasted time. I wanted it over as fast as possible, so together we struck Bianca from every angle.

I got Jack in on the fun without him realizing it. I said I wanted him to destroy the box of Polaroids we took together in college. Unsurprisingly, he struggled with the task. He still wanted us to be together. Burning those photos was probably harder for him than I realized. And there were more than a bunch of photos in there. He'd even kept some of the notes I used to leave him when we weren't together.

The destroyed box created a marvelous opportunity for me to sneak in a half-burned photo of the two of us. One where my face was missing. I already knew Bianca was trying to find the box she had spent years completely unaware of. So, when she found the burned Polaroid, she believed it was a photo of Jack and Nicole. She thought she was so clever with her 'hidden' cameras. I hacked into those within minutes of them coming online.

Despite being broken up, Jack and I have been in contact with one another for the past three years. Every text he sent me gave me hope and kept my love for him strong. This week was different. I'd been texting him more than normal and had met with him several times in person to talk about us. I was pushing him to reconsider getting back together, giving him one last opportunity for me to avoid dealing with Bianca my own special way. I could see in his eyes that he wanted to say yes, that he was torn, but he could no longer betray Bianca's trust. In fact, he said he was going to confess our long-standing affair in their next therapy session. He thought he could come clean with the whole truth and save his marriage. I told him to do what he thought was right, but I knew he wouldn't have the guts to tell Bianca something so damning.

With no other choice, I moved forward with my plan. I came to Jack one last time and said Nicole had admitted something awful to me about Bianca. Something to do with Kara. That got his attention.

Nicole had no idea how it would all end. She thought we were just punishing Bianca. She was a useful pawn in my game to win Jack over, and she played her part well. I almost felt sorry for her. But I couldn't risk leaving her alive. She knew too much. Plus, I saw the way she looked at Jack at the barbecue. She still had feelings for him. Especially after hearing my lies about Bianca.

Jack has no clue about any of it. He thinks Nicole killed herself from guilt and wrote the crazy note. He thinks he choked his wife to death because she had conspired with Nicole years ago to kill his sister. He even helped to convince the authorities that Bianca had up and left her family to run away from the crime she committed eighteen years ago. Given her recent and very public breakdowns, it wasn't much of a stretch for people to believe it.

It never is.

People are so willing to believe the worst things about each other. You just have to find what that thing is and run with it. I guess I sealed the deal when I anonymously paid some lowlife to drive an old A3 around town to harass Bianca. He did it for less than a thousand dollars.

After it was all said and done, Gabrielle helped as well, telling the police about the threatening note Bianca allegedly stabbed at Nicole's door. Darell Vargas also contributed and spoke to the officers who came to Maple Court. Apparently, Bianca had accused him of some things he had no part in. That was a nice bonus I wasn't aware of until the end.

"How are you holding up?" I ask Jack as we lie in Nicole's bed. Our clothes have been strewn about the floor. We are sneaking around again. I can feel the same heat between us that was lost when he broke things off with me. I did what I had to do, and now it's alive again.

"I'm okay. I just . . ."

"What is it?" I ask, placing a hand on his bare chest.

"I can't help but wonder if I made a mistake doing what I did to Bianca."

Her name grates in my ear whenever he mentions it. I shuffle closer and make sure he is looking directly into my eyes. "She got what she deserved. After what she and Nicole did to your poor sister, they got off lightly."

"I know they did. I do. I only wish I could shake this guilt. I thought getting justice for Kara would have made me feel better."

"It will. You just need to give it some time. You've been through something traumatic. No one expects you to bounce back as if nothing has changed. Your wife is dead, but she got the end she deserved. Frankly, so did Nicole. Sure, it would have been nice to see them both face life in prison for what they did, but it's over now."

Jack's gaze falls away from mine and returns to staring at the ceiling. There are cracks in the plaster, and the paintwork is peeling. The entire house needs a renovation. With a bit of love and attention, this old place could be whipped into shape and could be considered the best home on Maple Court. It's not my problem, though. Nicole's lawyers will have to work out what happens to number six. For now, though, it's the perfect location for Jack and me to meet up in secret. We have to keep things in the dark, at least for now. I still have the problem of my husband to deal with, but that clueless idiot will be easy to handle when the time comes. And the time will come. Maybe I'll do something about his painful mother while I'm at it. I see an unfortunate car crash in their future.

Bianca's body was simple enough to dispose of. I took care of that for Jack. He helped me load her into the trunk of her Subaru. I then drove it out to Lake Roesiger, making sure my identity was hidden the entire trip. A man I met on the dark web helped with the grisly task of making sure Bianca's body would never be found. I used Nicole's money to cover the cost. The entire process was anonymous and straightforward. Afterward, I felt a weight lift from my shoulders.

In a few months, Jack and I will be living under one roof with the four children. I will tell him all about Ethan and Olivia when the time is right. He will understand why I had to keep them a secret from him. Luckily, he's always been close by in their lives. As for Dot and Noah, I will tolerate them for as long as I need to. It will be a challenge considering who their mother was. They are lucky they have Jack's blood in them.

I wrap my arm tighter around Jack and feel the rise and fall of his chest. The coming months won't be easy, but we will face them as one. Soon, I will no longer have to be one of Jack's dirty little secrets. I will be good enough for him to show off to the world. Nothing can stop us now.

Jack tilts his head toward me and says, "Thank you, Ellie. For everything."

I smile up at him. "I'll always be here for you. Oh, and you know better than to call me that name. Tell me the one I want to hear."

"Okay, Nora. I love you." He cradles the back of my head in one hand and pulls me to his lips. We kiss. His lips are tender against mine as the world seems to fade away. No one can harm us. We are unstoppable. The scar that was once on the palm of my hand might be gone, but I plan on starting it again. Its significance runs as deep as my love for this man.

J + N Forever.

THE END

AUTHOR'S NOTE

Writing *The Ex* has been a deeply thrilling experience. This story of secrets, betrayal, and the delicate balance of relationships was inspired by my fascination with how the past can come back to haunt us, often when we least expect it.

First and foremost, I want to thank my amazing family — especially my wife and children — for their constant support and patience during my writing career. Your love is my driving force and the reason I never give up, even when the journey gets tough.

I would also like to express my gratitude to my editor, Siân Heap for all her hard work throughout the development of this book along with Managing Editor Kate Ballard. Also, a big thanks to the amazing team at Joffe Books, who have helped shape this story into what it is today. Your feedback, insights, and encouragement have been invaluable.

For those of you who have followed my work, thank you for your continued support and for trusting me to take you on this new journey. For new readers, welcome — I hope this book keeps you on the edge of your seat and makes you question the things we think we know about the people closest to us.

Finally, if you enjoyed *The Ex* or have any thoughts you'd like to share, I'd love to hear from you. Feel free to connect with me on social media or through my website. Your feedback and engagement mean the world to me, and I'm grateful for each and every reader who picks up my work.

Thank you for being part of this journey.

Warm regards,

Alex Sinclair

THE JOFFE BOOKS STORY

We began in 2014 when Jasper agreed to publish his mum's much-rejected romance novel and it became a bestseller.

Since then we've grown into the largest independent publisher in the UK. We're extremely proud to publish some of the very best writers in the world, including Joy Ellis, Faith Martin, Caro Ramsay, Helen Forrester, Simon Brett and Robert Goddard. Everyone at Joffe Books loves reading and we never forget that it all begins with the magic of an author telling a story.

We are proud to publish talented first-time authors, as well as established writers whose books we love introducing to a new generation of readers.

We won Trade Publisher of the Year at the Independent Publishing Awards in 2023 and Best Publisher Award in 2024 at the People's Book Prize. We have been shortlisted for Independent Publisher of the Year at the British Book Awards for the last five years, and were shortlisted for the Diversity and Inclusivity Award at the 2022 Independent Publishing Awards. In 2023 we were shortlisted for Publisher of the Year at the RNA Industry Awards, and in 2024 we were shortlisted at the CWA Daggers for the Best Crime and Mystery Publisher.

We built this company with your help, and we love to hear from you, so please email us about absolutely anything bookish at feedback@joffebooks.com.

If you want to receive free books every Friday and hear about all our new releases, join our mailing list here: www.joffebooks.com/freebooks.

And when you tell your friends about us, just remember: it's pronounced Joffe as in coffee or toffee!